Collateral
Damage

Collateral Damage

Sara Loggin

DREAMING BIG
PUBLICATIONS

Collateral Damage
Copyright © 2020 by Sara Loggin

Content Editor: Kerstin Stokes
Copy Editor: Katie Schmeiser
Editor-in-Chief: Kristi King-Morgan
Formatting: Kristi King-Morgan
Assistant Editor: Maddy Drake

Printed in the United States of America

ISBN- 978-1-947381-30-8

www.dreamingbigpublications.com

To all my brothers and sisters in EMS, Fire, Law Enforcement, Dispatch, and Hospitals, who work tirelessly day in and day out, through good days and bad. The good days are nice, but it's the bad days that teach you exactly what you're made out of. Diamonds are made under pressure. Keep shining.

To my teachers who saw a "rough around the edges" dreamer and encouraged me to keep writing, to keep pushing through the trials, and to reach for the stars until I had obtained my goals. I may not have looked like I was paying attention with my nose always in a book, but I assure you, I was listening to every word.

To everyone who contributed an idea or medical knowledge into this novel to make it as real as possible. Google is great, but it's so much better when there are people you can talk to, who will help make it more life-like. Thank you.

To my mom, Karen, who showed her starry-eyed 4-year-old daughter a picture of herself in bunker gear and introduced me to the world of "First Responders". For nurturing that hunger by raising me on all the medical shows we could find, and for always listening to me after every single bad call. Thank you for pushing me to never give up.

Most importantly, to my husband, Andy, for not only being an inspiration, but also for being one of those rare individuals in my life who has listened without judgment, spoken without prejudice, helped me without entitlement, understood without pretention, and loved me without conditions. None of this would have been possible if you wouldn't have taken a chance on a damaged young Paramedic and pushed her to her potential and beyond. I want to thank you also for your insight on the law enforcement aspects of this novel, and for making sure it was as close to procedurally accurate as possible, and for pointing out ways it could be better. You will forever be my knight in shining armor. I love you.

Preface

This novel is a compilation of fiction and non-fiction. I wanted this novel to reach out to people, to grab you by the heartstrings, and to make you feel what these characters are feeling. I couldn't have done that without living through many frightening days and troubling nights. Not all the details contained in this book are true to my own life, but I thought that would help to connect with you, dear reader. Enough truth to flesh out this novel, and enough fantasy that no single person could claim a character or a situation is purely about them.

Aaron's character has anchors in real life in an attempt to make him more "real" to readers. I wanted to make him as human as possible, and my imagination was far surpassed by reality in the things he says and does. Just remember that every villain was once a child, and it was a hard life that turned them onto the dark and winding path.

David is a melting pot of many officers I know, taking qualities from each one to make him into exactly the man I wanted for this novel. I hope his bravery, his kindness, and his emotions are true to life, and that you are able to love him as I do.

Meredith is also a mix of many medics I know and have worked with, in the hopes of making her a well-rounded and relatable character. She has faced many trials in her years, and it is my hope that how she handles the bad things may one day help someone in her situation to overcome them too. With that being said, if you are in an abusive relationship, I urge you to find the help you need. Help is out there, and nobody deserves to be mistreated. In the words of Tim, love shouldn't hurt. Visit: **www.thehotline.org/resources/victims-and-survivors** if you or someone you know needs help.

Being in emergency services for well over ten years, I wanted to use some of that knowledge and stored-up energy to turn this book from ink and paper into a roller coaster of emotion that would leave you on the edge of your seat, demanding answers until the very last page. I hope that I have left no stone unturned, and no question left unanswered, and I hope that you found the thrill ride you were after.

Chapter 1

"Don't you dare die on me! I haven't even told you I'm in love with you yet!"

The blood was everywhere - on her hands, her face, her hair, on the ground, turning the silty sand into mud that caked her boots and pants. It was too much blood, his face was too pale, respirations too shallow, his pulse thread and weak. She was waiting for her partner to bring the ambulance closer. They were disobeying so many orders, not to mention how many protocols to get him to safety, but she threatened to forcibly remove her partner's kidney if he didn't bring the rig here immediately, and he knew she wasn't kidding by the devilish glint in her fierce eye.

It was too nice of an evening for this to have happened. Too early in the shift. She had only come on an hour ago, and anticipated an easy night of catching up on homework and Netflix. The sun was still bright and warm, despite sunset creeping ever-closer. There was a gentle breeze that caressed her red hair, pushing it into her green eyes. There were several fluffy clouds floating lazily on their way to their next destination, no threat of rain in sight. A large tree stood nearby, the wind through its leaves creating a soothing sound that would have calmed her nerves at any other time. Across the street, a stray cat stared at the commotion, silver fur puffed up in agitation, and there he stayed until another loud sound frightened him away.

The bullet had ricocheted against his car and gone in below his left collar bone, just above his vest. The blood ran down the Kevlar vest, soaking his uniform shirt and hers. She was holding him up, cradling his head and shoulders, trying to help him breathe; keeping him elevated enough that he wouldn't drown in his own blood. She was ill-prepared at this moment for this sort of injury. All she had was a tourniquet, and there was nothing she could do with it here. Her slender, gloved fingers pulled softly at his vest, trying to see the wound and how bad it really was. His ocean-blue eyes fluttered open in a panic, hands raising up to defend himself, unsure of where he was, or who was touching him. He knew he was in a fight for his life, and wasn't about to go down easily. One calloused hand curled in a fist, the other still weakly holding his pistol. Her hand stroked his cheek, rough with stubble. His eyes took a minute to focus, but once they did, he smiled, and let his eyes drift closed again, hands relaxing, falling still once more.

***

"I have you. I have you," she crooned softly to him, this, among other sweet nothings, willing him to live; trying desperately to pass her will onto him.

His respirations seemed to steady for a minute, but then he began coughing. Frothy blood spattered the front of her uniform as she held him against her chest. She knew that if she didn't get him into her rig and to a hospital soon, he would likely die. He had a collapsed lung among other injuries she couldn't see yet, and if he didn't get it corrected soon, it would likely start putting pressure on the other lung, and could kill him. She wasn't ready to lose him. Not until she had a chance to tell him how much she loved him! This stranger she had only recently fantasized about.

They had met several years ago when she and her boyfriend had first moved to Elk Creek, while they were both working a nasty accident scene. There were patients everywhere, each one calling out for help, for relief from the pain and fear they were suffering with. This officer had her entire scene controlled, and gave her a report of each patient, suggesting which one was the most critical, and who could wait a minute. He helped her and her partner load them into the ambulance and stayed behind to help with the second-out ambulance as well. It was something she had never seen before from a cop.

She had gone out of her way to thank him for his help, and to help inter-agency relationships. She had noticed the agencies seemed vastly separated in their willingness to work together, and that was a shame - they were all brothers and sisters out here. Taking him in a thank-you card after the rig was put back in order, and giving him a nervous handshake, she gave him a shy smile and couldn't help but feel a wave of panic as he opened the card in front of her. She hated when people read things she wrote in front of her! He gave her a lopsided grin and gave her a calm, "You're welcome," as they parted ways.

They had met numerous times on scenes and at the hospital, and she had grown fond of him. He was handsome and quiet, but had a commanding air about him. He had always treated her with respect, and that was an intense draw to her. Simple kindnesses were something she didn't get often at home, so when she found them, she basked in them.

Home wasn't a place she enjoyed anymore. Not with the abuse her boyfriend, Aaron, continually dished out. She couldn't do anything right in his eyes, and in turn, he made sure she knew it. He wasn't often physical with her, but it did happen. He did raise his hands to her, leaving welts and occasional bruises in places that she could hide with her clothing. It made it easier for her to believe it wasn't happening. That, and if nobody saw it, nobody asked questions.

She muttered angrily under her breath, "Roberts...you had better get your ass here soon...I don't have much time..."

She knew he couldn't just blaze in, lights and sirens blasting with bullets still zinging off the car they were hidden behind. She knew she had gotten herself into a stupid predicament, but she knew that she was the only one brave (or maybe dumb) enough to dodge gunfire and try to save this man's life. The other crews would have staged several blocks away, waiting for safety to be more of a guarantee before they went in, and then, they would only be doing body recovery while waiting for the coroner. She had nothing left to live for with an abusive boyfriend at home and all her friends and family believing his lies, and so, she followed the second wave of officers into the scene to try and save a life despite their telling her to stay behind.

Somewhere behind her, she heard the diesel engine rumbling. It crept closer until it was hidden behind a building, as close as it could safely get without the ambulance being at too much risk for getting shot. She knew she was likely going to lose her job for this, but at the same time, she didn't care. This was something she felt in her soul that she had to do. Leaving him to die was something she wouldn't be able to live with, no matter the risk. Her partner crept closer as law enforcement took their turn shooting at the barricaded suspects, giving him a single moment to get to her. His face was pale, sweat running down it in rivers, and his breathing was as erratic as her patient's, and he was shaking from head to toe.

"What's the plan, Meredith?" he asked, nervously adjusting the top button on his uniform shirt. He was looking around, fidgeting like a ferret about to be fed to a very large snake. For a minute, the bullets stopped flying from all directions. Meredith peeked through the only window in the police cruiser that wasn't shattered, and turned to her partner.

"You aren't gonna like it. Grab one of his drag straps, and I'll grab the other. We're gonna haul ass to the rig as soon as our guys start shooting again. Are you ready?"

Tim Roberts, who had only been an EMT for a few months turned paler than their patient. He violently shook his head, which matched the rest of his trembling body, brown eyes wide in terror. "Are you fucking crazy? We're going to get slaughtered! Haven't you seen any war movies?

The bad guys shoot the guys trying to drag the injured out! My insurance hasn't even kicked in yet…I can't do this!"

Meredith nodded grimly. "I'm afraid that's our only option, unless you want to watch him die. And if we don't save this officer, I'm going to remove both of your kidneys and feed them to you." Her voice was steel and ice, no room for argument. Tim swallowed hard, trying to put the terror away so he could help his partner with her crazy plan. She turned to the other officers. "Boys! Cover us! We gotta get him out of here!"

Several officers nodded and got ready. There was logic behind her actions, though everyone knew it was stupid and foolhardy, likely to get them all killed, but they were willing to cover her, so she was going to take advantage. She had to save him. There was no question about it in her mind. As soon as they began firing again, Meredith, Tim, and their patient, who was now moaning in excruciating pain, headed as fast as they could toward the ambulance. It took them a minute to get there through the dirt and sagebrush, but once they made it, Meredith knelt down to cradle the fallen officer against her chest again.

"Roberts…get the cot down. I can't lay him flat," Tim muttered under his breath about tyrant paramedics and kidneys but wasted no time in bringing the cot to the ground. Together, they lifted the officer, whose bloody gold nametag read, "D. Price."

Together, Tim and Meredith loaded the officer into the ambulance. "Just drive, Tim. Get us to St. Victory. I can't lose him!" The tone of her voice bordered on panic, though he could see that she fought to maintain control. Hard to imagine the tough, A-type personality medic that drilled him daily about drug dosages, treatment modalities, and where equipment was stored in the rig could be so close to losing control. He jumped in the driver's seat, flipped on the lights and sirens, and drove away in a hail of rocks and dust without looking back.

In the back of the ambulance, while bouncing in a way that would make even the most experienced roller-coaster rider ill, she cut his shirt up the middle, and then the straps on his vest. Removing the heavy Kevlar, she could see the bullet wound. It was red, angry, and still oozing dark red blood. At least there was no arterial spray. That was a bit of good news. With a forced sigh to calm herself, Meredith reached across him for an occlusive dressing to cover the wound with. This, she taped on three sides, leaving the lowermost side open. Every time he took a breath in, the plastic dressing would close over the hole, pulled down as his body tried to "breathe" through the bullet hole, and with every exhale, any extra air in his chest would be allowed out through the open side of the dressing. Perhaps a primitive piece of equipment, but extremely effective nonetheless. Next, she started the biggest IV she could get and got a set of vitals while fluids ran wide open; then grabbed the pneumothorax kit. She had always wondered why it was called a kit when all it was, was a very large needle. Meredith stared at it for only a second before she readied herself for what was to come.

With shaking hands that would not steady, she found the landmark she was looking for, and inserted the needle deep into the tissue until she heard a reassuring "hiss" sound. That let her know that there was air in the chest cavity where it didn't belong, and it had been relieved. At least for now. She watched the monitor, relieved that his oxygen saturation began to rise, and once she had a free hand, put a non-rebreather with oxygen on him to help him along. Part of her felt bad knowing she had just bought him a chest tube, but as long as he lived, it would be worth it. Besides, if she didn't put the needle in his chest, he would have died.

While any other time, she would have been excited to strip him, now it was only a methodical assessment that all of her trauma patients received. She stripped his pants by cutting them up the seams. She didn't see any obvious injuries there; just a couple bruises to his knees, and when she felt for anything abnormal in his lower legs and thighs, she didn't feel anything shifting in a way it shouldn't, and he didn't cry out in pain. That was a good sign. His hips were stable, so they weren't broken. She felt around his abdomen, and he winced a time or two, but she didn't feel anything obvious that would indicate a big internal bleed. She asked him to squeeze her hands, which he did, but when she asked him to wiggle his toes, they remained stationary. A wave of fear crashed over her that he was paralyzed, and there was nothing she could do for him. Had she done something wrong to have injured something internally? Should she have wasted time putting a collar on him? Or a backboard? That would have taken several officers out of service to help them carry him, but would it have saved his legs? She talked to him softly, letting him know she was going to roll him onto his side to look at his back. With only her in the back of the ambulance, she was unable to keep his neck stabilized, and so, felt his neck. He had no sign of injury - no bones were crunchy or moving, he didn't wince in pain, and there was no bruising. Being certain he didn't have a neck injury, she rolled him toward her and held him the best she could with one hand while the other hand felt down his spine. He had severe tenderness about mid-way down his back. She could see dark bruising that seemed to be spreading with faint purple coloration. He cried out when she touched it, letting her know this was likely the area where the bullet stopped. Rolling him onto his back again, she checked his pupils, and was relieved that they reacted normally, so she believed he had no head injury.

"Price…tell me when your birthday is. Can you tell me?" Her voice was gentle; that of a mother talking to a frightened child. She needed to be able to assess his mental status to see if he was alert, or confused; to see if he was even aware of what was happening.

"May...twenty-first...nineteen...eighty." He was awake, alert, and able to speak, even though he wasn't able to talk in full sentences. It was a start.

"Any allergies?"

"Penicillin. And bullets." She grinned. His sense of humor was intact.

"Are you on any medications on a regular basis?"

"No."

His eyes were still closed, wincing with pain at every bump they hit. Meredith pulled out a vial of Fentanyl and gave him a dose. Nearing six feet tall, and built like a brick house, she knew the dose wasn't going to take the pain away entirely, but being conservative, she didn't want to give him too big of a dose to begin with. It's easier to give more, and harder to take it away once it's in the body. After administering the medication, she sat beside him, her hand unconsciously running through his short blonde hair. He looked like he was resting more comfortably, so Meredith didn't give more medication, but kept the syringe ready just in case he showed signs of increased pain.

The rest of the short ride in was uneventful. Meredith monitored Officer Price's vitals and lung sounds with no major changes noted. The fluids ran into his veins as fast as they could go through blood tubing, and before they were half finished, they had gotten to the trauma center. Rushing him inside with the help of her partner, Tim, Meredith called out a loud report to a room full of nurses, doctors, interns, and about twenty other people.

"This is Officer David Price, a 38-year-old male hit with a bullet that ricocheted off his car. It went into his left upper chest area. I was able to decompress once and his sats and ability to breathe increased. He's still at about a two-word dyspnea. He's gotten fifty mikes of Fentanyl that took the edge off. Blood pressure has been soft, but stable. Allergies to Penicillin, no daily medications. He has been able to move upper extremities without difficulty, but unable to move his lower extremities with no priapism noted."

With that, the thirty other people in the room descended upon the man she loved, but had failed to tell. Tears welled up in her green eyes and threatened to spill over. An intern walked past her, and gave her a brief, pitying look as she paused her hurried actions.

"It's ok. We'll take good care of him." As if Meredith were only worried about who was taking care of him.

No, her concern was for the man she loved who was hurt beyond her ability to soothe it. Meredith knew she would kick herself if he died before she could confess her feelings for him. She was utterly helpless and could only trust that this hospital and God could heal him. She had never been a devout Christian, but she took a minute to send a prayer up that David would be ok; that he would walk again.

Behind her, she could hear the doctors calling out injuries, demanding a chest tube, a foley catheter, Type O negative blood for now, and a type-and-cross so they could match blood, giving his body the type it needed to function properly. They were yelling for x-rays, CT scans, and something about possibly intubating. Her heart dropped. Hadn't they gotten here in time? They were going to save him…right?

Chapter 2

Tim was ready with a clean cot and required billing paperwork by the time she had composed herself again. It was amazing that he was so calm, and remembered something as mundane as billing at a time like this. Her mind was in a whirlwind, every emotion but happiness was threatening to consume her. They walked back to the ambulance in silence, and it extended past her mopping the spilled blood from the floor, disinfecting and wrapping up cables from the blood pressure cuff, the 12-lead, and the pulse oximetry. The silence stretched to her sitting on the bumper of the ambulance and breaking down. The sobs came soft at first, and then like a bursting dam. Tim stared for a minute before sitting next to her, wrapping an arm around her shoulders.

He was probably the only one who knew what sort of a predicament she was in, and why she had been so impulsive as to run into a hailstorm of bullets to get to the side of a man she hardly knew except in fantasy. She had told him most of the gory details of her relationship with her boyfriend of nearly twelve years. He was the only one who knew that she had nearly died at the hands of a man who swore to love and protect her.

Several tense minutes passed and when Meredith had composed herself again, they loaded the cot and hopped back into the rig. Without asking, Tim drove them to the nearest Starbucks, knowing instinctively that she would need caffeine to get through the rest of the shift with some semblance of sanity. He left her in the running rig while he picked up some fancy coffee creation with a name he never would have remembered if she hadn't text it to him several times throughout their partnership.

With a half-smile, he offered her the steaming cup. She took it in her hands and stared at it, lost in a daze of her own thoughts. Tim had never seen his partner act like this. Not even the worst days of abuse had left her in such a catatonic state. He awkwardly looked at her, trying to find the right words.

He buckled his seatbelt, checked the mirrors, and headed back to base, where he knew they were in for one serious ass-chewing from the captain, who had undoubtedly heard about this by now. His heartbeat was erratic, and he was sure it from fear, and not from the double-shot something-caffeinated he held in his own hand.

"That was a hell of a call, Mare. I know you've got a lot going on in your head, but I think talking about it would help. I know it always makes me feel better to go through everything." Tim waited a minute, unsure if Meredith was even going to reply.

"What if he dies, Tim? What if I missed something? What if I didn't do enough?" Meredith's voice shook with an emotion that Tim had hardly ever heard from his partner. It was uncertainty.

"Meredith, you did everything you could. We have been partners for long enough now that I know what you are capable of, and I have never seen you only give a little bit. If he dies it's because it was his time, not because you did anything wrong."

"I don't know if I can keep working if he dies, Tim. I'll feel like his blood is on my hands," she replied, trembling as she looked down at her hands, staring at the proverbial, metaphorical blood.

"Meredith, look at me," Tim told her with as stern a voice as he could muster. Meredith blinked several times before turning her head to look at her partner. "You are amazing at what you do. Don't second-guess yourself. It's only going to drive you insane. Trust me. Believe in yourself and see what happens."

The rest of the ride back to the station was near-silent. Meredith did not feel like talking, nor did she feel like taking her partner's advice and look to the bright side of things. She knew, deep in her heart, that she had done everything she could possibly do for David. Now it was in hands far greater than her own.

As they entered the common room, they were assaulted by the raucous voice of their captain.

"What in the *hell* were you thinking? You not only disobeyed protocol, but you disobeyed several orders from our cops! You could have been killed! And worse - you dragged your partner into it!" Captain Stevens yelled, making no attempt to mask his rage as his fist crashed down onto the rickety table, an exclamation point to his statement. They had barely walked in the door after restocking their rig when they had been ordered to sit in the hard chairs of the meeting room.

"In her defense, Cap, I don't have drag straps, so she didn't technically drag me anywhere, but we dragged out an injured officer who would have died there if she hadn't been so bull-headed. He *did* have drag straps." Tim tried to lighten the tension in the room the only way he knew how. Of course, it didn't work, but it was all he knew to do.

"And you! You were dumb enough to follow her! If it were up to me, you would both be packing your shit right now! But lucky for you, the board suggested only a suspension pending investigation and formal decision. So pack your bags. You're both on unpaid suspension for a week, pending the board's decision. You will be lucky to still have your jobs next week." The captain growled this last threatening statement, ominous as black clouds before a storm.

Without waiting for objection, Captain Stevens stood up abruptly, sending his chair crashing to the ground behind him, and left the room, doors slamming in his wake. Tim couldn't speak, and opened his mouth like a fish looking for its next meal. Meredith stared at the coffee cup that was still in her hands and remained silent. Tim turned and looked at Meredith.

"That could have gone worse, eh? I thought we were getting shit-canned, for sure!" His charming smile did nothing to lighten the mood or to make his partner smile. He sighed softly and put his hand delicately on her shoulder. "Let's go. I'll buy you some dinner before you go home."

A shudder ran through her at the word "home." She knew she would have to face him. She also knew the punishment that would likely come from her being suspended. She was going to get beaten for sure - a week's worth of lost income was going to be hard to deal with. He was going to beat her, and if she were lucky, she would be able to walk away without anything broken. Aaron just wouldn't understand why she ran into the hell-storm to save a man she didn't know (or so he thought). He wouldn't understand why she would dare to risk her life and paycheck for "just a cop." He would never understand why she would be in love with someone else, because, in his mind, Aaron was the perfect man. He would hit her if he even thought she was interested in someone else.

Meredith stood up and walked with Tim to the parking lot. "He's going to kill me," she whispered, voice quavering between fear and desperation. "I'm going to die." She blinked back tears, not for the first time today.

"Mer, come stay with me until you can find a place. Or my parents. They have a spare room, and won't charge you rent. Let us help you! We won't let him get to you again." Tim spoke gentle and soft, knowing this was a delicate topic. "You don't have to let him hurt you. That's not love, Mer. Love doesn't hurt."

She shook her head slowly, soft red hair cascading loosely around her shoulders, having come free from the hair-tie she had in it. "He wasn't like this when I first met him. He was kind, supportive, and a true gentleman. I don't know what changed." She was hardly listening to Tim, her mind unable to wrap around the changes that came on so gradually, she was astonished to look back and see how dramatic they were.

"He got you, Mer. He got his claws so deep into you that you think you can't leave, and now he's showing you his true colors. He's a narcissist. Borderline psychopath, I'd wager." Tim paused, waiting to see if Meredith was going to come to the defense of her crazy boyfriend. He was relieved when she didn't try to defend the man who had left her bruised on several occasions.

"Maybe you're right. But I still can't leave. He'll kill me. He told me if I ever tried to leave him, he'd kill me before I could go to the police." The last big fight they had was several months ago. She had raised her voice when he didn't bother taking the trash out, or washing dishes while she was at work, and had the audacity to demand dinner as soon as she walked in. He had struck her with an open hand and left a red welt across her cheek. Before that, he punched her in the arm for something she didn't remember now. It bruised with a fierce intensity that lasted for several days.

"So why don't you go to them now? You don't have to tell him you're going."

Meredith paused, a look of epiphany on her face. "Tim! You're a genius!" She threw her arms around him and hugged him tight. "I'll go to the cops, all right, but not to all of them. Just one." With a sly smile, she got into her truck. "He'll never know, Tim!" She had probably lost her mind with all the stress, but she had also just stopped caring.

Tim was left standing in the parking lot, dumbfounded as her truck's engine roared to life and she threw it into reverse, headed as fast as she could toward the hospital. There were still several hours left of her shift - the overnight shift, and Aaron was likely fast asleep, or so deep in his video games, she could walk home naked with thirty prancing men and he wouldn't notice. With a little hope in her heart, she allowed herself a single daydream - leaving him and starting a new life where she wouldn't be pushed, or screamed at, or hit anymore. A life where she didn't have to hide her feelings or emotions; where she didn't have to live under the thumb of a man who couldn't care less about her well-being.

Chapter 3

Aaron had been a great man when she first met him. He was kind, caring, opened doors for her, offered to pay for meals, and rubbed her shoulders and feet after a long shift. It wasn't uncommon for her to walk in to a candlelit dinner that he had prepared himself. He would help her with the dishes, and that often lead to their hands entwined in the soapy water with him kissing down the side of her neck. He knew that drove her wild. And after that, it lead to the most sensual love-making she had ever experienced. He was absolutely the perfect man.

But as their relationship progressed, the handholding became less frequent. The kisses turned into blatant demands for sex. The dinners became less made by him, and more made by her. Chores were neglected, unless she did them all on her days off. It was a slow transition, though. So slow, she hardly noticed. Until she looked back and realized what she was missing. There was an empty feeling in her heart that she had ignored, and at times, filled with a tub of Ben and Jerry's finest chocolate ice cream.

She hadn't been allowed to go out with her friends as often, either, because Aaron was convinced she was out seeing other men, and as a result, her support group wasn't there when she came to this realization. She had also come to realize that when they had all hung out together, he had often dropped little comments about her "being crazy", or "overreacting", so when she tried to talk to her friends, they took on the same mindset - that she was blowing everything out of proportion. Aaron was fun to be around, paid for meals or drinks, and he always treated them with respect. There was no way he would ever be cruel to her. They started blowing her off, as she had been forced to do the same to them in order to please Aaron and his darkest desires.

Aaron had a dark side that nobody else could possibly know about. He was a great actor. He had everyone convinced that he was the perfect family man, and that Meredith was the problem. He convinced them that she was lazy, slovenly, and the world's worst wife material he had ever seen, but he was convinced that he, super hero that he was, could turn her into a woman he would marry one day. Her family adored him for this; for taking on such a "challenging" woman and making her

18

great. They seemed to have forgotten that when she was growing up, she kept her room clean and organized, her homework was always done on time, and she had always received top grades. She could have gone to Harvard if she had wanted, but she had discovered that her calling was being a Paramedic. She loved to be able to help people in their time of need.

His darkest secret, (even darker than being a narcissist), was that he was a swinger with a violent streak. When it was just the two of them together, he forced himself upon her time and time again. The only respite she received was when she was at work, and even then, he would text her and tell her exactly what he was going to do to her when she got home. She was forced to play along with his game, or else face the consequences. His favorite torture was to blindfold her, tie her hands above her head and use heavy leather crops on her.

When used correctly, they aren't so bad. He had been gentle when they first started this venture. He had made the suggestion that he saw it once, and was curious how it worked. They started with small things - a feather, a string of pearls, different sensations and different feelings. And then as they progressed, he brought in heavier items - light crops, a small cat-o-nine-tails, and then into heavier leather and scarier toys. It didn't matter how many times she would ask him to stop, or how many tears she shed, drops of blood spilled, or how she thrashed about trying to free herself, he would get more excited, more violent, more forceful. She had learned to be stoic. If she didn't cry out, he didn't get worse. Not that he was any gentler beforehand, but at least he didn't amp it up a notch.

She often went to work with bruises that were hidden by her uniform. She was embarrassed by them; afraid to tell anyone. Who would believe her, anyway? He had convinced them that she was clumsy and had a tendency to self-harm, but refused to seek help. He had convinced all her friends and family that she was only attention seeking, and that's why there were only bruises, instead of obvious cuts or worse. She suffered in silence most of the time.

Until her partner had tossed her a bag of saline that hit her chest just right and she cried out. Aaron had been particularly rough, utilizing teeth and hot wax against her the night before, and then striking her with a closed fist when she didn't react the way he wanted her to. Tim stared at her with a confused look, and she broke down.

"Whoa! It's just saline, Mer! Are you ok...?"

"It's bad, Roberts. You won't believe me. Nobody does."

"Meredith...you know I won't judge. Talk to me, and let's see if I can help you."

"You can't. He has everyone convinced I'm crazy. He beats me, but if I went to the cops, he'd kill me. You don't understand. It's not just that he walks up and hits me. It's about sex. He's violent." She couldn't meet Tim's eyes as tears poured down her face. "He does things intentionally to hurt me. I tell him to stop, but then it gets worse. I don't know how much more I can take."

Tim was silent for a moment. "Why can't you leave him? You can stay with me, or my parents until you can get a place of your own. Nobody deserves to live in a place that hurts them. Love shouldn't hurt, Mer." He had never been in a position like Meredith was in, but he truly believed it. Love shouldn't hurt.

She sniffled as a rogue tear slid down her cheek and then detoured across her lips. "He was such a good man when I met him. He changed so slowly, that I feel stupid for not noticing. How could I be so blind?"

"Don't feel stupid. That's what people like that do. They change so minutely, that it's impossible to see until it's too late, and you're caught up in their web. They use every tactic they can think of - manipulation, guilt trips, removing anyone who might want to help you; kicking your legs out from under you after tightening the noose above you… It's not your fault."

Chapter 4

Meredith blinked several times, and the memory was gone. She had missed the turn off for the hospital, and drove around the block until she found the lighted sign that read "Emergency Entrance." She pulled in and parked, staring at the dated building for a minute. What if something bad had happened to him? What if he was...*no*. She couldn't even bear to think the word. If he was gone, she would have no reason to continue. No hope of a better life, or of finding a man who might just care for her. She would feel the crushing reality break every bit of resistance she had left, and she would simply give up.

She had found herself slowly falling for him. David Price was a tall, handsome man that had every woman he came into contact with falling over themselves, vying for his attention, but he never really seemed interested in any of them. She wondered if she was stupid to think that she was any different. He had short blonde hair, the darkest blue eyes she had ever seen, and a smile that made her heart stop every time he flashed it. She doubted he had any idea what he did to her, but she didn't care. It was a feeling she hadn't felt in quite a long time, and she relished every single minute of it.

Meredith had just seen him a couple days prior. They were on a horrific accident where a patient had been ejected, thrown some fifty feet from the small truck, and the other patient pinned inside the vehicle with life threatening injuries. Alcohol bottles and beer cans littered the scene, so she was sure they had been drinking, and likely, partaking in other drugs. Alcohol meant the blood was likely to be thinner, and they would bleed more. This made any severe bleeding more of an emergency than normal. She worked hard to free the trapped person with the help of her fire department guys while another crew worked on the other patient.

Officer Price had stood back and was making sure nobody ran up to the scene, or attempted to harass the crew who was working to save to lives. He watched, amazed at her ability to control the chaotic event. Everyone was working together at her command, with nothing left in question. When she barked an order, someone jumped to attend to it. It was impressive.

They had met again at the hospital. He needed a blood draw from both patients to see if alcohol and drugs were involved in the accident, and if so…, how much. She took a moment after the patient had been somewhat stabilized and joked with Price about their superstition of using the word "quiet". Everyone in emergency services knows you don't use that word. It was like trying to eat a hot meal, taking a shower, or using the bathroom. You just don't do it because Dispatch knows, and when Dispatch knows, they send you on awful calls. He shook his head and grinned. "If I find out who used that word, they're gonna get tased. This is my day off."

They joked back and forth for a few more minutes before Meredith was able to get into the room and get the blood draw for him. She initialed where he pointed on the paperwork and then he was gone. Only after he left did she have a minute to look in a mirror. Her hair looked like a wild-haired Einstein stuck a fork in a light socket. It was everywhere and then some. There was sweat and dirt coating her otherwise plain face. She sighed and smoothed it out the best she could, knowing the only thing that would fix it was a shower and a very aggressive brushing, and maybe a small miracle.

She didn't know how she had walked through the hospital's front doors until the receptionist asked in a very irritated manner, "Miss! Can I help you?" Meredith started and blinked several times before she realized where she was. Blushing and nodding, she spoke softly, as if hearing her voice above a whisper would break her (and she feared it would).

"I'm looking for David Price. We just brought him in a little bit ago by ambulance?"

The receptionist tapped away at her keyboard for a minute and looked up, confirming she was in uniform and that it was for the local ambulance. "He's in surgery right now, but will be in the ICU once he's finished. I suggest waiting in the ICU waiting room. Second floor." She quickly returned to ignoring Meredith, as if what was happening on her computer screen was so much more interesting. Perhaps it was.

Meredith nodded and headed for the elevators. She had taken them hundreds of times when transferring patients to this hospital from smaller rural facilities. The elevator seemed to know her rush, and it took its sweet time, stopping at every floor from the sixth on down to the first. When it finally opened, she nearly bowled over several residents who were animatedly chatting away about some interesting case or other. A quick apology was muttered and she jumped into the elevator, jamming the "2" button several times before the doors groaned to a close.

It took an hour, she felt, to get to the second floor, but once she got there, Meredith checked in at the nurse's station, asking to please be advised once Officer Price was out of surgery and in his room. The nurse nodded, not paying much attention, and muttered that she would come fetch her once he was settled. It was going to be several hours, she thought, but it could be more, or it could be less. Meredith's nerves were so frazzled, she had to walk away before she said something she was likely to regret once she was calmer.

Meredith took a seat and stared out the window. The last of the sunlight had faded. The clock on the wall ticked its way past 10:00. She had only been on shift for four hours. It felt like an eternity since they had gotten the call, had responded, gotten suspended, and that she found herself here. Her stomach tied itself in knots with anxiety. What was going to happen? Was he ok? Would he walk again? Her mind began its panicked spiraling out of control again, and Meredith didn't realize she was rocking back and forth until a little old lady sat down next to her and placed a wrinkled hand on her knee.

"First time in the ICU, isn't it, dear?"

Her voice was warm and comforting; exactly the way a grandmother's voice should sound when speaking with a child. Her eyes held the wisdom of all her years, and there was a mirth deep inside them that seemed out of place for such a dismal, depressing room. The waiting room itself seemed to suck the color out of everything but this lady's eyes. The curtains were a dingy tan, and the faded carpet used to be blue with purple and darker blue patterns, but now just showed the walking path for nervous, pacing families.

Meredith jumped and turned toward her, nodding as an apologetic smile came to her dry lips. "Yeah. A friend of mine is in surgery, and he'll be here as soon as he's out. He got shot. The bullet collapsed his lung. I'm really worried, he wasn't able to move his toes. What if he's paralyzed? Or worse! What if he dies? I couldn't bear it."

The old lady listened as Meredith's words came out in a mad rush. "God will do what's best for him, no matter what it is, and with a friend like you, I'm sure no matter what happens, he will be in good hands." She paused. "My husband is here too. He's dying. It's hard to know that the person you've loved for over fifty years will be gone one day. But I trust in my faith. I know that one day, I will see him again when I get to the pearly gates, and we will both be young again. He won't have to worry about cancer and organ failure, and I won't have bad knees and eyes." She smiled a dreamer's smile as her eyes closed, imagining that reunion, ignoring the pain that would come before it.

Meredith hung her head, feeling guilty that she was worried about whether or not Price would walk again when this woman's husband was going to die. "I'm sorry. You must think I'm insensitive and foolish."

The old woman chuckled softly and shook her head, silver hair catching the fluorescent lights and glittering like snow-covered diamonds. "Of course not. We all face our challenges, and there isn't one that is greater than another. I imagine you have never dealt with anything like this before, and I have been here for the past several years, on and off. Charlie is such a brave, strong soul, but he's tired. I imagine your friend will be strong and brave, too. Just be there for him. He's bound to have good days and bad days where he wants to yell and stomp his feet, and days where he just wants to sulk and stare out the window. Listen to what he's telling you, and pay attention to what he's not, and I'm sure you'll be just fine. And if you believe in God, say a prayer or two for him. It helps." She smiled a knowing smile.

"Meredith Thomas?"

Meredith jumped up as a nurse called her name. "I'm sorry, ma'am. I have to go." The old lady smiled and struggled to her feet, hugging Meredith with arms that were stronger than she would have thought, then shooed her toward the nurse who had a soft expression of understanding. It was unclear if she had felt the pain of the waiting room, or if she had worked here long enough to know what people went through.

"He's out of surgery and in his room. We still have him on a ventilator, and there are several wires connected to him. I don't want you to be surprised." This nurse was kind and soft, leading Meredith through the hall toward the room that would reveal everything. She didn't have the harried look of someone with too many patients and not enough hands. She looked relaxed and calm, and exuded an air of confidence. Meredith relaxed slightly despite the fact that her heart was still racing, and her stomach was still tied in several knots.

"How is he?" the apprehension was evident in her voice, however.

"He's stable for now. The doctor put in a chest tube, and the surgeon was able to repair a bone in his back that the bullet hit. A fragment struck the spinal cord. We aren't going to know the extent until we are able to wake him up after we stop the sedation and take the breathing tube out, though the report says the cord looked good. But for now, we're leaving him on the vent so we can manage his pain, and give his spine some time to heal before he starts moving about."

Meredith exhaled, unaware that she had been holding her breath. They passed several rooms with patients groaning in pain, or on ventilators with the mechanical sounds seeming louder than they should have. Several rooms reeked of old urine, and Meredith wondered why, in an ICU, they didn't clean it or do something about it. She wrinkled her nose and kept walking. The rest of the hallway smelled faintly of a lemon cleaner that did nothing to mask the smell of sickness. It was disconcerting, but it seemed like a good distraction if you were looking for one.

Finally, they got to a dimly-lit room with chipped and worn white tiles, old, yellowed shades were pulled down over the window, giving the room a claustrophobic feel. The ventilator made its woosh noises as it breathed for the man she didn't recognize lying in the bed. Every time she had seen him, he had been strong, brave, and very much alive. His blue eyes twinkled and had little wrinkles that proved he was a happy-go-lucky man. They had shared jokes and conversations in passing, and had been on hundreds of scenes together. He wasn't supposed to be like this. This wasn't right...this couldn't be the same man. She paused and the nurse put a hand on her shoulder in an attempt to reassure her, or stop her from running...she wasn't sure which. Meredith steeled herself with a heavy breath and walked the rest of the way in, pulling up a chair next to the bed. She looked at the LCD screens, monitoring his vitals, his heart, his breathing, and arterial line readings. The arterial line was better able to monitor all of his vitals in real time, instead of there being a delay. Nothing was alarming, so that was a good sign.

She slipped her slender fingers into Price's cold hand and sat there, uncertain. The nurses had all silently left the room, so it was just her, Price, and the machines. Unconsciously, her thumb stroked the back of his hand.

"Hey Price. It's Thomas. I don't know if you can hear me, but I wanted you to know that you're not alone. You were shot, and we dragged you out to bring you to St. Victory. They said the bullet went through your lung and hit your back, but they say you're gonna be ok." She knew it was probably a lie, but what else was she supposed to say? "I got suspended for a week, but it was the best thing I've ever done with my life. I'd do it again if I had the chance to do it over, though I think if I knew it was going to happen, I'd tell you not to go in." Her voice was fierce, but soft. She wanted him to know that she regretted nothing. Even if it meant getting another beating once she got home. "I'm sorry I couldn't do more for you. But with my suspension, I will be here every night until it's over. I hope you'll be home before then, resting comfortably without nurses harassing you every hour." She smiled ruefully to herself, knowing he wouldn't be home any time soon. Not after the trauma he sustained. At this point, she was mainly just talking to ease her nerves. She was afraid of the silence, scared it would press too hard down on her and force her to break down again.

A slew of nurses came in and tried to make her leave. "Visiting hours were over several hours ago. We extended you special courtesies because you're in uniform. But he needs his rest."

Meredith shook her head. "I can't come during the day, and I don't want him to be alone. Please. He has no other family, or they would be here. I don't want him to wake up without a familiar face, and have no idea what happened to him. You won't even know I'm here, and I'll let him rest. I promise."

The charge nurse pursed her lips and looked like she was about to forcibly remove her, but changed her mind with the desperate tears that welled up in Meredith's green eyes. "I had better not hear a peep from you, or you're gone. Do you understand?" Meredith smiled and nodded enthusiastically, but didn't say a word as the charge nurse turned and left the room.

"You hear that, Price? They're going to let me stay with you at night. But you need to get some rest. I'll be here watching over you."

Chapter 5

They were at a Halloween party, her and Aaron and about a hundred strangers. Everyone was in costumes ranging from skimpy to elaborate. Their hostess was in a gorgeous Victorian era dress, and her host was in similar era, but a man's suit. She had only been with Aaron for about a year when he started this new thing - swinging. She had never heard of it before, having been raised by a fairly conservative family. She didn't even get "the talk" until school determined they were old enough to learn about the birds and the bees.

Aaron had dressed her in a "sexy fireman" outfit that was barely long enough to cover her butt. She was extremely uncomfortable, but thought the compliments he gave her made it better. He told her how amazing it made her look, and with the heels she was wearing, made her legs look unbelievable. He had a hard time keeping his hands off her, and that's what she thought love was supposed to be. She was enjoying the attention from him, and for a minute, felt even better about the costume.

They walked into the room and all eyes turned to her. If it had been a cartoon, there would have been wolf-whistles and eyes popping out of heads. She pressed herself closer to Aaron, who was dressed as a plain old boring fireman. She never did understand why he forced her to dress up like this when he didn't bother. She chalked it up to he just wasn't interested in the holiday, but wanted her to enjoy it. She wished she would have known the real reasons behind his behaviors. Maybe she would have left him sooner, before the emotional damage could really take hold.

They sat down at the bar and ordered drinks and snacks. The bartender was a vivacious black woman with beautiful hair and a dazzling smile. Meredith immediately took to her, and they stayed chatting while Aaron went off, likely to go find a couple he could snag with Meredith as bait. It was always the thrill of the chase for him, seeing who he could get interested in her. He usually went for the guys with the hottest wives, because how could he possibly be with someone less than a 10? It was a travesty to even think about it.

Several minutes into a simulating conversation, Aaron tapped Meredith on the shoulder with a couple in tow. The man looked to be nearly fifty, but the wife was a *beautiful maybe forty-something. She was fit and absolutely stunning, and Meredith could see why Aaron was interested. He held a hand out to her, and Meredith took it, immediately whisked away to one of the rooms that were open for adult activities. She cast a forlorn look over her shoulder to the bartender who simply waved with a smile. The woman had no idea how torturous this was to Meredith. Maybe she would have done something.*

Once inside a small room, equipped with a bed and an overstuffed red armchair, they sat down and started talking about inconsequential things - their likes outside of the bedroom, dislikes, careers, families. It seemed odd that everyone was there for sex, but they feigned interest in life outside of such. Meredith was still uncomfortable with the whole thing, but didn't say a word. She didn't want to upset Aaron - she wanted him to love her for being adventurous, and besides, he wouldn't lead her into danger. He loved her! Maybe this was just his way of trying to get her to open up, to not be so shy. There had to be a benefit for her, too, or he wouldn't do it. Right?

More time passed, and with nods between the two men, Aaron went to the stranger's wife, and her husband approached Meredith. He gently led her to the bed in the dimly lit room and began to caress her. She looked in a panic at Aaron, but he was too busy doing his own thing to notice. She decided that he wasn't mad, so it was ok. Slowly, things progressed to undressing, and beyond. Meredith was uncertain, still, and confused. Why was this such an enjoyment? Wasn't it breaking their relationship? Weren't they supposed to be faithful to each other? Why was this ok? She swallowed down the urge to panic, and fought the desire to fight off the strange man. He wasn't doing anything wrong, but she was extremely uncomfortable, and all she wanted was to go home; to go back to when things were normal.

Before she could truly argue or ask him to stop, the stranger was done, and so was Aaron. The two men quickly dressed and spoke a little more, as their women got dressed a little slower. The rest of the party was much the same - mingle, drink, eat, look for candidates. Aaron exchanged numbers with several other guys before they left for the night. All he could do was brag about how amazing it was, and how next time will be even better because he'll have more freedoms at home when the next couple came over. Meredith sat in silence, offering an occasional noise to let Aaron know she was listening. She felt dirty. Used. Worthless. She didn't see how Aaron could find enjoyment in what they had just done. She felt like she had committed a sin so vile that even God wouldn't want her anymore. She resisted the urge to cry.

Once they got home, Meredith went straight to the shower, but she couldn't wash away the feeling of a stranger's hands and mouth, no matter how hot the water got. She shed a few tears for the dirty feeling, but even that didn't cleanse her soul. She must have gone through half a bottle of rather expensive body wash, but still, she could feel his grasping fingers on her; his wet mouth; hear his moans of pleasure as he used her body. She shuddered as she turned off the water, wrapping a towel tightly around herself.

She crossed the hallway into her room to find Aaron laid out on the bed. He was naked, and clearly waiting for her. She shook her head slowly. "Not tonight, Aaron. I'm not sure I'm up for it."

He sat up slowly and then stood, gently leading her to the bed. He pushed her onto it and removed the towel. "I wasn't asking, my pet." There was a dangerous look in his eye as he caressed her in a way he hadn't touched her before. It was a mixture of possession, guilt, lust, and a hint of love. She assumed seeing her with another man drove him mad, and he wanted to know that she belonged to him. He was gentle at first, her negative answers to his questions seeming to spur him on, faster, deeper, harder. "Did you enjoy that? Having other men look at you?"

"Not really...I'm not sure it's for me, Aaron. I just want to be with you."

He became a little hungrier in his movements. "You didn't like having a stranger desire you? You didn't like driving him mad to the point he had to have you?"

"No. I really didn't. I really just want to be with you."

Again, he became hungrier, and angrier, more possessive. It was to the point that he was almost hurting her. She winced in discomfort, and that only drove him further.

"Aaron...stop. That hurts!"

He continued harder until he was done, then leaving her curled up on the bed, bleeding only slightly, crying softly so he wouldn't hear. She didn't want to make him feel guilty, still believing that he was capable of feeling guilt, or any emotion that would imply he cared about someone other than himself. He left the room and she heard the shower turn on, hot water cascading down into the tub until he stepped in. She cleaned herself up and crawled under the blankets, pulling them tight around her shoulders. She had never felt so dirty in all her life. What was she getting herself into?

Once Aaron got out of the shower and crawled into bed, Meredith tried to talk to him about it, to tell him she couldn't do that anymore. It was wrong and a severe invasion of what should be private between a man and his girlfriend.

"I think we just haven't found the right couple yet. Once we do, you'll really like it. You'll see," he gently chided as his head nestled deeper into his pillow. Within minutes, he was softly snoring, and Meredith stared at him, in shock that he could sleep so well after that train wreck of a night.

Chapter 6

A monitor shrilly beeping pulled her from this most recent memory (or perhaps nightmare). Her eyes widened and she looked at the monitors, trying to decipher what it was that was making noise. A nurse came in and silenced the alarm in a nonchalant manner.

"Is he ok? What was that? I must have dozed off and didn't see what alarmed."

This nurse was not the same one who had led her to the room. She seemed harried, busy, and not wanting to answer questions, but she paused just long enough to do just that. "The vent alarmed. He's over-breathing it a little. It's no big deal. We'll just increase his sedation and pain control to keep him comfortable. It's not uncommon...just means he's strong and fighting the medications."

Meredith sat there on high alert, staring at the numbers as they changed on the monitor. She watched the nurse as she punched a few buttons on a pump, and adjusted a couple settings on the ventilator. Everything seemed to even out and the machines stopped their alarms. Meredith was able to relax in her chair and watch the easy respirations of David Price.

"It looks like she got the machines straightened out now. I bet you'll be able to rest easy. You do just that, and I'll keep watch over you." She again nestled her hand under his, studying them. They were large by comparison. Scars on his knuckles - she imagined he did mechanics on his off days. She smiled as she imagined him in an oil-soaked tank top, drinking a beer while staring under the hood of his truck. He was a man - of course he had a truck. He would be tinkering around, fine-tuning it so it ran smoother. Or whatever men did when they were tinkering under the hoods of their trucks. Admittedly, she had no idea. She was lucky she was able to change a flat.

Her hands had taken on a will of their own, and she found herself rubbing his right shoulder and chest, doing anything she could just to touch him. Her heart ached for him, wanting desperately to talk to him, to make sure he was as comfortable as he could be. She knew that no matter what she did, he was going to be in pain. For one, he had a foley catheter in his bladder, a chest tube in place, and a spinal surgery. All she wanted to do was soothe his hurts.

An hour or two passed before she knew it, and Meredith found herself resting her head on the bed near his arm. She could smell his deodorant mixed with blood, iodine, and sweat. It didn't take long for the adrenaline dump to wear through her system, and she was asleep. It was a fitful sleep, full of nightmares and restlessness.

When her eyes opened again, the first rays of morning light were filtering into the room. In a panic, she jumped out, finding all the tight muscles and kinks in her neck, and searching for a clock. It read 5am. She sighed in relief and sat back down for a minute and tried to work the knots out of her stiff neck. Sleeping hunched over like that was not the most comfortable.

"Morning, Price. I need to get going in just a little bit if I'm going to get home on time. I may already be in trouble, but you don't worry about that. I'll be alright. You just focus on getting better, and I'll be back tonight to see you."

Meredith sat there for a few more minutes, stroking his hair and murmuring softly to him. Moments later, a uniformed officer walked in and stopped mid-step, surprised to see someone else in the room. Meredith blushed furiously and ducked her head. She wasn't expecting to get caught leaving the room, especially by an officer that obviously knew David.

"I was…just leaving. Thought I'd stay with him, being suspended and all."

The on-coming officer shook his head and grinned. He seemed to sense her emotions, but didn't say anything about it. He merely shook her hand on the way out and took up the post at Price's bedside. Meredith was thankful that she didn't have to explain herself to him. It felt awkward enough that she was here and wasn't family. Meredith felt like she had been caught doing something naughty at school, despite having done nothing wrong. She took her time entering the elevator and walking to her truck, letting the night replay in her mind as she climbed into her car, taking several minutes to just breathe, trying to decompress.

The drive home was especially painful despite the warm sunlight and cloudless sky. Her mind kept up its ridiculous, out-of-control pace, and it took all her concentration just to keep her truck between the lines. Even when she ran calls all night, she was never this tired. She didn't know how she was going to explain things to Aaron when she got home, but hopefully, she wouldn't have to.

Pulling her truck into the drive, she turned it off and sat there for a minute, staring at the two-bedroom, white-with-red-shutters house with the wood fence surrounding it. Steeling herself, she got out, gathered her bag and headed inside. Aaron was still in bed, thankfully. Meredith set her bag down, and headed into the bathroom to shower away the night and crawl into bed. The hot water hit her, but didn't wash away the memories of the night before. She wanted to succumb to the emotions and lose control, but at the risk of Aaron coming in and asking questions…she choked down the hysteria.

After showering, Meredith crossed the hallway into her room and slid under the sheets. Aaron was awake and rolled over to begin touching her. Meredith stiffened. She knew she wasn't in the mental state of mind to deal with his abuse today. Especially when she was already at risk of serious punishment if he found out she was suspended. She was afraid her body would break if he did anything else against her - raised a hand, or attempted to force himself on her. She just knew she would crack in half and die.

"You're warm. Come here and warm me up." Aaron's sleepy voice was sultry and thick. Meredith obeyed and moved closer to his prying hands.

"I had a pretty hard night, Aaron. One of our officers got shot and we wound up taking care of him. It was a long night." She hoped that this would be enough of an explanation to why she wasn't interested, but she knew that once he was, he had no "off" switch.

He paused a moment. "I'm sorry to hear that." But he didn't stop his searching hands from pawing at her breasts, slipping lower to her stomach, and finally, to that little place that she normally enjoyed having touched. Once he found what he wanted, he continued on until unwillingly, her body betrayed her. He smiled and moved so that he could enjoy himself, slowly sliding himself into her. To her surprise, he was gentle, much like he was in the beginning of their relationship. She wanted to weep with relief, but held it together - barely. He even had the grace to hold her afterwards while she fell into a fitful sleep.

Nightmares terrorized her for the few hours she slept, each one worse than the last. She dreamt that Price died, that it was her fault for not moving fast enough, for not putting a collar on his neck, and for not putting him on a backboard. She watched him bleed out in front of her, his depthless blue eyes full of blame and cold hatred. The next one, Aaron found out about her suspension and beat the hell out of her. He was ruthless and cruel, telling her how she was no good, that she would never amount to anything, and that he only stayed with her out of pity.

He hit her again and again, until she could feel her body breaking beneath his hands. She woke up crying from that one, looking around the room with her hands raised defensively for the next blow to fall. When it didn't, she laid back down. She was in a cold sweat and figured that she wasn't going to be able to get back to sleep after that. Meredith laid in bed for a time after, trying to calm her thoughts; trying to convince her stomach it didn't need to be in a knot, that she didn't need to vomit. She tried to tell herself that it didn't matter if Price lived or died - he wasn't hers to worry about. She tried to tell herself that Aaron wasn't going to hit her again, and that he wouldn't find out about her suspension. She knew all of these things were lies, but still, she tried.

Slowly, she got up and stretched, trying to decide what to do with the rest of her afternoon. Aaron was busy with doing his own thing outside, so Meredith went into the kitchen to make lunch. She settled on some macaroni and cheese and a ham sandwich. She made one for Aaron too, and peeked her head out the door to yell at him to come eat. She sat down to her lunch and began eating. She was still in a daze, trying to understand everything that had happened over the past few hours. She had been at the station a short time, had done rig checks and was settling in to work on some studying. She enjoyed going over protocols when she had down-time to ensure she was ready for whatever call came next. The tones dropped for a standby of a barricaded suspect with hostages. They had thrown on their tactical vests and headed to the staging area. Radio traffic had screamed about an officer down, and she wasted no time in jumping out and running closer. The officers who were furthest back told her to stay away, it wasn't safe. She could see an officer lying on the ground. He wasn't moving. She ignored their commands and ran in through a hail of gunfire that wasn't aimed at her and found it was the same officer she was slowly falling for. They got him out of the scene and to St. Victory. He survived the surgery and the night.

Meredith was anxious to get back to him. She had to see for herself that he was still alive, that he was ok. She still had several hours before she could leave "for work," so after eating, she cleaned up her spot at the table and started to sweep up the kitchen; anything to keep her hands and mind busy. Aaron had just walked in and sat down to eat.

Chapter 7

"I think I almost got that old car ready to start."

Aaron had been working on an old project car for several months now, and was hoping to have it running by the end of the summer.

"Just a few more tweaks and things, and I'm ready to try it." He grinned.

He was an extremely handsome man when he wasn't trying to break her spirit. He had dark brown hair and darker eyes, a strong chest, and arms that would be better suited on a knight in shining armor than this asshole. But they used to comfort her, protect her from her demons, and all the evils of the world. It was times like this that Meredith remembered why she fell in love with him in the first place. He looked so harmless.

She smiled and moved to the back of his chair, rubbing his neck and shoulders.

"I'm glad to hear it. I know it's been one hell of a project for you. Maybe we can cruise it soon."

She was excited to see the old car on the road again. She had never really been a car person, but it would be nice when that project was over and he didn't have to stress over it. That was a source of contention in their relationship. When the car frustrated him, he usually took it out on her, picking a fight just to get his anger out.

"I think I'm going to pack a lunch for tonight. I noticed my pants are getting tighter." She rolled her eyes, hoping he wouldn't notice that she really hadn't gained weight. He wasn't one to bring her food, but in the off chance that he got a wild hair, she wanted to put a stop to it before it happened. She was looking for conversation - anything to let her know if he had figured out her suspension. If he didn't question lunch, he didn't know about it.

"Yeah, I thought so. It's ok. We'll hit the gym and get you back in shape." He winked. Nope...he hadn't noticed that she was lying. She sighed softly, half in relief, and half in annoyance. Only a few more hours left until she could see him again. She put together a small lunch - just something to keep her going through the night while she sat with him. She didn't want to leave his side once she got there. After it was made and ready to go, she could feel herself getting fidgety, looking for something to remain busy until she could leave.

Laundry seemed like a good idea. There was a pile of it staring at her from the end of the bed, and there was a pile of socks and underwear in the bathroom. She wondered if it would kill Aaron to put his dirty clothes in a hamper, but had given up on trying to train him. She had decided that men were not meant to be trained, at least not by her. Maybe if she was more like him, and was half as good with a crop, she could whip him every time he threw a sock on the floor. She giggled at the thought.

"What are you laughing at?" Aaron asked with a quirked eyebrow.

"Huh? Oh, sorry. Just thinking of something dumb my partner said last night. We went to get coffee and there was a cop car parked in the spot behind the delivery truck. He was saying the cop was waiting for it to move so he could pull it over and confiscate the donuts." Quick thinking had always been a strong suit.

"I bet it was a fat cop too, wasn't it?" Aaron didn't much care for cops. Not since he had gotten a speeding ticket. Of course, he never did any wrong, and the cop was just out to get him. That's what he told the judge when he tried to fight it in court, and inevitably lost. Meredith forced a chuckle and a nod and left the room to gather the rest of the laundry.

Once the washer was filling, she turned to the sink. No matter how many times she washed the dishes, it seemed there were always more to do. She wondered if there would be a money-saving venture in just buying take-out every night. It would save on water and dish soap, dishwasher soap and sponges, and her hands, for sure. Aaron crept up behind her and wrapped his arms around her before sliding his hands down her arms and into the hot, soapy water. He twined his fingers with hers and kissed the back of her neck. She could feel goosebumps rising where his lips met skin. She didn't want to feel this way, but it was so nice.

"I wish you didn't have to work nights. I miss you when you're gone." It was the sweetest thing he had said to her in months. Unfortunately, she knew he only meant he missed having her there to have sex with. But instead of picking a fight, she leaned back against him and pretended that she was back in the beginning, when things were good. For a moment, she felt conflicted. She was supposed to love him forever, and only him...but she was also falling for another. Why was this happening to her? Had the bad days begun to outweigh the good? Before she could start thinking along that line, he kissed the back of her neck one more time and let go of her, pulling away.

"I'm going to finish that car." He dried his hands on a towel and left. Meredith felt like she had been punched in the stomach, unable to breathe. Why was he being so kind today? Was he on drugs? Or was he maybe just having a really good day? Was he actually a good man that she was misreading? Was she really the problem in their relationship? Was that why he was so mean to her? She began to think that maybe that's the problem. Maybe she was too independent and that hurt his feelings, and the only way he knew how to deal with it was to lash out.

The hours passed slowly, but she was able to accomplish much in that short time. The laundry and dishes were done. The floors swept and mopped. And dinner was in the oven. She had been craving lasagna for several days, and decided that today was the day to make it. A good, hearty Italian meal always comforted her. By the time she had gotten dinner started, Aaron had come in and washed his hands. He'd cracked open a beer and sat down to a movie before dinner was ready. Once it was on the table, they ate.

"Tomorrow. I think that car will be ready. I've replaced most of the lines, and the spark plugs, and fluids. I've looked at the belts, and most of them look ok, and the starter looks decent." He grinned broadly at this. "I think we'll be cruising her to car shows in a couple weeks."

Meredith smiled again. "That's awesome! I can't wait. Does that mean it's time to start looking at primer and paint? I'd love to see it a deep cherry red." She could just see it. An old, gorgeous red car and Price in the driver's seat, herself sitting in the passenger seat, wind blowing through the open window, her hair flying behind her, joy etched on their faces... Wait...where did that come from? She looked at Aaron, but of course, he can't read her mind, so no harm done.

"I was thinking black. A stunning dark black with maybe some metal flecks in the paint that will make it shimmer and catch the eye." Of course, he was thinking of picking up their "flings" in this new car. Meredith forced a smile to her face again and nodded.

"That would be nice," she said, flatly. She couldn't hide the disappointment in her voice, but luckily for her, Aaron wasn't paying any attention.

After dinner, she rinsed their dishes, put them in the sink, and put a big piece of lasagna in a Tupperware. It was going to be dinner after her sandwich and chips while she sat with David. Packing a few more snacks, Meredith set her lunch bag on the table and headed back to the room to change into her now-clean uniform. Underneath the scent of Gain detergent, she could still smell a hint of blood. She was sure it was just her imagination, but just in case, she spritzed on a little Victoria's Secret perfume.

With a quick kiss and the promise to be home in the morning, Meredith jumped into her truck and headed toward St. Victory feeling every bit as free as a convict who knew the law was looking for them. It felt like hours before she was pulling in to the parking lot. She moved to the back of the lot where she would have to walk further, but her truck would be more hidden. She took a look around, just to be sure there was nobody watching her (they were all too busy with their own lives to care about a stranger) and walked inside.

Chapter 8

The elevators moved a little more quickly today, and before she knew it, she was standing at the ICU nurse's station.

"Meredith Thomas here to see David Price." Her voice quivered slightly, but she stood tall and proud, an easy expression on her face. She was the picture of confidence, even if she didn't feel like it.

"Room 2113, on the left." The nurse didn't look up from her phone. Must be a good Candy Crush day, Meredith thought. She didn't complain - the less people that saw her, the better.

Quickly walking down the hallway, she ducked into room 2113. The curtains were open today, letting the sunlight brighten the dismal room. There was a TV on the wall, but nothing on the black screen. The ventilator was still attached and still humming along. The monitor showed his vitals were stable, and the numbers from the arterial line seemed the same as last night. There was an officer dozing in the same chair she had recently occupied, so she crept in and sat on the other side. She looked at the chest tube and saw that it had drained some blood during the day. She crinkled her nose, imagining how painful that must be. She had seen videos of how chest tubes were placed, and knew it was a barbaric procedure, despite its necessity.

The dozing officer snored himself awake and looked around, as if he had forgotten where he was. Meredith giggled and that caught his attention.

"Aren't you the girl who was here last night?" he questioned, looking her up and down as if that would tell him anything.

"Yeah. I pulled him off the scene. Got suspended, so I thought the best way to spend my days off would be to hang out. I didn't see a ring, so I'm assuming he's not married." Meredith was good at fishing, and if she were being honest, wanted to know how much of a chance she had with him.

"Naw. Divorced. She was a nasty bitch, if you ask me. Cheated on him time and again, drained his savings, and ran off with a dentist. Can you imagine? A dentist!" He curled his lips in disdain, shaking his head.

Meredith shook her head. Her own dentist had a receding hairline and Superman underwear that hung out of the scrub pants he just couldn't be bothered to pull up. "That's shitty. I couldn't imagine. Well, I'll hang with him at night during my suspension, so he won't be alone. Do you know when they're going to extubate?"

"I don't know a damn thing. Doc said something about wanting him to stay in a coma for a little bit so they could keep his pain under control. I'm not sure what that means."

"Got it. Sounds like they want to give him enough pain meds to sedate a horse, and if he isn't on a vent, he won't be able to breathe on his own because the meds would knock him out. Not a bad idea, I guess. I'm Meredith, by the way."

"Lowfield. Paul Lowfield. This guy trained with me way back in the day. I owe a lot to him. And to you, apparently. He'd be dead if you wouldn't have come in."

"It was worth it, and I'd do it again; just the same as he'd do for me if I were in his shoes." She shrugged. She had never seen herself as anything heroic - it was just her job. She did what needed to be done.

"Unlike this poor bastard, I have to go home and listen to the girlfriend nag that I was gone all day and didn't check in enough, and oh God, I missed a lunch date. You take care, and one of us guys will be back in the morning." He firmly shook her hand and grinned, rolling his eyes at the drama of his situation.

Once Lowfield was gone, Meredith sat in his empty chair. She took David's hand again and was about to talk to him when a nurse came in and began fussing with machines. She drained the foley "He's got good kidney function and making a lot of urine…that's definitely a good sign!" the nurse murmured to herself; and the chest tube: "Poor thing is still draining some blood. I hope he recovers quickly!" and did some neuro checks.

"He's pretty sedated. We don't really want to see any movement yet. Maybe tomorrow he'll be off the vent, depending on what the doctor says." It seemed to take her ages to pay attention to Meredith, who didn't mind being hidden in the background.

"You must be his supportive wife? He's a lucky man to have such a devoted woman to stand beside him through this. Not too many spouses will do that," she almost sounded jealous to believe that Price was married, warily eyeing Meredith, trying to look for a ring without being obvious about it.

Meredith was taken by surprise with the nurse's statement, and all she could do was shake her head. "No, ma'am. Not his wife. Just a friend. I don't believe he's married." She liked the thought of the word "wife," but she was supposed to marry Aaron one day. If he ever decided to propose, that is. He just wasn't the marrying type, he kept telling her.

"Well either way, I've been told you've got special privileges and as long as you're good, you're here overnight. If you need anything, please let us know." She left the room on her way to check other patients. It must have been a busy night with how fast she left the room, or maybe she was off to spread the latest gossip - the sexy officer down the hall was *single!*

"You hear that, Price? They're still going to let me stay with you. You won't be alone while you're here. I promise it." She stroked his hand. It felt dry and cold. Meredith pulled a blanket up and covered him with it. He shouldn't be cold, it was hot in his room. Was that normal? Should she tell the nurse? Did she just leave it alone? What if she just crawled in bed beside him to warm him with her body heat? She shook her head, smiling ruefully. "Quit daydreaming, girl," she told herself, as a warm blush crept up her neck.

The night passed slowly again with no major alarms or issues. She napped on and off, and was allowed to warm her lasagna dinner in the nurses' break room. She promised to bring cookies as a "thank you" for them sharing their break room with her. She returned to Price's side to eat, and then wondered if he was hungry. How did he eat if he was on a vent? Did he even need to eat? She decided that if he was only on a vent for a day or two, they wouldn't feed him, even through the IV, since he had fluids and things running. The doctors would want his stomach empty in the event that he needed to go back into surgery sooner than later, so he wouldn't have any sort of tube straight to his stomach to feed him, either.

Meredith pulled out her phone after dinner and wasted some time on Facebook and surfing the net for what the "normal" values were for arterial lines. It wasn't something she was taught in school, and she wanted to know that he was ok. She kept the page up on her phone after she had researched it. She looked at the art line he had in place. It would be there for a while, that way, they wouldn't have to keep poking his arteries to get blood gasses and make sure his electrolytes and things were normal. And it would keep a close eye on his vitals. All the numbers on the screen looked good, so she relaxed. She continued to look up injuries associated with a gunshot wound to the chest, and what could happen to the body with the velocity of the bullet. It did nothing to calm her worries, but she felt confident that because he had survived the night, that he would recover well.

"Please make a full recovery, Price. I haven't told you - how could I? - but I have a thing for you. Like…a lot. I want to be able to talk to you, to see you on scenes again, to know how you feel - if you feel anything for me. Please get better." She cooed similar things to Price as her fingers caressed the back of his hand, willing him to get stronger, to survive this ordeal. Meredith fell asleep to thoughts of "what if."

Chapter 9

Near the early hours of the morning, Meredith awoke again with nightmares. She reached under the blanket to grab Price's hand and found it notably warmer. To her surprise, she felt his fingers tighten minutely around hers. She stared at him intently for a moment, watching the steady rise and fall of his chest with the ventilator. He wasn't moving anything else, and he wasn't fighting the tube. His vitals were stable. Was it just her imagination?

"Price, can you hear me? Squeeze my hand if you can hear me." He squeezed again. "You're in the hospital - at St. Victory. They have you on a ventilator to help you breathe - you had some surgery to fix your back and lung. I'll let the nurse know you're awake, I don't want you uncomfortable with that tube."

He squeezed again when she tried to pull her hand away. She sat back down and stared at him again. His eyes were still closed, and he looked peaceful, but why was he awake? The medication he was on should have kept him in a coma for a while still. He wasn't fighting the equipment, and his vitals hadn't changed, so she thought that maybe, just maybe, he was ok for a few minutes. She reasoned that if he were in pain or severe discomfort, his heart rate would be steadily rising, and she would see different waves on the ventilator's screen to show he was trying to breathe on his own and having a hard time. It would show if he were coughing - a natural reaction to having a plastic tube shoved down your throat. He must be doing ok, then.

"I have to leave in a couple hours. It's about 4am. One of your guys should be here before I leave. Nobody wanted to leave you alone." He squeezed again. She let her imagination believe it was him saying he didn't want her to go. She smiled at the thought. "I'll be back again tonight, David. I'll stay with you at night until my suspension is over, and then I have to go back to work. But for a few days, at least, I'll be here with you."

She talked to him with idle chatter. Just enough so he wouldn't feel left in the dark. She talked briefly about wanting to leave Aaron, but not having the strength to do so, and the car she was hoping to be cruising in soon. She talked about the ice cream shop on the way to and from work that she enjoyed when she had a minute to stop and get a cone. She talked about wanting to have a family with a nice house, a picket fence, and a dog, and having backyard barbecues with the neighbors on weekends. She spoke about the way her mother believed Aaron's lies, and how her father had died when she was very young. The rest of her time passed quickly, and before she knew it, Lowfield had returned.

"Girl, you keep talking like that and you'll wake him right up." Paul chuckled, eyes twinkling with humor.

"He's been awake. Well, sort of. He's been squeezing my hands for a while. I need to let his nurse know to check on him and make sure he isn't in serious pain. Other than that, it was a very boring night, which was nice. How was your girlfriend's nagging?" she winked.

"Oh, you know. I was home late, and gone all day, and I forgot the milk. Same shit, different day. But she made a mean beef roast and homemade bread. I can't complain too loudly. Anyway, you go home and get some rest. You look pretty tired."

"I am. But it was a good night, I think. I'll see you tonight."

Meredith left the room with one last glance at David. He looked so peaceful that all she could do was smile and wait patiently for the rest of the day to pass so she could be with him again. At the nurse's station, she found the only nurse who wasn't so deep in her phone she didn't look up. "Hey, David Price has been squeezing my hand. I think he's awake. No other movements or anything," she reported softly.

The nurse nodded. "I'll let the doctor know as soon as I see him." She didn't seem too concerned by it, so Meredith left it alone with a smile and a nod.

Meredith left the hospital with a small sense of elation that Price still had neuro function intact. If he was able to squeeze her hand in response to her questions, that meant he was able to hear, understand, and respond. That was a fantastic sign. She could only hope that he had movement in his legs as well once the sedation was removed. The walk down to her truck was full of these thoughts. What kind of therapy would he need? Did he have anyone who could help him? He was divorced, and it sounded ugly, so no wife. Nobody said anything about kids, so she figured there weren't any. What about parents? If he had parents, they would be here, right?

The drive home droned on, and the events that followed were much the same as yesterday. She got home, showered, crawled into bed and had nightmares. They were less intense than the day before, and she was able to get a few more hours of good rest. When she woke, most of the chores were done from yesterday, so she didn't have much to do after packing a lunch for the night, and eating lunch now. She opted to forego the self-imposed homework of reading up on the latest medical studies and work protocols and put on some Netflix and catch up while Aaron was outside with the car, tools banging, and swearing loudly over the sounds of her show.

Nearing the end of her time off, she heard the old car start. First, it sputtered, and then it roared to life. She jumped up, threw on some shoes, and ran outside to take a look.

"Aaron! That's amazing!" It was idling a little high and backfiring, but considering it hadn't run in so long, it was a small issue. "I can't believe you got it going!"

He grinned. "Now all it needs is a quick tune-up to get it idling better, some tires, and paint, and she'll be good as new. We might want to redo the interior one day, but for now, it'll work," he said, full of pride that he had, with his own two hands, gotten this car running again.

They discussed the car for a few more minutes before Meredith went back inside, gathered her things, and headed out to work a minute early. She wanted an ice cream cone, now that she'd started thinking about it, and she was anxious to see if David was extubated yet or not. She knew better than to call and find out, especially with Aaron being home - he would want to know who she was calling, why she cared, and what business it was of hers, anyway. She didn't want to fight with him. It had been a good couple of days.

Chapter 10

Pulling into the back lot of St. Victory again, Meredith was floating on air. She had a few good days in a row with Aaron, and he hadn't found out about the suspension, and David was doing better. If things kept going like they were, she should be winning the lottery any day now. She nearly bounced to the elevator and pressed the button for the second floor. Entering his room, she saw a couple nurses making adjustments to the machines and fixing his tubes. She was also surprised to see that he had been extubated sometime during the day.

"Thomas! You're back!" Lowfield greeted her like an old friend with a half hug and a smile. "They extubated this morning, just shortly after you left. He's been in some pain, but doing well considering. They figure the chest tube will come out in a day or two, and then they'll see what to do about rehab."

"Rehab?" Meredith asked, excitement trying to creep into her voice and her heart. That was great!

"Yeah… he's still not able to move his legs. The doc says the steroids should help with the swelling, and that should help get him on track. After that, they'll move him down to a step-down unit, and then into a long-term rehab unit where they will focus on getting him back on his feet."

Meredith was devastated at the news. She had hoped that meant he was progressing toward walking, but instead, he was paralyzed. "Was it something that we did wrong in the field?" Her voice was filled with apprehension. This was her worst fear, that she had done something wrong to paralyze the officer.

Lowfield shook his head. "No. They said after the bullet hit his lung, it went into his spine, sending a piece of bone into the spinal canal. It was pressing down on the cord for a little bit, but that's what the surgery was for. To fix it and fuse the bones together so there wouldn't be greater injury. I don't know better details - it's all medical crap that's over my head anyway. But he should be back on his feet within six months to a year. They were pretty optimistic," he finished with a half-smile that put Meredith's heart at ease.

After a few more pleasantries, Lowfield left to return home, and Meredith sat beside David. He was just waking up and turned his head to look at her. A slow smile spread across his dry, cracked lips as he realized who she was.

"Hey you. You've been here for a while, haven't you?" His voice was raspy and rough, not the smooth baritone she was used to hearing from him. Even as it was, it still sent a shiver down her spine as she imagined what it would sound like if he told her he loved her. She imagined she would simply melt like an ice cream cone in June.

"Yeah. I didn't want you to be alone." Her own voice was sheepish and soft. Suddenly, she wasn't as brave as she had been while he was in a medically induced coma. This was different - he was awake now. He could respond to her thoughts. What if he didn't feel the same way she did? What if he told her she was just a stupid little girl with a stupid little crush, and she needed to go back to her dolls and toys? Could he be so cruel? After all, he wasn't Aaron…

"That's sweet of you. Pauly said you'd been here every night since I got here. Also said you did a damn good job dragging me out. Guess I owe you my life…so…thank you." His gaze was intense, his eyes even deeper blue than she had ever seen them. She could feel herself falling into them - stars and hope and promise; but she knew it would be for naught. She was under the thumb of a man who didn't see her as a person. She ducked her head again, lest she get trapped in those eyes forever.

Aaron's eyes were unreadable in the full moon's light. The stars littered the sky and there wasn't a single cloud to be seen. Everything was perfect, as it should be. They had driven up into the mountains to enjoy the view and maybe some nighttime action. They were in the bed of his truck watching for shooting stars. Her head was in his lap, and he was stroking her hair, murmuring softly about love and forever and promises that she had no idea he would never keep.

"Meredith, I want to marry you one day, but I want it to be perfect. Will you wait for me until we can have things work out the way we want them?"

"Of course, Aaron. I want it perfect, too." She smiled up into the darkness. The thought of walking down the aisle with a perfect man like this made her giddy and dizzy. She imagined an outdoor wedding with their families both in attendance; bright sunlight filtering through the willow trees. She knew that there would be butterflies fluttering about, and they would find a cousin or someone who could be the most adorable flower girl imaginable. They would write their own vows that would be heartfelt and unbelievable; something they could frame and hang above the mantle; something they would tell their children and grandchildren about one day.

Imagining their children was another thing that gave her great joy. She knew that they would have at least two. A girl and a boy. They would be perfect and would know how to cook, and change a tire; they would hold doors open for women and the elderly, and would have excellent manners. She would read them all the classic books that she had loved as a child, and would read them poetry. They would know how to use a dictionary, and have a vocabulary unlike any other. They would get into great colleges and have successful careers and raise families of their own. She just couldn't wait until life was perfect and they could try for their first child.

They stayed there for most of the night, until the sunlight began to crest the horizon. They went home and stayed in each other's arms for hours, curled under the blankets, listening to the birds chirp their excitement for the new day outside their window.

Only recently, Meredith had asked Aaron about having a child. They had been together nearing twelve years, and they hadn't talked about it in so long. He had told her that she was an unfit mother; that she was too moody and refused to obey his orders that were designed to keep her safe. That she was too headstrong, and in order to have a baby, she would have to be willing to follow his every word to ensure their child grew up to be safe, sane, and perfect. All she heard out of that entire conversation was "unfit mother." It struck a chord so deep in her heart, that she could feel it bleeding, and doubted it would ever be the same again. What gave him the right to say such mean, hateful things? She wasn't a bad person. She worked hard to provide for herself and for him, and would do the same to provide for their child.

She had changed the topic then, afraid if she said one more word about it, that she would start screaming obscenities at him, risking another beating. She was so angry, so hurt, that she wanted to lash out and fight him physically. She knew she would never survive if she ever raised her hand against him, even in defense, but the thought still made her feel better.

Chapter 11

"I was afraid you weren't going to make it." She glanced up, risking looking into his depthless eyes again. They were still staring at her, but there was something deeper than just a vague curiosity. It was closer to admiration, or maybe the beginning of interest. "You were in bad shape when we got you here," she admitted. She had feared that he would choke on his own blood before she could get him to the ambulance; that he would bleed out before they could get to the hospital; that he wouldn't make it through surgery with the extent of his injuries.

He reached out to grasp her hand. His was so big and warm, she felt small and weak by comparison. "If it wasn't for you, I wouldn't have made it." His voice deepened, full of gratitude and astonishment. He had never imagined that he would ever be struck down - especially when he was wearing his vest.

She couldn't stop the fire that was building in her stomach, slowly at first, like a match, and then exploding like it was thrown into gasoline. She was consumed by the moment as she felt a rush of bravery steel her spine and ran her thumb over his fingers. It was comforting to feel his strength, his vitality. She couldn't quite meet his eyes for fear he would see her vulnerability. She felt very vulnerable right now; like a kitten in the presence of a junkyard dog, not knowing if that dog was gentle or not.

"But you can't move your legs. I feel like that's my fault. I didn't do enough for you. What if…what if you never walk again?" She chanced a glance at him. His dark blue eyes reflected some pain, but he hid it well.

"It's not your fault. The doctor said the bullet hit my spine just right and a fragment went into the spinal canal. I heard Lowfield telling you the same thing. There was nothing you could do. And besides - they have me on enough steroids and things that I'll be dancing out of here in no time. Don't you worry about it one bit. I stand by it…well…I sit by it - you saved my life. I would have suffocated in my own blood if you hadn't stormed in and pulled me out." He squeezed her hand, and she looked up, surprised at the firm touch. "You're a damn hero."

"Price…I…"

"It's ok, Meredith. I just wanted to thank you. That's all." He smiled and slowly pulled his hand away. She almost panicked and grabbed it back, but held her composure. She wasn't sure if she saw disappointment in his eyes or not, but imagined she did. All she wanted was to hold his hand forever; to lean in, kiss his pale lips until they weren't dry anymore, and stay with him forever. But instead, she was a frightened child sitting beside him, desperately screaming in her head for his touch. Her mind reeled, wanting to know exactly what it must feel like to have his hands glide down her ribs to her hips, and what it would feel like for those same hands to grip her ass firmly and pull her closer…stop!

They spent several more hours talking about little things. His goals for recovery and returning to the police force, her goals of getting the car (now running!) on the road, and her darkest desire: ice cream. They shared hours of laughs and stories until he began to yawn.

"I'm sorry! I should be letting you sleep! Get some rest, I'll watch over you." Her voice was soft again; intoxicating; like whiskey and velvet. He smiled and adjusted himself in the bed.

"You're a guardian angel, aren't you? I'm dead, aren't I? What did I possibly do to deserve someone like you in my life?" again, his voice was full of wonder. She was amazing to still be here, let alone just checking in on him. Had it been any other medic, they would have dropped him off at the hospital and never thought twice about him. This woman was something special.

She blushed and ducked her head again, unable to hide the smile. "You put your life on the line every day. I figure the least I can do is watch over you while I'm suspended. I can still come tomorrow, but my days off…I have to be home. I'm sorry." The frustration and sadness was evident on her features. She didn't want to be at home. She wanted to be with him, watching his progress, making sure he wasn't lonely, or in pain, or hungry. She wanted to tend to his every need, but instead, she had to be home with Aaron, and tend his needs; a man who hated her very existence.

"What are you sorry for? I get it. I mean, I don't get why you'd rather be here than relaxing at home, no matter why you're off duty; but I'm not complaining either." He grinned. "I don't imagine my company has been that stimulating, you know, being in a coma and all."

"I felt like I needed to be here. I was…worried about you. I didn't want you to be alone and wake up alone in a hospital. Do you not have anyone who could be here with you?" she questioned slowly. She didn't want to dig into anything he didn't want to talk about, unsure of what other hurts he had in his past.

"I appreciate that, Meredith. Really. But don't worry so much about me. I'm a survivor. Take care of yourself, and see me when you can. If you want to, that is. And when you're not here, Pauly is around, or one of the other guys. I'm never alone." He didn't mention anything about family, and she stored that away for later. It felt like a sensitive topic for him.

She nodded enthusiastically in response to his asking if she wanted to be here with him. Of course she wanted to see him. She wanted to wake up with him and go to bed with him. To feel the strength in his touch, and to know the gentleness of his caress. She wanted to stare forever into his eyes, to untangle the mysteries that were just below the surface. Another brave streak filled her and she grabbed his hand again, holding it delicately, as if it would break if she were too rough.

"Get some rest, David. I'm here. I'll watch over you."

He smiled again, and nestled back against his pillow, making the final adjustments before his eyes closed. In minutes, he was snoring softly, body entirely relaxed. She imagined the pain he must be in, between the chest tube that hadn't been removed yet, and the surgery. The bullet would have likely done some severe damage to his body, shocking his entire system. The fear he must feel of not knowing for sure if he would walk again. The loneliness of being here without any family. She wondered how she would take it, and came to the realization that she wasn't strong enough to do it - she would give up. He was even stronger than she first imagined.

Morning came faster than she anticipated. With a heavy sigh, she stood up and stretched out her sore muscles, feeling several things in her back pop into place. She used to think the bed at work was rough, but after this, the hard mattress would be heaven by comparison. She yawned and picked up her bag as David opened his eyes. He smiled warmly and patted the bed next to him with his right hand. Meredith sat down, giddy with emotion.

"You stayed all night?"

She nodded.

"Thank you," he said, his brow furrowed. Nobody had cared about him like this. He wasn't sure if it was "too much", or "just right."

Meredith looked at him, and there was genuine gratitude shining on his face. He looked perplexed and confused that she had stayed, as if he'd expected her to run away in the middle of the night. She had told him she'd stay, and so she had. Besides, she didn't have anywhere else she could be.

"I'll be back tonight. It's supposed to be my last shift on duty for the week, then I have four off. I wish I could stay here with you. I don't want you to be alone."

"I'll miss you too, but I'll see you soon…right?"

She nodded again, not trusting her words. She felt on the verge of hysterical tears that she wouldn't see him for a few days, but then, there was still tonight. "I have to get going, but I will be back tonight."

"I look forward to it, Meredith." The way he said her name set her soul on fire. It burned so hot that she was afraid to look down and see herself turning to ash. She hadn't felt this way in so long, she had almost forgotten what it was to have someone say her name that way.

Before she could let her heart run away with her, she stood up gently and smiled, a promise that she would be back in less than twelve hours.

Lowfield wasn't back today. It was another officer that didn't look nearly as friendly, nor did he give her the time of day. She walked past him with her head down, hands shoved deep into her pockets and walked slowly to her truck. She hated leaving David. She wondered if there was a better way. Was there even a way she could stay with him? Sure there was - leave Aaron after first making sure David cared for her, and wanted a girlfriend. It sounded like his divorce had left a pretty sour taste in his mouth. But then, who was talking marriage? She shook her head, mentally telling herself to calm it down. She was moving way too fast, even for her own liking.

Chapter 12

Pulling in the driveway, she saw Aaron was already outside. She wasn't sure what he was doing, and had a pang of terror that he found out about her suspension, and was about to punish her severely. She began shaking as she stepped out of her truck and waited for the blow to fall. Instead, Aaron walked up to her, threw his arm around her shoulders and pointed at the old car.

"I thought we'd take a ride and look at paint for the old girl. I think she needs to feel the open road again. We'll get a nice lunch at that seafood place you like, and spend a day of it. What do you think?" his tone was light and airy, full of a fondness she hadn't heard in years.

She was taken aback - he hadn't found out about her suspension and the fact that she'd been spending her nights with the wounded officer? She thought about it for a minute. What if this was just a ruse to get her somewhere and actually kill her? Tim was the only one she had ever told about the abuse he put her through, and there was no way he knew about Price, or he wouldn't have been able to contain himself, and would have barged into his hospital room. She gave a meek smile and nodded.

"That sounds like a good time. As long as I'm home in time to get to work, I think it's a great idea. Let me shower and change real quick."

Meredith grabbed her favorite pair of jeans - the pair that made her butt look fantastic (Aaron thought they did, anyway, and frequently told her so, but he was biased), and a flowery shirt that she always thought made her green eyes stand out and sparkle in the sunlight. She jumped in the shower and hurried through it so they could get on the road. Once she was dressed, she combed her hair back and twisted it into a French braid. She always liked the look of her hair after it dried like this - when she let it back down, she had beautiful curls that framed her face.

Together, Meredith and Aaron jumped into the car he had just gotten running and headed up the mountain pass toward the city. It was only an hour away, so they would have plenty of time to get their shopping done, and whatever other bumming Aaron had in mind. She was excited at the thought of a good day with him - even though she was still conflicted about what to do about David. Maybe it was just a passing thing; a fantasy created over a shared trauma. Maybe that was all it was. She tried hard to convince herself that was it. Things like that happened all the time. People bonded over a horrific event, and then, when the emotions wore down, they were back in their normal lives. She didn't have to worry about leaving Aaron - she wasn't going to fall for David.

The drive up to the city was gorgeous. The sun was hitting the trees and mountain peaks just right, setting everything on fire. A red-tailed hawk circled overhead, probably in search of his breakfast. They spent time listening to the radio that sometimes picked up a station, and chatted idly when it didn't. They talked about past ideas and future plans. Most of those plans were about the car and how to finish fixing it up.

"Aaron…what do you think about getting married? We've been together for almost twelve years, and we had such beautiful plans." She was testing the waters, trying to see what his frame of mind was. Was he ever going to marry her?

"I think we should slow down a little bit. I mean, with your job not paying the greatest and my looking for steady work, I don't think we can afford it right now. Besides, I thought we had a good thing going like we are? I thought you were happy with what we have? Why change it?" He began to implement guilt tactics to make her feel bad, which inevitably worked.

"I am happy…I just thought you still wanted to get married like we planned." She knew she wasn't happy and never would be. Not with Aaron, anyway. She wasn't ready to admit this to herself, and knew if she admitted it to him, he would hurt her.

"I do, babe, but I told you - I want it to be perfect. And it can't be perfect if I can't give you everything you deserve. I want you to have that fairy tale wedding you've always pictured in that head of yours."

She sighed softly and looked out the window, heart breaking into pieces. "And what about our kids, Aaron? Are we still planning that? I'm not as young as I used to be when we first met."

He chuckled softly. "No, babe. We don't need kids. How would we be able to make trips like this with a screaming brat? Besides, I thought you wanted to have your career? You can't do that if you're a mother. Especially if I'm working too. Who will watch the kid? Besides…you said it yourself. You're getting older. What if you don't have the energy to keep up with it?

I can't do it all. Not working and raising your kid and doing everything I do."

More bullshit excuses. She began to daydream about David again, wondering if he'd want kids, and not lie about being "too old" or want his "freedom" more than happiness. Meredith began to imagine what it would be like to have a man who did his share of the housework, who made her dinner, who did what she imagined a partner should do. Her daydream continued until it circled back around to Aaron, and his inability to help her with the things that needed to be done.

Aaron didn't do chores all that often, and when he did, he made sure to text her pictures of what a "clean house is supposed to look like." He rubbed it in that she was inadequate, and always would be. She had come to the conclusion months ago she didn't truly want to be married to him - not if this was the way it was going to be, and she didn't want a kid with him if he was that disinterested. She would hate to saddle an infant with a father who couldn't care less.

"Maybe you're right." It was all she could say to keep the peace, tears welling up in her eyes.

The rest of the ride passed in awkward silence, but Aaron didn't see it as awkward. He was never wrong, and had merely shown Meredith the value of his "practical thinking." She was upset that he was acting this way - like his needs were more important than hers. There was no compromise, no offer of a "meet in the middle". It was his way and that was it. It hurt to realize she was with a narcissist, for that's exactly what he was.

Once they got to the auto parts store, they walked in together, hand in hand. She compared his cold hand against David's warm one, and decided that David's hands were bigger, more calloused from working, and were more likely to wipe away her tears than to point angry fingers at her. She imagined that he would gently guide her, instead of pulling her along to submit to his will, as Aaron was currently doing. He dragged her to the paint section so they could look at the available colors, dodging several sales associates on the way, who looked like they were desperate to help someone. They must work partially on commission, Meredith thought. She sent them all apologetic glances, half hoping one of them would rescue her.

"I really like this black. It's got the metallic flecks I've been looking for. What do you think?" Aaron asked, though he wasn't really looking for her opinion.

Meredith shook her head. "I still like a dark cherry red. Like this one." She picked up some paint that was close to what she had in mind. It even had the metallic flecks he was so concerned with. "I think this will really turn heads and make an impression at car shows," she said, imagining what everyone would say when they saw the car.

"Everyone has a red car, Meredith. This black will put us in the winner's circle every time." He wasn't going to back down, and the only way to avoid a meltdown in the middle of the store was to agree with him.

"Ok. Fine. We'll go with the black." She shrugged and put her hands in her pockets.

"Don't sound so disappointed. You'll see. It'll be perfect," he chirped, thrilled to have gotten the "validation" he wanted. She had to fight back bitterness at that word. Perfect. Like the perfect wedding they were supposed to have? And their perfect child that should be ten years old by now? Yeah. She was really fed up with *perfect*.

They checked out (she was stuck paying for it, of course), along with several tools that Aaron insisted he had to have, and returned to the car. She no longer saw it as something that would bring her peace, but something that was trapping her with Aaron. This car was a symbol of his dominance over her; of his self-proclaimed superiority. She would see the color he chose and forever be reminded that she had no say in her own life. She was a prisoner, unable to leave him for the binds he had slowly wrapped around her. She was *stuck*.

"Aaron...I want to be a flight medic. I've thought long and hard about it, and I think I truly want to fly."

"Why would you want to do that? Aren't you gone from home enough? Imagine all the schooling you'll need, and the trainings, and meetings, and you'll never be home. You might as well tell me you want to break up," he retorted with an edge to his voice that bordered on dangerous.

She stood there as if she had been slapped in the face. "I don't want to be gone from you, Aaron. But this would be a chance at better pay, better insurance. We wouldn't struggle so much. It could be good for us," she reasoned.

"We aren't struggling. We're doing fine. And when I find work, we'll be doing even better. There's no need for you to go back to school. I think the stress of it would be hard on you. Not to mention all the new things you'll have to learn to be able to use the equipment and stuff. I don't think you're experienced enough for it."

She was so hurt, she wanted to break down, but that would only prove his point even harder. Besides, what did he know about the experience she had? His experience was about how to lose jobs, not advance in them! "I looked it up. School is online, and I'd only have to be gone for one weekend at the end of it for the hands-on portion. Ground school is usually a week or two, and you could come with, since you're not working. You can hang out and see new places and explore new things. Maybe we'll even find an area we like better than here." She was excited at the possibilities; at the thought of a better life without struggling to make ends meet; at the idea of a new start.

"Why would you want to leave here? My family is here. Why would you want to leave my family?"

"Aaron, it was only an idea. Of course I don't want to leave you or your family." Never mind the fact that she left behind everything she knew so he could get the most amazing job as a mechanic that he only kept for a month before a temper tantrum led him to throw a wrench through the window of a customer's new car. His parents had moved down to help them with their finances until Meredith was able to work enough to cover their bills. Of course, he told his parents he was working, and that she was only "part timing" it for "spending money." If they only knew the extent of their son's lies.

"I mean, if you really have to, then go do it, but when you fail, I don't want you to come crying to me about it. I think it's a terrible idea. Besides, where will we get the money? We don't have extra for that!" Didn't he just get done saying they were doing fine? Besides…if she was the one paying the bills, shouldn't she have some say about what she did with some of her money?

"No, that's fine. I'll just put it on hold." She was visibly deflated, but tried hard to hide it. She didn't want to fight with him. Not now. Not ever. It felt like it was inevitable, that no matter what she did, it was never going to be good enough for Perfect Aaron. *"Forget I brought it up. I'm sorry."* He waved it off, as if he was doing her a favor by not continuing with the conversation.

Chapter 13

They headed next to Red Lobster to enjoy an early lunch before heading home. The conversation was upbeat, at least in Aaron's mind. He chattered about the car, about how amazing it was going to be when it was painted and had a new interior. He then changed the subject slowly to the same gripes he always had when he wasn't getting the attention he wanted from her - about his goals and wishes; that he wanted to open up his own mechanic shop so he could charge what he wanted and not have to worry about getting "stiffed" by his employer, and about how he wished Meredith would be a little better at housework, and help him, that he just couldn't do it all by himself.

She'd had about enough today. "Aaron…I do most of the chores. I'm paying all the bills. I'm not going to school because you want me home more; but if I'm home more, the bills don't get paid. I need some help. I need you to find work, or do something. I can't keep doing this!" She gestured as if "this" meant paying all their bills and keeping up with the house. She wasn't sure if it meant just that, or if she meant the entire relationship. Apparently he didn't know either.

"Are you breaking up with me? Is that what this is all about? You don't want to be with me anymore? I should leave you here and let you figure it all out since you're so fucking smart."

Meredith put her head in her hands, trying to steady her nerves. This was not how the afternoon was supposed to go. "I don't want to break up with you, Aaron. I just want you to help me like you used to. You used to help me with dishes, or make dinner once in a while. You used to hold me just to do it - no sex necessary all the time. You used to just love me for me. I miss that." Her voice took on a broken edge. She was at her breaking point; about to lose herself in tears. She begged herself to not start crying in public. She didn't need the spectacle. She was also desperately trying to get him to understand that she wasn't leaving him; all she wanted was help.

The argument continued as they walked into the restaurant and sat down, ordering drinks and appetizers. Once the waitress was back with their drinks, they ordered their meals. The waitress looked uncomfortable at the awkward air between her customers, but made a valiant attempt to ease the tension by offering specials and deals to them. In the end, they ordered their favorites, and waited for it to arrive.

Lunch was eaten in silence. Meredith knew Aaron was fuming, looking for a way to punish her in public that wouldn't land him in jail. She could see the cold hatred in his eyes, the calculating thoughts that he didn't try to conceal. She knew the ride home was going to be awful, but the thought of seeing David again was going to be worth it. No matter what Aaron did to her, she was still going to see the man she could imagine herself with for the rest of her life. She let her mind wander while they finished eating, about what the conversation would have been like if it were David sitting across from her. They would have compromised on color and selected something they both liked, and could both enjoy. They would be talking about redoing the interior, and about what car shows to enter. They would have discussed how to handle situations with their child in school - bullies, homework, sports. They would have laughed and giggled and enjoyed themselves.

Crawling back into the car with Aaron was frightening. He was completely silent, and she was tensed in preparation for the physical assault or verbal ear-beating she knew was coming. Except it never came. He remained silent and ignored her completely. Part of her was relieved to not have to hear him complain about her the whole ride home, but part of her was afraid of what was coming next. Was he going to explode once they got home? Was he going to throw her out? Would he throw her things out while she was at work? Why would he give her the silent treatment? It continued until they got home, and then continued some more.

Meredith changed into her work uniform, packed her lunch and her backpack, and walked up to Aaron, expecting a hug and a "good night". He didn't even look up at her. She didn't understand the angle he was playing at, and it frightened her more than his abuse ever did. She knew she was leaving a little early for work, but with the way he was acting, she was too afraid to stay at home and see what happened next.

"I'll see you in the morning. Have a good night, Aaron. I love you." But did she really? She felt like she'd reached the end of a long, dark road, and the sun was just beginning to shine again.

He remained still with no indication that she was even there. Her heart broke a little more as she walked out the door, a hot tear sliding down her cheek. Was this relationship even worth saving? Was she fooling herself into thinking that Aaron could possibly be the right man for her? She couldn't afford to move out and still pay her bills. She would feel too guilty about leaving him with nothing. What would he do to keep a roof over his head? Feed himself? Keep the lights on? There was no way she could just leave him with nothing, even if that is exactly what he would have done to her if the situation were reversed. But then again, he had his parents who could take care of him, coddle him, and stroke his ego. They would tell him how she was so bad for him, and how he never needed her anyway, despite the obvious fact that he did need her.

Meredith crawled into her truck, and put it in reverse. Her mind was speeding through too many thoughts at once, and she nearly hit the mailbox. Swearing softly, she corrected the truck's angle, and drove steadily toward the highway.

Before she knew it, she was back at St. Victory. She stepped into the elevator with a defeated air about her. She'd had enough time to pick up the cookies she promised the nursing staff, and dropped them off at the nurse's station. They swarmed like sharks around a wounded fish and dug in, thanking her with mouths full of crumbs. Muttering a "you're welcome," Meredith slunk into David's room. She ignored the same surly officer who had ignored her earlier and sat down beside David. She watched the nurses as they went about their business and made idle chatter before leaving to check on their other patients. David was grinning ear to ear when they finally left.

"Look!" She looked up at him, pointing at his feet. He scrunched up his nose and then wiggled his toes. "See?!" It was hard to not be just as excited - it was infectious, and the miracle she needed to salvage the night. She could feel the joy welling up inside her, threatening to pour out of her eyes in the form of happy tears.

"David! That's awesome! I'm so excited for you!"

"I know it's not much, but the doctors said with some rehab and maybe another surgery in the future, I should be able to walk again. He was impressed. Told you I was amazing." He chuckled, his deep voice full of life and happiness. Meredith's grin broadened and her heart was full.

"That, you did. So are you ready to blow this popsicle stand yet? Let's go, I got the truck out back." She never understood where that saying came from - "blow this popsicle stand", but it seemed fitting.

"Of course. Pull it up front and I'll just run down the stairs and catch up with you before the nurses even realize I'm gone," he chortled, an amused look on his face.

They shared a laugh and a couple eye-rolls. "You just settle down there, cowboy. Let's get you on your feet before you try to run away with me." Meredith giggled, and then realized how bold that statement was. It was, obviously, too late to take it back, but when David didn't say anything, she decided it wasn't too far. Good. That meant there was a chance.

"I thought you were married?" he asked softly.

"No. I've been with Aaron for quite a while, but things aren't the same, you know?"

"Ah. You lost the spark. Been there, done that." David gave a knowing nod.

"Not just the spark, but the whole thing. But it's not something you need to worry about. I think you need to focus on getting better. So let's stay on that, shall we?"

David wrinkled his nose at her. "Maybe that will help me to get better? Knowing more about you? Tell me more about your Aaron," he pried delicately. He wanted to know everything - she had hinted several times she was unhappy with him, but hadn't ever told him why. Not that he was able to ask while he was in a coma, but still. He was curious.

Clearly, she did not want to talk about him, having several fresh mental wounds that were deep. She was afraid that if she started talking, she would reveal all of his dark secrets, and that would be exceptionally bad for her in the end. "He's...great. A real great guy. Was a mechanic, but between shops right now. Has aspirations to open his own shop, but needs to get back on his feet first. Speaking of, how are we going to get you back on your feet?"

"I already told you. More medications, therapy, and maybe another surgery. How long have you been with Aaron?" David deflected the question about his own health and continued to ask about her life.

"Almost twelve years. Aren't you afraid of the surgery, or any of the complications?"

"And you aren't married? Any kids?" He was unknowingly getting too deep into questions for her. It was starting to break her down, little by little. She didn't want to shatter in front of him. He had so much else to worry about. Her eyes began to shine with unshed tears that she blinked back. No. She wasn't going to cry. If she started, she knew she wouldn't ever stop. She would sob uncontrollably until she simply died of shame.

"No. He doesn't want to marry me. No kids. I'd make a horrible mother, being so focused on my career and everything." She let her watery green eyes drop to the blankets as she picked at the fuzzies that were there from several years of abuse, blood, bleach, and washings.

David's strong hand covered hers. "I'm sorry to hear that. What an awful thing to say to someone you love. And for the record, I doubt you'd be a horrible mother. You seem like you'd do pretty well." He was able to pick up on the fact that Aaron thought she'd be no good at motherhood. David could see the hurt in her eyes, could feel it radiating from her broken heart. He wanted to heal her, but knew there was little he could do from his current position. Especially with his own heart being in pieces.

Meredith shook her head slowly. "I'm not sure he loves me anymore. I'm just a convenient familiar, but really. I'd rather focus on helping you get better. I'll be off for the next four days, but I'll be back if I can drag my partner in on my next shift; but is there anything I can bring you in the meantime? Reading material? Snacks? Strippers? Are they letting you eat normal stuff? Or are they keeping you on one of their fancy hospital diets?"

"I would kill for an ice-cold beer and a fat ribeye served up by a scantily-clad woman. But all I could really use is some company when you're available. Lowfield and the guys are great, but they just want to talk about work; about how the case is going, about taking down the suspect who shot me, about charging him and getting justice and blah, blah, blah. I'd rather talk about anything else right now. So that's why it's refreshing that you're here. You're happy to talk about anything else."

"Well…I don't know anything about the case, except what the media is showing, so that limits my ability to talk about it. Did the doctors say when your chest tube would be coming out? I imagine your lung should be healed enough to pull it soon."

He winced at the mention of it, fingers unconsciously reaching over to touch the protruding tube. "They said tomorrow, I think. I can't wait for it to be out. It's irritating and it hurts like hell. I can't wait to get out of this bed, too. I think my ass is numb?" He chuckled. He wasn't feeling much from the waist down, despite being able to almost wiggle his toes. Meredith rolled her eyes, but couldn't help but smile. It was good to see that despite it all, his sense of humor remained intact.

"I'm not sure there's much I can do about a steak or your numb ass. But I can stop by as often as possible. I'll see if my partner is willing to come by on the start of our shift. I'll see if I can sneak you some snacks in. Anything in particular?"

He thought about it for a moment. "I do have a weak spot for 3 Musketeers."

"Done."

The rest of the night passed with similar idle chatter. It was the sort of conversation that was meant for getting to know one another, even though neither of them said anything about it. They both knew there was something there; something hidden between the lines - but then, was it really that hidden? That didn't mean they had to act on it. For now, they were both enjoying the ride and the company.

The hours passed quickly, and the late hours of night turned into the early hours of morning. "You'd better get some sleep or the nurses are going to ban me from coming in again. I may have made friends, but that charge nurse does look pretty mean. Especially when she's not holding a coffee cup."

David grinned and waved his hand, as if shooing away the thought. "I'm not afraid of her...I know I could take her if I had to. Besides, she can't deny her patient what he needs to heal. It's unethical. Or something like that," he winked and chuckled quietly. While he was confident about his ability to talk his way out of any nurse troubles, he didn't want to test the limit.

Meredith laughed again. She hadn't been this carefree in quite a while. It felt nice to laugh with someone. How long had it been since she had been able to just sit and have a conversation that wasn't strictly about putting her down, or making her feel inferior? Too long, she knew. It was a dangerous game, this coming to see him every night. She knew her heart was slowly falling for him, and that wasn't good for her either. First, if Aaron found out, he would probably kill her. Second, who knew if he was even interested in her? Maybe he was just being polite by letting her stay with him. Maybe he was just lonely and needed company to keep from going mad, and there wasn't the connection she thought there was. Could she really be fooling herself that badly?

"Can I ask you something?" Her stomach was in knots, but she had to know. She didn't know how she was going to get the words out, or if he would answer honestly. She didn't know if she was going to vomit on the off-white tile floor or simply disappear from embarrassment. But she knew that no matter what happened, she had to try. She had to know if she was wasting her time, or if there was even the remotest possibility that he could be interested in her.

"Of course. What's up?" He looked interested in what she had to say. That was a good sign. Right?

"Is there...do you...am I..." she exhaled forcefully, trying to get her brain to cooperate with her tongue. "Does it bother you that I'm here? Is there a connection between us...or...?" She risked a quick glance at him, and couldn't decipher his reaction. Oh no. She had pissed him off. She had ruined any chance of being with a man who didn't seem like he would beat her. He was going to tell her to leave; to never come back and forget everything she had done. She was terrified of that look.

"It doesn't bother me one bit. I quite like the conversation. As for the connection..." he paused, causing the knot in her stomach to explode into trillions of drunk butterflies. She was waiting for the axe to fall now. He paused. That meant it was going to hurt. "I just got through a really nasty divorce. I mean, it was ridiculously ugly at the end. Do I think there is a connection? Yes, yes I do. But I'm not "there" yet. Does that make sense?" He reached out to hold her hand, but she pulled away, convinced he hated her.

"I'm sorry. I should let you rest…" She stood up to leave.

"Sit down," his voice was the perfect combination of firm and gentle. Meredith sat. "I didn't ask you to leave. You haven't done anything wrong. I'm just not at a point where I'm ready to explore any feelings yet. Stick around a while, and we'll see where things go in the future. I want to be fair to you, and I can't give you what you need if I'm still hurt and pissed about my ex-wife." He offered a reassuring smile and reached out again to take her hand. She let him. His rough thumb ran over her slender fingers.

His eyes were liquid fire when he looked at her. They were dark, full of desire, with a hint of fear. She wanted so badly for him to kiss her, but he had just said he wasn't ready. She could feel the butterflies becoming even more erratic as she imagined what that kiss would be like. Sultry, deep, passionate. It had already taken her breath away, and it hadn't happened yet. She knew the real thing would kill her.

"Let's just take it slow and see what happens," he suggested. His voice had dropped low, as if he had read her thoughts and felt the same way about that first kiss.

Her voice was almost inaudible as she whispered, "I really need to go. I can't be late getting home." She knew Aaron would question it. Heaven forbid a shift ran a few minutes long.

Price held her hand a little tighter before letting her slip away. His stare remained intense, begging her to stay, yet being afraid at the same time. Meredith had a hard time understanding it - he was so big, so strong, how could he possibly be afraid of her? She was tiny by comparison, and certainly no threat to his heart. She had no desire to hurt him, or as Lowfield had said the last one did, to run off with a dentist. He was the only one she wanted to run off with. She gave him a fleeting smile before she haltingly left the room.

Lowfield was just on his way in when she bumped into him.

"Sorry, Paul. How's it going this morning?"

"Hey Thomas. Good, I guess. Broke up with the ball and chain…I mean, *girlfriend*." he shrugged, rolling his eyes. "How's our favorite gunshot victim doing this morning?"

Meredith blushed again, afraid that he could see the night's conversation in her eyes. "He's in good spirits. Was able to move his toes a little. That's a good sign. Sorry to hear about your girlfriend. I hope it wasn't too devastating? Hey…would it be ok if I text you while I'm off to see how he's doing?"

"Sure. Give me your number and I'll shoot you a quick text. You know I'm here all day, and if I'm not, I can find out how Price is doing, no problem." He pulled out his phone and input the number Meredith gave him. He sent a quick text her so she would have his number, too. "And don't worry - the girlfriend was crazy anyway. Possessive and demanding I spend more time with her. She said I liked to hang out with the boys too much. Apparently she doesn't understand that cops have a brotherhood - we stick together no matter what." he shrugged.

"Thanks, Paul. I appreciate it."

Chapter 14

The drive home this morning was especially nerve-wracking. Meredith's mind was anywhere but driving. She nearly missed several turns on her way home, imagining what that kiss would have been like, had Price pulled her near, eyes closed, lips delicately crashing into hers…

It was dark behind the restaurant where Aaron had parked his car. The only light was from a distant, buzzing streetlight that didn't fully illuminate the area. In the distance, a late-night train blew its horn, causing her to jump. She was young and inexperienced, had never been in a situation like this before. They had met when her boss asked her and her partner to take the rig in for maintenance. He had been working as a mechanic. He was handsome, polite, and knew his way around a vehicle. It had impressed her to the point where she talked to him for a short time after the maintenance was done.

Several sly smiles and offers of dinner, and she caved. She had never been invited out to dinner before, and didn't know what to expect. But he told her he would pick her up after her shift and they would go out to a nice place, enjoy a good meal, and see where the night went.

She was filled with naïve excitement, talking in giddy tones with her partner the rest of their shift. They had discussed allowing him to pay for the meal, or whether she should pay for half. If she should offer a movie, and if so, should she buy tickets and snacks, or should he buy snacks if she bought tickets. They discussed whether or not a kiss at the end of the night was appropriate, and how far it should be allowed to go. They discussed everything imaginable before the next crew came in. This was back when she was working days, allowing her to enjoy something of a night life.

He looked nervous as he opened the car door for her. He stuttered as he asked her if it was alright to take her to a local restaurant. They had the most amazing ribs he had ever tasted, and wanted to share that with her. She nodded and smiled. She had never been on a date before. She was just a baby - only nineteen years old. She had no experience in the ways of dates, men, love, or etiquette. She was as scared as he was during the drive, trying to make small talk and figure out what was expected of her.

Once they got to the restaurant, they went inside. Aaron held the door open for her, and was nothing but a true gentleman. They ordered dinner and talked more about life, goals, plans, and dreams. They ate dinner and laughed the night away. When they had finished, they walked back to the car where they stayed talking, making plans to see each other again. Meredith found him charming, sweet, and she was excited at the thought of seeing him again.

Eventually, Aaron drove her home. He opened the car door for her again, and then walked her to the front porch. It was like a scene from an old-time movie where the man will put his jacket down so the woman can cross a puddle. They talked for a few more minutes before he slowly leaned in for a kiss. It was wetter than she expected, as if he had just eaten a sour candy. He was pushy, as if he were afraid that she was going to change her mind. He seemed to not know what to do with his hands, and first they started at her hip, and then the small of her back, and finally near her shoulders so he could pull her closer. She could feel his excitement, but she just wasn't ready. She pulled back.

"Aaron..." she was breathless, her voice hardly above a whisper.

"It's ok...I'm sorry." He stepped back to give her some space. Immediately, she felt endeared to him for being so understanding. How had she found such a good guy without even looking? Was this what they meant when they said you shouldn't look for love? Maybe that was good advice, after all.

Meredith spent the rest of the night with thoughts of him swirling in her head. She pictured the future, possibilities, a family happily playing games, and barbecuing. She was young and naïve enough to picture life in suburbia with the entire white picket fence dream home and a mini-van. It was supposed to be perfect.

She imagined the kiss with Price would have been gentle. There would be no grasping hands that were lost on her body. She imagined he knew his way around a woman's body, and would know exactly how to hold her. She imagined he would gently press her against his patrol car, his hand behind her head, softly cradling it while possessively kissing her. It would leave her knees weak, her eyes closed for fear of it only being a fantasy, and her breath caught in her throat. She could scarcely imagine anything better than that first kiss. Except maybe the second kiss.

Only, he can't walk now, so there would be no pressing her against the patrol car. And she wasn't sure what the etiquette was for kissing a man in a hospital bed...

"Meredith!" Aaron's voice was annoyed and loud, and only then did she realize he had been calling her name for several minutes. "What in the hell has you so preoccupied? Are you planning on coming in the house, or are you going to stay out there all day?"

She gave a sheepish grin. "Sorry, Aaron. I was thinking about my night, that's all. Got lost in thought." He would positively kill her if he knew exactly what she was thinking about. It was a good thing that he couldn't read her mind, and even if he could, he wouldn't worry about it - he was too self-centered to care about her thoughts.

"Whatever." He went back inside and closed the door. Meredith grabbed her bag and headed into the house. Immediately, her senses were assaulted with the tantalizing aroma of bacon. She smiled a broad smile as she saw the table loaded with bacon, eggs, toast and jelly, orange juice, and coffee. It looked like a breakfast fit for a king.

"That smells amazing!" It was an attempt to make peace with him.

"It was, like ten minutes ago. Now it's cold, but whatever. Go eat, shower, and go to bed. We'll figure out what to do in the afternoon when you wake up. You're off for a few days, right?"

"Yeah. I'm off for four days now. What are you thinking?"

"Let's paint the car and see what we can find for a new interior. I'd like to find seats, and something to fix the dash, if we can find it. But go get your daydreaming done, and then maybe you can pay attention to me."

His acidic words left a stinging in her chest, but she fought hard to ignore it. She sat down to her cold breakfast, put her plate in the sink, and then headed for the shower. While the hot water cascaded down her back, she imagined what it would be like to have Price holding her, his hands in her soapy hair, pulling her body close to his. She wondered what it would feel like to have his strong arms around her, protecting her from all the evils of the world. She allowed herself to daydream while covering herself in the remainder of her lavender-scented soap. What would it be like to have someone waiting for her outside the shower with a warm, fluffy towel and a loving smile, the way she did for Aaron? What would it be like to have someone care for her the way she cared for others? She began to wonder if she would ever know that feeling. For now, she felt the crazed wings of the butterflies in her stomach; her new constant companions.

With a heavy heart, Meredith got out of the shower, dried herself, and slipped into a pair of shorts and a t-shirt so she could get some sleep before the rest of the day played itself out. All she could do was hope for no nightmares, and no more fighting.

Meredith calmly walked into the bedroom, a new daydream in her mind. What if she talked to Aaron the way he talked to her? Treated him just as brusquely? Raised a hand to him just because she was irritated? Made threats because he was being "difficult?" Would it still be acceptable? Would he allow it because he had done it to her so long? What if she just walked out? Grabbed her important papers and a change of clothes and just left? Where would she go? Tim said she could stay with him or his parents until she could find a place. But what if she couldn't find a place? Should she work on that first? Could she really leave him?

No. Probably not.

As she began to drift into dream, another scene unfolded. David would crawl under the covers beside her, broad arms wrapping around her and pulling her tightly to him. He would kiss the back of her neck and simply sit there, holding her in a cocoon of safety and love. There would be no pressure for sex, but the offer would be there - and she doubted she would say no to him. It would be amazing - gentle and slow, a dance of exploration and learning, of velvet touches and whispered desires; there would be no secrets, no pain, nothing but a mutually shared bliss.

With those thoughts filling her dreams, Meredith slept better than she had in days. When she woke suddenly, however, Aaron was beside her, invading her dreams, insistent that she "tend to his needs," as he put it. Without any reason to deny him, she rolled over. His hands began to paw at her shorts, as if ripping them off was his goal (and maybe it was, though she didn't see the point of it. All it would do was cause her unnecessary pain, though he enjoyed that, too). He was especially rough with her today, taking no time to ensure she was ready for him. Today was going to be one of those days.

She wasn't really in the mood for his sweaty body to be holding her down, forcing her to his will. She didn't feel like faking enjoyment with him, because if she didn't, he was going to punish her. She didn't want to deal with the bruises when he bit her, and the cramping and pain after he forced himself on her. Without thinking about it (let's be honest...her mind was on David), she twisted her body, searching desperately for a moment of respite. Maybe it was the lack of sleep, or maybe it was the fact that she had just been having a steamy dream about David that had been interrupted before it finished, but she gave several heavy sighs and used every trick she could think of to get him to come quickly that she could get back to sleep. The bedside clock said it had only been a couple hours since she had laid down.

"What's with you today? You're acting like it's going to kill you to have sex with me." Aaron's acerbic words had an edge of jealousy. She knew it was dangerous territory - if he thought she was cheating, he would get worse, and definitely more abusive. He seemed to believe that if he left his mark on her, no other man would want her. She didn't need that right now.

"I'm just tired, Aaron. It was a long, busy night. And you hurt me." Her own tone was guarded, afraid to let him know too much.

"Hurt you? You don't say anything! You expect me to know when I'm too rough, but I can't read your mind, Meredith. Like you haven't figured that out by now. Who are you fucking that you can't be bothered to care about me anymore? To talk to me and tell me what you want? To tell me when you like something I do?"

Here it was. He was convinced she was cheating. She rolled her eyes. "I'm not with anyone else, Aaron, except your other personalities. I don't have time for anyone else. I go to work, I come home. That's it. There is nobody else."

He glared at her, a threat imminent in his eye. "If you are so busy that you can't spend a minute to actually be here with me, maybe you should leave." His tone had dropped low and frightening. "Maybe then you would see what it is I actually do for you. You wouldn't be here if it wasn't for me," the threat was thinly veiled.

Well, obviously. She would probably have been in a normal relationship with a normal man. She would likely have two children, a minivan, a suburban house payment, and a dog. She wouldn't keep looking over her shoulder to see if the jealous shadow was behind her or not, and she certainly wouldn't hate the thought of sex! The idea of moving out was becoming more and more appealing - even if David was never interested in her, she could be free of Aaron and his abuse. Could have a place to call her own, and it would be her refuge.

"I'm not looking to leave you, Aaron." Lies. "I love you, you know that." More lies. "It's just that you get too rough sometimes." Sometimes? Did the man know what gentle was? Did he ever do anything without the intention of hurting her? She doubted it. "I'm just tired right now, and that makes me a little cranky. Let me rest a little more, and we can talk through this, ok? I'll make it up to you tonight." She didn't want to. She wanted to just get up, pack her bags, and leave. But how could she?

"Whatever, Meredith." He stormed out of the room, slamming the door behind him, causing a picture on the wall to swing wildly before it settled back on its hook.

There was nothing she could do to make this situation better right now, so instead of trying, she snuggled down in her blankets and closed her eyes. Her breathing slowed to a level and before she knew it, she was dreaming, but this time, the dreams were not about David. They were about monsters trying to kill her with their gnashing teeth, and raking claws; awful, faceless monsters that she knew instinctively had a name. Aaron.

Several more hours passed with fitful nightmares until she awoke again. Meredith was not looking forward to having to have a talk with Aaron, nor was she looking forward to his childish attitude and silent treatment. She thrived on validation, and having the one person who matters most to you ignore you was a torture worse than anything he could physically put her through.

Pulling on a pair of clean jeans and a non-work-related t-shirt, Meredith yawned, stretched again, and left the safety of her bedroom to find Aaron. She was not surprised to find him on the couch watching a rerun of an old

MMA fight. She sat beside him and patiently waited for a commercial to come on. She delicately slid her hand into his.

"Aaron. I love you. I want you to know that I'm not seeing or doing anything with anyone else. I will try to tell you when you're too rough so we don't have this problem again. I don't like when you're upset with me."

The problem was that she had told him he was too aggressive; too forceful; too rough. She had used every synonym she could think of to get through to him that he hurt her every time they had sex. It was too much for her. She wasn't sure how much more she could handle of this, especially his childish reactions.

He ignored her, and with another heavy sigh, she got up, went into the kitchen, and began to root around in the cabinets to find something to start for dinner. It looked like it was time to go grocery shopping again, as all she could find that was remotely appetizing was a pizza in the freezer. Pizza it is, then. She had bread, butter, and garlic, and decided she would make garlic bread to go with it. He always enjoyed garlic bread.

"How about we put on a movie tonight? I'll run and get us a couple drinks and we'll make a pizza. We'll have a nice stay-in date night. What do you think?"

"Sure. Whatever you want." His tone did not imply that things were even remotely ok between them, but at this point, Meredith was beyond caring. She put on a false front to avoid further conflict, but at this point, if he were to start screaming at her, she would simply stare at him blankly. She was over it.

"I'll run to the store quick and get us some drinks, you pick out a movie, ok?"

He gave a nod of his head - the only indication that he heard her, or cared about what she said.

***

Meredith put on her shoes, grabbed her keys, and left the house without looking back. As soon as she was out of line of sight from the house, she pulled out her phone, and pulled up Lowfield's number and a blank text. *How's it going today? Any changes?*

Several minutes passed before her phone beeped with a reply. *No change. He's doing good. Wants to get out of the hospital. Getting mad that he can't move more.*

Meredith could understand that. He was a very fit, muscular man, so that implied he was active. To be stuck in a bed where he not only wasn't allowed to move, but couldn't move would be a fate worse than if he had died out in the field. Sadness filled her - all she wanted to do was make him feel better, but there was literally nothing she could do.

Sucks. Keep his mind busy. Talk about anything but work. Meredith was trying to reply only at stop signs and red lights, knowing the dangers of texting and driving. She had seen numerous accidents where people had been hit, or had hit someone innocent because they were too busy with their head in their phones to drive their cars. She didn't want to be one of the statistics.

Like what? Romance? A certain medic? The reply made her laugh out loud and shake her head. Damn Lowfield.

No. Like movies or something. Go get him a 3 Musketeers.

They bantered back and forth for several more messages, and by that time, Meredith had run out of stop signs and had arrived at the store. Walking inside, she grabbed a six-pack of Bud Light and a bottle of Stella Black wine for herself, and checked out. Before she knew it, she was back home. The tension was starting to diffuse by then, as Aaron looked at the beer and smiled, nodding approvingly. As if she wouldn't remember his favorite drink, or the fact that drinking made him forget he was mad at her. They had been together so many years, she couldn't forget it if she tried.

It was too early for dinner yet, so Meredith went about and picked up the house. The floors had been neglected, and they were full of dirt from walking in and out from the garage and the vehicles. Once the sweeping was done, she filled up a bucket with hot water and Pine-Sol, and set to work. A short time later, the house was smelling refreshing and clean, and she was ready to start the pizza.

"What movie did you decide on?" she asked as she slid the pizza into the oven.

"I thought we'd watch *It*. The new one. I've been dying to see it, and it's been out for a while now. I want to see how it compares to the original one." Aaron had always loved horror movies. Meredith nodded. There was no response needed - she could make any suggestion in the world, but unless it was his idea, it wasn't going to be acceptable. And this time, she didn't mind - she had been wanting to see it as well.

Once the pizza was hot and ready, they sat down on the couch, under a blanket, with a beer and a glass of wine, and Aaron put It on. The lights were dim and the sunlight was fading fast. It didn't take them long to get sucked into the movie. Meredith didn't hear her phone buzz with another message.

The movie was over relatively early, but Meredith was still tired from the poor sleep in the morning. "What do you think? Do you want to watch some TV in bed before we go to sleep?" She stood up and took the plates to the kitchen while Aaron thought for a moment.

"Yeah, why not."

She folded up the blanket and left it on the couch, retrieved her phone and went into the bathroom to brush her teeth. She opened her phone to see a message from Lowfield.

They found a pocket of infection in his back. Putting him on antibiotics. Can't move his legs again.

Meredith nearly dropped her phone in the sink. An infection? How bad? Was he paralyzed for good now, or could they fix it?

How bad? Prognosis? Her fingers were shaking as she typed out the response, having to erase several extra letters in annoyance. Why couldn't she just be steady?

Antibiotics. Minor infection, caught it early. Then steroids again after.

She felt a little better knowing it was only an "early" infection. That means they caught it soon enough to treat it, and hopefully it would be gone after the antibiotics. She finished brushing her teeth and rinsed her toothbrush. Taking a lung-filling, steadying breath, she shoved her phone in her pocket and crossed the hall into her room.

Meredith plugged her phone in, making sure it was on 'silent' mode, and the screen was facing down, just in case Lowfield sent any other messages. Quickly, she changed back into shorts and crawled under the covers and nestled into their refreshing crisp coldness. Aaron was watching as the news played a story about a happy reunion of a lost dog and its young owner. She settled down against her pillows and then rolled over and laid on him. He grunted as if annoyed, but allowed it. She thought how magnanimous he was to allow her to express her affection this way. It wasn't as if she was often allowed such luxuries.

The news switched then to the story about David getting shot, and how one of the suspects was killed on scene. They were really dragging out the story for several days; Meredith wondered why, instead of just playing it for the normal two days and then blasting it all over social media.

The hostages were a single widowed mother and her three young children. They were unharmed, other than being utterly terrified and probably having nightmares about the entire ordeal. The motive was something along the line of money; the suspects believed her deceased husband had left her more money than she knew what to do with, and they were going to relieve her of it. Meredith shook her head. How sad - to target a single mother. To target anyone is a crime, but this was especially heinous. She was sad that the suspects were killed, too, before they had the chance to face justice for their crimes, but glad that they didn't have the chance to hurt anyone else. The news mentioned one last suspect who wasn't killed, and would be facing charges, but she knew that no matter what the judge threw at him, it wouldn't be enough for his crimes.

Slowly, her eyes fluttered closed and she didn't have nightmares, much to her surprise. She slept well, dreaming of lost puppies returning home unharmed, and single mothers with happy, safe children. Her dreams were tranquil, each slipping into the next of bright colors, of joyous reunions, of smiling faces. She was warm, content, and filled with peace.

Chapter 15

When she woke, she didn't remember any of the night's dreams. Maybe that was for the best, she thought, since they were normally nightmares. Aaron was awake, waiting for her to wake up. He was looking at her, a half-grin on his face as the sun shone in and lit him up like something angelic.

"Let's go do something fun today. Want to go rent a couple ATV's and we'll hit the hills?" the tone of his voice was enticing. It was light, excited, and filled her with anxiety.

Why was he wanting to go out for a day? That was unusual. Meredith yawned broadly and then answered him. "Sure. That sounds like a good time. I'll pack us a couple lunches." She was unsure why he had the sudden mood shift, but she decided to make the best of it. No point in panicking over nothing and ruining a perfectly good day.

They got up and Meredith worked on making several sandwiches and snacks. Once those were packed, she gathered a couple bottles of water and threw everything in a backpack. She knew it would be a long day, but hopefully, it would be well worth it. It had been so long since they had been out without fighting. She hoped today would be one of those days. Together, they jumped into his truck and headed out, animatedly chatting about hoping to see wildlife, and maybe, if they were out long enough, the sunset. Aaron mentioned a beautiful lake he had been to once in his youth that he hoped they could find again.

Somewhere in the middle of a particularly good run of 90's hits, Meredith's phone rang. She was filled with apprehension and dread when she saw it was Captain Stevens. She didn't need this now - she was planning on having a good day…what if he fired her? Aaron would kill her. She could count on walking home and having her things thrown outside, if he didn't really kill her first. She felt ready to vomit all over the floor of Aaron's truck when she answered.

"Hello?"

"Thomas. It's Captain Stevens. Have I caught you at a bad time?"

She wanted to say yes - to not call again until she could find a place of her own and be free of the abuse she was afraid was coming. "No, sir. What's up?"

Aaron looked at her with an eyebrow quirked. Who deserved the distinct honor of being called "sir?" She mouthed the word work to him. He rolled his eyes and returned them to the road.

"I've had a very long several days, between talking with the ambulance board, and several phone calls from the Chief of Police. It seems Chief Barnes is throwing a fit about your suspension. They want you back on your normal shift, and told us that we would not be docking your pay for the suspension, whether I like it or not. It seems that he has pull with the board as well, and they are backing his decision, despite my arguments against it. He has also decided that you and Roberts would both be receiving commendations this Friday at their annual fundraiser event. It starts at 7pm in the ballroom of the Elks Hotel. I'd recommend writing a speech and wearing something formal. You got damn lucky this time, Thomas. You had better keep your ass in line from now on."

Meredith was stunned. Not only was she not getting fired, but she was getting a commendation from the Chief of Police? In *front* of people? It was an even bigger shock to realize that Friday was two days away. She had two days to not only find a dress, but to convince Aaron to wear a suit, be on his best behavior, and accept the fact that this was happening, on top of writing a speech? She knew it was going to be a challenge, as this wasn't something he was going to be willing to participate in. David would, if he were able to; but the sad fact was that he was in the hospital with an infection, and he wasn't hers to bring along.

"Yes, sir. Thank you, sir. Will I see you on Friday?" she asked, excited, anxious, and worried all at the same time.

"Of course. I'll be there to represent the rest of the department. I'm assuming there will be a lot of people there. This is their biggest fundraiser of the year, and thought it was a fitting time for this commendation. I'd plan for a long night. Now, I need to go call Roberts, too. I will see you on Friday." His tone suggested it was final, and there would be no arguments.

"Thank you, sir."

She ended the call and stared at her phone in silence for a moment, stunned to a point of being unable to speak. Her heart was fluttering in her chest, as if it didn't know if to stop completely or go faster.

"Are you going to tell me what that was about, or am I going to have to guess?" Aaron asked, his tone bitter and sarcastic.

"Sorry… Captain Stevens said that Tim and I are both getting commendations for our part in pulling the wounded officer off the scene."

It killed her to not use his name, but she didn't trust herself to say it without breaking down, or having an inflection of something more than "just a work colleague". She also knew if she started using his name, Aaron would be sure they were together, and had been for quite some time. You don't just know somebody's name without sleeping with them, despite the fact that they work together on a fairly regular basis.

"Why the hell would they do that?" he asked, tone on the verge of outrage. Why would they reward someone for such blatant stupidity?

She stared at him, incredulous. "Because they feel it was above and beyond the call of duty. They feel it is deserving of their commendation. And it is their annual fundraising gala, so I'm guessing they are hoping to raise some extra money. I know they've been trying to buy a K9 for a while." She shrugged and then looked out the window, a smile creeping across her face.

"Sounds like a scam to make money on your ass," he stated, a dark look contorting his features.

Meredith ignored the comment. It didn't matter what he said. She was proud of what she had done, even though she didn't feel it deserved any special recognition. She was happy just being able to talk to David when she had the chance. Maybe he would be there. She doubted that after only a few days in the hospital he would be allowed to leave, no matter how much progress he had made. Especially with this new infection, but it was a nice dream anyway.

"Either way, I have to be there. When we're done in the hills, we should find us something matching to wear. What do you think?"

Aaron made a non-committal sound in his throat. "You're actually going to make me dress up for your thing? I'm not getting an award out of it."

"Aaron - it's one event; one night. You can wear a suit for me, just once, can't you?" It wasn't like she was asking him for anything big - just to support her for one night. "Please?"

"Fine. I guess we should do that instead of the day I had planned then. Maybe we can spend a day having fun tomorrow," he retorted angrily. How dare she have something that was more important than him or his ideas.

"We can still do this today. We'll go clothes shopping tomorrow. We'll have two date days." Meredith tried to sound excited for the ATV's still, but to be honest, she was entirely focused on this gala now.

She wondered what she should wear, if she should go all out and have her hair done, or leave it down. Should she wear heels? She couldn't walk in them very well, but if she was only expected to stand there, she could manage. Did she get a long dress or a short one?

Billowy and flowing, or conforming to her shape? So many questions and decisions!

"It's fine. We'll just go a few more miles into town and see what we can find." He was clearly upset, and now that he had his heart set on being angry, there was no changing it. There was no reason they couldn't spend the day doing what he wanted, and spend the day tomorrow finding a dress and a suit. Meredith knew better than to continue arguing with him, however.

They continued driving, passing up the ATV rental place. They passed several little shops until they arrived in the next town. Pulling up to the mall, they parked the truck and got out. This wasn't the place she had in mind for finding a suit and a dress, but then, maybe Aaron knew something she didn't.

Walking inside, Meredith slipped her hand inside Aaron's. He held it, but it was clear his heart wasn't in it. They passed several happy couples, smiling, giggling, and animatedly chatting. Meredith felt a pang of jealousy that they weren't one of those couples. It had been so long since they were nauseatingly in love, and not afraid to show it to the entire world. They passed by one couple who were enthusiastically kissing near one of the jewelry stores. Maybe they had just gotten engaged. That's what it looked like.

"We'll try JC Penny's first, since we're here." Aaron's voice was flat, as if he were already bored. Meredith nodded, trying to hold back the tears. Why couldn't he just be excited for her? Just once? Was it really too much to ask?

They searched for a short time before Aaron was able to pick out a black suit. "Let's see what we can find you for a dress so I know what color tie to get."

Heading over to the women's section, Meredith had her eyes on a beautiful pink ombre dress. It was light at the top, and dark at the bottom, and it was covered in sequins. Meredith looked at it and smiled. That was the one she wanted. Aaron took one look at it and shook his head. "I'll never find a tie to match that. Why not this red one?"

He pointed to a knee-length red dress. It was plain, ordinary, and more suited for a fancy family dinner than a police gala where she was going to be recognized. She crinkled her nose, and found a fair compromise. It was emerald green and had several layers that would complement her body. She tried it on in the fitting room and was excited at how well it fit. She spun around and it fluttered against her legs when she stopped. Yes - it was perfect. She stepped out of the fitting room to show Aaron, but he had gone to look for a tie that would be a close match. Disappointed, Meredith changed back into her jeans and t-shirt and found Aaron moping around the tie selection.

Together, they picked out a tie that would match her dress. Meredith suggested they find a necklace that would go with it, and Aaron reluctantly agreed. "I don't really want anything expensive. Maybe just a little pendant so my neck doesn't look so naked." She grinned. He shrugged as they paid for their purchase and headed down to the jewelry store where they had seen the kissing couple.

Meredith looked in the display cases for several minutes before she found an emerald pendant that would not only match the dress, but add a little bit of elegance to her outfit. The price was right, and so she asked the lady behind the counter to please box it up for her. Aaron agreed that it was beautiful, and a good buy for the price.

"I do have to admit, you know your way around a deal." He seemed to be in less of a bad mood. Maybe that was the key - buying him things. Despite being a little bitter with the thought, Meredith was having a good time spending the day with Aaron. It was nice to just be away from home and the responsibilities that went along with it. Out here, she didn't have to do dishes, sweep, mop, or fold laundry. Out here, she was free to just enjoy herself.

Leaving the store with their gala attire, they decided to not eat at the food court ("I don't want food poisoning," commented Aaron), and decided on a small burger place they had passed just down the road.

"I still don't know what the big deal is about you dragging this cop to your ambulance. It's not like you don't do it every day," he said, rolling his eyes again. His tone suggested disdain for the fact she had done something heroic; at least in the eyes of the law enforcement community.

"It's not the fact that we did it. It's the fact that it was such a dangerous scene. It wasn't like walking into a nursing home and putting granny on our cot. This was a hot scene. And if we wouldn't have pulled him out, he would have died. They are making such a big deal about it because he survived due to something we did. We had a direct impact on this man's life," Meredith explained again. She stared at him for a moment, almost daring him to argue with her. She didn't want a fight, but she was tired of him belittling her job and the things she did.

Aaron didn't respond to her explanation. He was more interested in the greasy bacon burger that had just been placed in front of him by a busty waitress, and then, staring at the waitress' tight, round ass as she sauntered away. She knew she was good looking, and wasn't afraid to exploit it.

"What about her? We could take her to a hotel here, have a little fun, and then go home. Wouldn't even have to worry about cleaning the sheets." Aaron was still staring even after she turned the corner into the kitchen.

"No. We're here to spend a day together, not take a rogue waitress to a seedy hotel." Meredith pursed her lips and then concentrated on eating her fries. They were soggy with a hint of "undercooked" in the mix. Even excessive amounts of salt didn't hide how bad they were. Disappointed, she gave up on them.

"You're going to lighten up one day and let me have some fun. We only get to live once!" Aaron complained as he took a large bite of his burger, grease spilling onto the plate.

Meredith rolled her eyes and shook her head - not for the first time today. She could only hope that they only lived once, or if they got another go-around, if she could choose another man to start her life with. It turns out he wasn't the best first choice she could have made. Jeffrey Dahmer would have been a better choice.

Chapter 16

It was another one of his swinger parties. Halloween again, she remembered. He had her dressed as a slutty nurse, skimpy skirt barely covering her butt and shirt cut so low on both ends, it was hardly a shirt, while he was in second-hand hospital scrubs that covered everything. She was uncomfortable at the way the men stared at her, commenting on how they could use a "little nursing" and other such catcalls. Aaron didn't mind - he had his eye on their wives.

Several conversations later, he was dragging her toward a private room…no; it was a small theater with hardcore porn playing. Luckily, the sound was turned down. There was nothing more irritating to her than fake screaming. On the bright side, the chairs were comfortable, even if she wasn't.

Several other couples were already in there, just starting their evening. Meredith wasn't interested, but had no choice in the matter. It was either submit willingly, or have no choice, and then be punished for it later. She was growing to hate the pain that sex inflicted. She had always thought it was supposed to be a pleasing time between partners. She had also thought that sex was supposed to be shared between one man and one woman only. She could even accept gay and lesbian couples in that; but she hated the thought that she was being passed around like yesterday's newspaper so Aaron could do dirty things with other women.

Aaron was torn between watching the big screen, and watching the couples. Obviously, they didn't mind an audience, or they would have gone to a secluded room. He kept trying to slide his hand up her thigh, but she kept irritatedly pushing it away. He had assumed she was playing coy with him, and only tried harder. Before long, she silently stalked out of the room, and it only took him a moment to figure out she was gone. He jumped up and followed her, grabbing her arm and stopping her.

"Where are you going?" he asked with an edge to his voice.

"I'm done with this. I feel dirty. I want to go home. This isn't right, Aaron."

"It's just a good time, Mer. Really. Let's go have a good time, and then we can go home," he nearly begged, reluctant to give up the potential to sleep with someone else.

"Let's get something to eat and see how it goes, I guess."

She felt defeated. She wasn't going to be able to get out of his "thing" he had planned. Her heart broke as much as her spirit. She lowered her head and pulled her arm away from his hand, fighting the urge to break down and cry.

"Sure," he said, almost bouncing with his excitement.

They walked to the bar and ordered a couple appetizers. Aaron picked a corner table at the end of the bar to sit at to wait for Meredith to finish eating. She stayed at the bar - there were too many people to risk walking around with a plate of food, and she really didn't want to be around Aaron more than she absolutely had to.

The food she ordered was too greasy, undercooked, and over-salted. She picked at it, trying to quell the frustration in her stomach. Several bites later, she was feeling queasy. A single woman had appeared out of nowhere, and was animatedly chatting with Aaron, who was eating up the attention. He had his hand on hers, and was grinning from ear to ear. She knew that look - it was the "I'm a good guy, fall for me," look. It worked all too well on her, and Meredith didn't want it to work on another poor woman. Meredith abandoned her plate, walked to the corner table, getting bumped into by two people who didn't even look up, and sat next to Aaron.

"Meredith! This is Stella. She'd like to come back to the room with us." The girl smiled warmly. She was a homely creature. Not pretty, but not ugly. Meredith nodded a greeting at the woman, shaking her hand. She had a limp handshake that Meredith couldn't stand. She didn't want to be outwardly rude, and instead, spoke softly, leaning closer to Aaron so only he could hear her..

"I'm not feeling real well, Aaron. That food is making me sick, I think."

"Oh," he replied, a hint of irritation and something akin to sadness in his tone.

She thought that tone was one that suggested she won - that they weren't going to have a threesome. That she would have a "night off" from his wishes. She felt a small amount of excitement start to well up in her breast. She had won! She didn't know how it had happened, but she was thanking every lucky star and saint she could think of.

"She's going to come back with us for a little bit, and then she'll go home," he continued.

"Aaron...I really don't feel well!"

"She won't be there all night. Really. You'll be ok," he finished, completely ignoring the fact that she looked ready to vomit all over him. And she would have too, if she were able to vomit on command.

Meredith was heartbroken as they walked to the door. Together. The three of them walked out to the parking lot where the girl climbed into her car, and they got into their truck. Driving slowly as to not lose Stella, they arrived at the hotel. They parked in the back and walked in together with Aaron and Stella walking in front, and Meredith trailing behind. She went into the bathroom to change into her pajamas while they wasted no time getting started. She could hear them giggling above the sound of the water she ran to brush her teeth.

Meredith crawled into the empty bed next to the couple, too angry to want to be anywhere near Aaron and his latest conquest. They were kissing intimately, and all she could do was turn up the Lifetime movie she had found. It wasn't her first choice of movies, but compared to what was happening in the next bed, she would have happily watched reruns of Barney the Purple Dinosaur.

Aaron kept looking over at her, beckoning her to join them in the next bed. Meredith shook her head, pretending to be intently watching the movie. She refused to acknowledge his outstretched hand, which was usually his unspoken demand that she would join him. She refused to be part of this game tonight.

Between the woman who was happily taking her place, and the greasy food that was threatening to make a comeback, Meredith was struggling enough to not vomit all over the white comforter. What a funny thought - a comforter on a bed. It brought her no comfort now, knowing her boyfriend was raucously having sex with another woman not six feet away from her.

Aaron was about to come and wasn't shy about exclaiming it, making sure both women heard him. She hadn't heard a peep out of Stella, and assumed she hadn't gotten that far yet. Once Aaron was done, he rolled over and waited only a moment before he pulled off the condom and threw it in the trash. Stella looked at him with intense sexual frustration. She had come here for a good time, and instead, was leaving unfulfilled. That was Aaron's way. Meredith wanted to console the poor girl, to tell her that was normal; to go find a real man; but before she had the chance to fully form the words, Stella was up, getting dressed, and leaving without a word. She slammed the door behind her.

Aaron then crawled into bed with Meredith, pressing his still-naked body against her and tried to hold her, hands pawing at her chest, wet mouth trying to drag hers closer in a claiming kiss. She tensed.

"Are you mad at me?" he asked, incredulous.

"Yeah, actually I am. How many times do I have to tell you I'm not interested? That I don't feel well? And you still brought her back to the room and fucked her!" Meredith didn't try to lower her voice in her anger.

"I thought you would relax once she was here and be able to enjoy it! You always enjoy it. I can't believe you're upset with me!" Aaron had a whipped puppy tone to his voice now.

The old guilt trip. It almost worked, but after several years of putting up with this behavior, Meredith's soft spot for it wasn't so soft anymore. She shrugged and ignored him, letting herself fall into a fitful sleep, not caring if Aaron held her or not.

Chapter 17

When the morning dawned cold and rainy, Meredith was glad Aaron had no intention of going out to ride ATVs anymore. He was sulking, but would get over it eventually, she reasoned. There would be other days that weren't miserable where they could ride ATVs all day. Instead, when he got up, he made a fire in their wood stove and started on breakfast. This morning, he made smoothies, pancakes, bacon, and eggs. Meredith was slow to rise, taking advantage of some alone time to stretch out in bed, and send a quick text to Lowfield, asking how Price had done the previous night.

I think he misses you. Told me about your commendation. Congrats!

Meredith grinned at her phone. *Thanks. I'm pretty stoked. Will you be there?* She hoped he didn't think she was flirting with him. She liked him, but she wasn't interested in him. He was definitely more the "big brother" type. She was just curious how many familiar faces she would have against a sea of strangers.

Wouldn't miss it.

Aaron opened their bedroom door and Meredith started, then smiled. "You scared me."

"Breakfast is almost ready. Are you going to be long?"

She shook her head. "Naw. I'll throw on some pants in a second and be right there." She stretched out one more time in an attempt to show him that she had only been lounging before slowly standing up and stumbling into their closet. She rummaged around until she found a pair of pajama pants and traded her shorts for them. There was a wet chill in the air today, but walking into the living room provided enough heat to warm her through. He was better than her at building fires that were fast to warm the house. For that, she was thankful.

She sidled up behind Aaron and wrapped her arms around him from behind, her chin resting on his shoulder. "Thank you. This looks great!"

He gave a non-committal noise and then moved, forcing her to let go of him. She sat down at the table and waited for him to sit before she started eating. She was many things, but rude wasn't one of them. Several bites in, she stopped and smiled. Aaron had few redeeming qualities, but being the world's best bacon cook was probably her favorite.

"I don't know how you get the bacon perfect every time, but I'm glad you do." She looked at him and grinned, then took another bite.

"I just watch it and flip it when it starts to brown, before it gets all nasty and black on the edges. If it gets there, you've had it in too long." He shrugged. "Bacon isn't hard."

"No, it's not, but I like yours so much better than mine," she said, trying to lighten the foul mood he seemed to be in.

After breakfast, Meredith got the dishes washed, dried, and put away while Aaron fed the fire. They had decided it was a good day to just veg out. Meredith curled up on the couch with a notebook, ready to work on her speech, soaking in the heat from the fire while Aaron put on some video games. She looked at the blank lines and tried to write an adequate beginning several times. Frustration began to build, and she growled softly.

"What's got you upset, babe?" Aaron asked. It had been a while since he'd used that nickname for her. She wasn't sure if it was because he cared, or he wanted to catch her off guard.

"I don't know what I'm supposed to say in this speech. Captain Stevens said I was expected to give one." She tapped her pen against the paper. It was mocking her, she was sure of it.

"Just say that you're awesome and did what anyone else in your position would have done. It is your job, isn't it?" he was only half joking.

"No. This was above and beyond. That's why they want to make a big deal about it. It's hard to know what to say without sounding like I *want* to be thanked. I really don't, but since I don't have a choice, I need a good speech," Meredith whined.

She scribbled down several beginnings and crossed each one out. How could she sound like the modest, caring girl she was without sounding like a pompous ass? Every beginning sounded like she was digging for a compliment. In the end, she crumpled up the paper and pulled out a clean, new page.

First, I want to thank you all for being here to support our law enforcement. I know it means a great deal to them to have so many of you backing them. Second, I want to thank Police Chief Barnes for inviting me and my partner to this event as guests of honor. I truly do feel honored.

Was that a good start? Did it sound stupid? She stared at it, rereading it a million times before deciding it could be worse. Besides, it was only a rough draft.

I don't feel I deserve this commendation. I did what any Paramedic in my position would do. I heard that one of my brothers had been seriously injured, and I jumped into action. He would have done the same for me, or for any of my coworkers, so it only felt right.

She groaned out loud. This sounded stupid. Resisting the urge to throw the entire notebook across the room toward the crackling fire, Meredith set it down and pulled the blanket up around her neck and shoulders. She watched Aaron play soldier and kill the bad guys for a while, until her eyes drooped closed and she found herself dreaming.

She could hear the bullets zinging all around her, flying over her head, ricocheting off the vehicles she was trying to hide behind, and when they hit another human. The sound was a dull thud. She could feel the reverberation as each body was struck with a high-velocity bullet. She could see the wounded all around her, reaching for her, each one begging for help. They knew she could be their salvation; their only hope for survival! But why wouldn't she help them? Her eyes fell upon someone familiar - David. She reached her hands out for him, and just when she was about to touch him, Aaron's angered cry woke her with a start.

"Son of a bitch!"

"Huh? What happened?" She sat up frantically, but was still half asleep, thinking he had been wounded, and that she should get up to assess him.

"I lost the damn match. I was this close to winning, too," he cursed again.

"Just retry it. You'll get it." She wasn't sure what you were supposed to say when someone lost a video game. Truthfully, she didn't much care - it was only a video game. He was still fully neurologically intact. Not a single bullet hole in his body. She snuggled back into her blankets, trying to recall the dream, or at least the part where she was about to touch Price's hand. She found she missed him more than she should, and that worried her, but not enough to stop thinking about him.

Sleep avoided her, so instead, she allowed her mind to wander where it would; first wading, and then leaping headlong into dangerous territory. In her mind, David walked up and sat beside her, and then curled up behind her, pulling her so close, she could feel his heart beating against her back. He whispered things to her…mostly about how he loved her, and how they would be married soon, and then would start their perfect family. It was heartbreaking how simple her fantasies had become. When she was young, all she wanted was a rich man to take care of her for forever; to buy her a fast car and a big house. Then, she wanted a man with a nice car who would show her the world. Then a man with a nice house who would share it with her. And now, all she wanted was a man who treated her well, and kept his promises. A man who wouldn't hit her or belittle her.

Some time passed and she dozed on and off through the afternoon. Aaron wasn't in any hurry to turn off his games, so she had nothing else to do until late afternoon rolled around and it was time to make dinner. She sat up and pulled out her phone to look up recipes. They still needed to get groceries, but she figured she could scrounge up enough ingredients to make something decent. She looked through the pantry and the cupboards until she had several ideas in mind.

Meredith settled on some homemade macaroni and cheese. She knew she had a couple chunks of cheese left that needed to be used soon, and this was perfect. It was cold out, miserable, and comfort food was absolutely called for. Especially with all the nightmares she had been having lately about not just Aaron, but about losing David. She got up and got all the ingredients prepared. It didn't take too long to boil the noodles, or make the sauce, and in the end, she was able to turn out a bacon-bit, cheddar, Gouda, and Colby macaroni and cheese.

She called Aaron to eat and during dinner, they discussed tomorrow night's gala event.

"I haven't been able to write a single decent line for this speech. What should I do?" she asked him, genuinely looking for some help.

"Wing it, I guess. You're pretty good at that," he replied, among mouthfuls of macaroni.

She couldn't tell if it was a compliment or an insult, so she gave him the benefit of the doubt. There was no point in starting a fight.

"Thanks. I guess I'll have to. I don't know what else to write that doesn't sound stupid or fake," she said, upset that she was unable to find the words she needed.

They finished eating dinner with other small talk, and plans for the evening's dance and dinner. Aaron, of course, took the conversation to the exact place Meredith was hoping it wouldn't go, and in record time.

"So what happens if we find someone who's interested in playing with us? Do we bring them home?"

"Aaron...can we just have one night together that isn't about other people? Enjoy the eye candy, but let's just go home together. Just you and me. I think we'll both be too tired by the end of the evening to really want to do anything with anyone else, anyway. And, these are the husbands and wives of people I work with. I don't want to do anything with someone I work with," she retorted, trying desperately to not have an angry tone slip into her voice. Her blood was hot and she was, in fact, angry, but again, she didn't want to fight with him. Not the day before the gala. What if he hit her? She would bruise, and likely have to lie desperately about what really happened so he wouldn't get his ass kicked by a room full of police officers who hated the thought of a woman getting abused.

"Always gotta spoil my fun, don't you? Well...let's just see how it goes, I guess. Maybe after dinner, a few drinks, and some dancing, you'll be feeling frisky. Who knows...you might even find someone you want to bring home," Aaron said with a wink. Meredith highly doubted that. She hated bringing strangers into her life for Aaron to have sex with and then discard. It made her feel cheap. The thought of him doing that to a coworker was worse - even a coworker that she didn't work next to every day. Chances are, whoever it was would see her on a scene somewhere, and that wasn't something she was willing to face.

They decided to crawl into bed, under the warm covers and watch a movie to finish out their night. Jumanji was replaying on one of the movie channels, so they decided that was a good movie to end the night on. Meredith was captured by the humor of it, and Aaron was deciding if he was better looking than the Rock or not. He pointed out every flaw he could find (he made them up when he couldn't find them), and pointed out all of his self-perceived strengths. Meredith rolled her eyes and laughed.

"Yes, Aaron. I would absolutely pick you over the Rock any day," she said sarcastically, grinning.

He chuckled softly. "Not gonna lie, I would absolutely pick Madison Iseman any day. She's gorgeous." He didn't stop to take into account Meredith's feelings as he continued. "I mean, she's got a nice face, but have you seen her ass? My God. It's perfect." He made several other vulgar references between himself and her rear end, but Meredith forced herself to ignore it. There was no point in getting upset. He would never understand, and it wasn't as though he had a remote chance of getting with the star. If she had to choose between a serial killer who specialized in gorgeous stars and Aaron, she would absolutely pick the serial killer. "And that chest of hers was forged in Heaven for men to appreciate. Let me tell you...I appreciate!"

Soon, the movie ended, and Meredith fell down to a dark, dreamless sleep underneath her blankets that were pulled up around her neck.

Chapter 18

When morning came, it was bright, with an air of anticipation. She couldn't wait to get to the gala and have a good time. She wasn't looking forward to the speech, however - maybe they would forget it about it, she hoped. There was always a chance they would forget about her entirely, and she could just be there to eat and dance. That would be nice.

The day passed faster than she thought was possible. Before she knew it, she realized if she didn't shower and get ready soon, she was going to wind up going to the fundraiser in her pajamas. She told Aaron she was going to shower. She turned on the water, got undressed, jumped in, and promptly cranked the heat up hot enough to rival a cold bath in hell.

She soaped herself and then shampooed her hair. She liked the feeling of the shampoo; it made her hair soft and silky, and it was always shiny when she blow-dried it. Meredith was struggling with how she was going to put her hair up. She wasn't really good at hairstyles, but figured a nice French braid would be practical, and still elegant.

After drying herself, she spritzed her hair with leave-in conditioner, and started to blow-dry it. Once it was barely damp, she twisted it into a French braid and then pinned it up. The end result was no runway model's hair, but it was still beautiful in her eyes. With a smile, she crossed the hall to her room and pulled her dress on. Returning to the bathroom mirror, she took a look and was surprised by what she saw. Instead of a gawky redhead, she saw a beautiful young woman who was proud of her accomplishments and was ready to be recognized, despite the fear she felt. It was going to be a magnificent night, and there was very little that would deter her from believing it.

Meredith left the bathroom again to check on Aaron and found him dressed and ready. He was exceedingly handsome, especially when he chose to dress up and wasn't belittling her. Meredith straightened his tie and smiled. "You sure are a handsome man."

"I know." He gave her a lopsided grin. It was endearing, and she hated that fact. She wanted to be mad at him for his earlier behavior. She wanted to hate him for all of his previous sins against her, but in a moment like this, she couldn't bring herself to be angry.

Aaron opened her door for her, and gently shut it as they hopped into the truck and headed to the hotel. Traffic was lighter than usual, so they made it in record time. Aaron was particularly quiet, just listening to the radio, leaving Meredith with her thoughts. She was still trying to find the words for her speech, and instead of finding words, she was finding she had a large knot in her stomach. She was nauseated, dizzy, and half contemplating asking Aaron to return home. She knew that once she got to the ballroom, she would calm down - she would have no choice.

They pulled into the parking lot of the Elks Hotel and hopped out. Meredith looked around to see the hundred or so cars that were there for this event. It didn't make her stomach calm down any knowing there were hundreds of strangers who were going to be listening to her give a speech she had not prepared, and not practiced, about an event that was more than just her "doing her job." She felt too close to it, too on edge, and too afraid of breaking down to remember how close to death David was.

Walking in together, Meredith saw several of her coworkers in the hallway. She smiled and waved, and when she saw Tim, she made a bee-line for him, an agitated Aaron in tow.

"Tim! Can you believe it? This is the craziest thing in the world!"

He nodded. "Yeah, I thought we were getting fired after that suspension for sure!"

Aaron gave her a suspicious look that Meredith carefully avoided. She gave Tim a dirty look that he caught on to very quickly. "I'm nervous for this speech. How about you? Were you able to get anything written down? Captain said we had to say something," he asked, letting his nerves show a little.

"No. I tried for hours, but I just couldn't get anything that didn't sound stupid. I'm freaking out a little bit," Meredith replied, a waver in her voice.

"Roberts! Thomas! It's time to get you situated in the ballroom. Come on."

"What did your partner mean about this 'suspension?' You were at work all week...?" Aaron asked, a definite jealous and dangerous edge in his voice. If he found out that she was with another man for an entire week instead of being at work, he would kill her; a room full of cops or not.

"They wanted to suspend us for saving the officer, but changed their minds. They were just upset because it was a bad scene. Go find yourself a seat, Aaron. I'll see you soon!" She gave him a quick hug and a peck on the cheek and followed Tim and the Captain into the ballroom, glad to be away from him.

Tim and Meredith were led onto the stage and sat down in two of the empty chairs toward the middle. Meredith's green eyes scanned the room for any familiar faces, and grinned when she saw Lowfield amongst the other officers. She waved, and he waved back, grinning widely. He gave her a thumb's up before being distracted by another officer.

Before long, Police Chief Barnes stood up and ushered everyone to fall silent. His presence was commanding, and there was not a person in that room who was truly willing to defy him. There was still the noises of several people coughing, sneezing, and screeching chairs as they moved around, however, but not one voice rose up above his.

"Friends, families, and generous donors! I would like to thank you for coming out to support our police force while enjoying a night of dinner, drinking, dancing, and, of course, donations! But before we get to the food and fun, we have several awards to hand out," he started. He had a deep voice that Meredith imagined could be soothing if he were talking to a child, but frightening if he were doling out punishments.

There was a polite round of applause as Chief Barnes paused.

He went through several different awards given to his officers, each one receiving a medal of merit, or a lifesaving award, one retirement, and a couple advancements in ranks. There was a round of applause and cheering as each award was called, after each story was told. Meredith listened aptly to their speeches, hoping to find something to say that they hadn't. She wanted this to be a speech to end the night on.

"And lastly, but certainly not least, I have two commendations to give. As I know you have all heard by now, one of our officers was seriously wounded in the line of duty. He was with his team when he was shot in the chest by a barricaded suspect. While knowing the dangers they were facing and continuing on despite the danger, Officer David Price is here today." Chief Barnes paused and the hall exploded in applause, several cheers, and whistles. Meredith's head whipped toward him, eyes wide, and a feeling of hot lava in her stomach. She had hoped he would be here, but hadn't actually expected him to be!

Price was wheeled by a nurse up a ramp that Meredith had not seen earlier due to her nerves. Her heart stopped when she saw him dressed in a suit and tie. He was the most handsome man she had ever seen, and Meredith had seen some extremely handsome men. Her green eyes were alight with an inner fire that she couldn't (she wouldn't) extinguish. She wasn't sure she even wanted to. Her mouth was dry, and her heart was fluttering in a way it hadn't in several years. He looked at her and smiled a warm, grateful smile. There was a look in his eyes she couldn't quite distinguish - she thought it was the same feeling she had in her stomach.

Once he was on the stage, Chief Barnes shook his hand and handed him the microphone. Price cleared his throat and began his speech.

"I shouldn't be here today to give this speech, but I'm very thankful that I am. While trying to peacefully resolve a conflict between several armed suspects and several hostages, numerous bullets were fired by the suspects. One of these bullets ricocheted off the car I was taking cover behind, and struck me just above my vest. This bullet punctured my lung and then lodged itself in my spine," he started slowly, but then gathered momentum as he felt more comfortable telling the story.

The crowd took a collective gasp, and it looked like everyone was at the edge of their seats, waiting to hear the rest of this story. It was the best story they had heard all year. Chief Barnes could practically see the pocket books being pulled out. Price paused a minute to take a few deep breaths - his lung hadn't fully healed, but it was pretty close. He was trying to not start coughing.

"I don't remember much after getting shot, except a pair of soft hands holding me up so I wouldn't choke on my own blood, and a voice telling me that I was going to be ok." He paused and glanced at Meredith, who was blushing furiously. "I was close to death when she got there, and from accounts told to me by other officers on scene, the two medics who are here with me pulled me to safety." He paused and took another steadying breath to keep his voice from quavering. "When I woke up, I heard several accounts of what happened, and from what I understand, without the quick actions of Tim Roberts and Meredith Thomas, I would be dead."

The crowd was silent for a moment, taking in everything Price had just said before they erupted in more cheers and applause, loud enough to temporarily deafen everyone on the stage. Meredith's face had turned from a dark blush into a deep red that she couldn't hope to hide. She felt like Rudolph trying to guide Santa's sleigh with her face. Tim was beaming beside her as if he had just won the billion dollar lottery.

Police Chief Barnes took the microphone back from Price. "I'd like to give our two recipients a chance to say a few words as they receive their Commendation." He handed the microphone to Tim first. He looked humbled, yet still proud as Price handed him the framed certificate and firmly shook his hand.

"I honestly don't know what to say, and believe me, I've thought about it since my Captain told me about this. I am deeply honored to be receiving this Commendation, and don't think I could have done it without the leadership of my partner. We knew we had to do something, or we were going to lose a brother. My partner and I weren't about to let that happen.

Our training kicked in and we reacted - the same as they would have done for us if the situation was reversed." He fell silent and smiled, standing between Chief Barnes and David for a few moments while they were bombarded by hundreds of camera flashes by new fans and media members. Tim didn't mention the fact that he was scared beyond belief, or that he questioned every decision she made. It made them both look like a better, stronger team this way.

Price then handed Meredith the other framed Commendation and shook her hand, but his fingers lingered just a second too long on hers. She felt the blush creep up her neck and back into her cheeks again. She nearly dropped the microphone as Tim handed it to her. She stared at Price for a moment before looking out at the sea of strangers. For a moment, she was struck speechless. There were so many faces and each one was waiting to hear her side of the story.

"I'm humbled to receive this Commendation. In truth, I was just doing my job. We were paged to stand by for the same scene when we heard radio traffic that the threat was escalating. They had called in for the SWAT team, but they were more than an hour out. The threat was too great to wait for them by that time. Next, we heard there were shots fired and shots exchanged, and then traffic for an officer down. The radio exploded with chatter then, trying to find out where he was, and whether he was alive or not. I heard the location from other officers, and I just reacted. I couldn't leave a brother to die. EMS and Fire and Law Enforcement spend a lot of time picking on each other and sharing jokes, but in the end, we are all one big brotherhood. I thank God that He gave me the ability and level-headedness to know what needed to be done in order to get Officer Price safely to the trauma center. I want to thank the officers who covered us so we could safely get in and out of the scene to take care of one of your own. It is an honor and a privilege to work with the finest officers I have ever met. I also have to give my partner his due thanks for being there when I needed him, without question. It was an intense and scary situation, and without him, I couldn't have done it either." She turned and hugged Tim, tears welling up in her eyes again. They had bonded even more over that traumatic event.

The crowd thoroughly enjoyed the speech, and in the end, Meredith looked out over a standing ovation. She then stood between Barnes and Price for her turn to endure the camera flashes, and then waved Tim over as well. Together, the four of them stood for several more photos before Barnes took the microphone back.

"On behalf of the city of Elk Creek, I am honored to work beside such magnificent Paramedics who strive to be the best they can be, and even more. Without you, we would have lost one of our finest. You both have done your department, your families, and your city proud." With that, the caterers began to serve plates of steaming dinner to each table. The room smelled delicious - warm rolls and brisket.

Meredith took the chaotic moments to find Price, who had not yet been wheeled down the ramp. "You're here! I didn't think you would be cleared to leave St. Victory for weeks!" she exclaimed, thrilled beyond reasoning to see him.

He grinned. "It wasn't easy. Chief Barnes had to promise the doctor that he would keep a nurse with me at all times, and if I had any issues whatsoever, that they would whisk me back to the hospital. I'm sure he had to sign in triplicate, the same promise, have it notarized, and filed with the Department of Justice. It was one hell of a process, let me tell you!" He chuckled softly. "I'm glad to see you," he added, his sultry voice low, hand wanting to reach out for hers.

Meredith was about to say something else when she felt a hand at the small of her back. Aaron loomed beside her, impatiently awaiting an introduction and the entire reason he showed up here: dinner. She was preventing him from eating, and that was a serious offense.

"Officer Price, this is my boyfriend, Aaron. Aaron, this is Officer Price." There was a tense moment between them before Price offered his hand for Aaron to shake.

"Pleasure to meet you, sir. I'm awful thankful your girlfriend was on duty that day. She really knows her stuff, and her ability to remain calm under pressure is unbelievable," he said warmly, looking at Meredith with nothing but admiration in his eyes.

"Yep. I'm pretty proud of her, myself." He let his hand wrap around to Meredith's hip to pull her closer. She wrinkled her nose and quickly returned her face to a neutral expression. He had never once told her he was proud of her, and had never once thought to care about what she did. He was simply trying to make himself look better in the eyes of Price, and to try and establish a sense of "dominance" over him. Meredith saw right through it, but refused to acknowledge it.

Barnes showed up at that moment and told the group that they were all going to be sitting at the same table - with the Police Commission, EMS board, and Price. The group slowly moved to their table with Barnes wheeling Price in his wheelchair down the ramp. Meredith tried to stay near him to finish their conversation, but Aaron was stuck to her like a jealous dog with a bone. She sighed softly and sat down between Tim and Aaron. Her frustration was building, but she fought to hide it. Here wasn't the place for a melt-down, no matter how much she wanted to do just that.

Dinner went smoothly with both the Commissioners and Board asking several questions of Tim and Meredith. They tried asking David questions about the event, but he politely reminded them that he had been unconscious, or at best, semi-conscious for most of the event, and was unable to contribute much. Aaron tried to push his way into the conversation, but when both the Commissioners and the Board ignored him, he sulked in silence beside Meredith. The commissioners promised they would find money in their budget to increase police training, and to try and do more training together with EMS. The two boards spoke together about finding money for better equipment, and maybe setting up a tactical EMS group. The talk continued through the meal.

Once dinner was finished, Chief Barnes announced that the dance would then begin, and the silent auction would last until thirty minutes before the end of the dance. The band, who had been setting up since dinner, began to play a lively tune that had people flocking to the floor to dance. Meredith remained near Price, and insisted that Aaron go enjoy himself, she wanted to finish her conversation. Aaron had found a woman he was interested in and wasted no time in trailing off to the floor to pursue the woman, leaving Meredith to a moment alone with David.

As soon as Aaron was off to the dance floor with the woman who had a slit in her dress clear up to her hip, she knelt beside David and smiled. "I'm glad you're here, but you shouldn't be! You're going to overdo it, and end up staying in the hospital longer than you need to," she worried.

"I had to see you. Chief asked me if I was up for it, and I told him yes. Besides, I've had enough steroids and antibiotics to kill all disease known to Mars. I'll be fine for one night." He shrugged and slid his hand slowly over to touch her shoulder. His dark blue eyes scanned the floor for Aaron to ensure he wouldn't create bigger problems for her. "You look beautiful, by the way. Absolutely stunning." He grinned, letting his hand fall down to caress her ribs. Aaron was too busy trying to set up a "date" with the woman to notice anyway. Meredith sighed softly and leaned closer.

"Thank you. Part of me was really hoping you'd be here. I've missed you the past few days. I'm sorry I haven't been able to see you…Aaron is pretty possessive, and I don't want him to think there is something going on." She gave a rueful smile. If only Aaron knew.

"But there isn't anything going on." David gave her a mock innocent stare, eyes wide, and a wink in return.

"Exactly. But if he thinks there is, it'll be a huge pain in the ass. He's one of those guys, you know?"

David rolled his eyes. "Yeah. I understand. You don't have anything to worry about from me. I'm happy just being able to see you." David pulled his hands away, and returned to his air of innocence.

Meredith nodded and then looked up as the song ended and she saw Aaron walking toward them with the girl in tow. Her heart fell. All she had wanted was a single night to just be herself. To accept this recognition and enjoy it. One night where she didn't have to pretend to be happy, or please Aaron's sadistic desires.

"Meredith, are you ready?" The girl hovered in the background, watching Aaron, and trying to pretend she wasn't waiting for him. David looked between the three of them and leveled his gaze on Aaron. It was clear he wasn't happy, but he didn't say anything that could cause her any grief later. He averted his eyes to avoid staring at Aaron with a look of disgust.

"Not really...I'd like to stay for a while. The night is still young, and I haven't even danced yet! Besides...we just got here," she replied. Why would she want to run off so Aaron could enjoy himself with another woman? She was enjoying the night right here - and in her mind, this was her night.

Aaron began to say something, a demand that she grab her coat or something similar when David couldn't hold his tongue any longer. He spoke up, voice cordial and even, eyes leveled on Aaron.

"If you'd like, I can arrange a ride home for her as soon as she's ready. It wouldn't be a problem at all."

Aaron stared at him for a moment, weighing his options. On one hand, he didn't want to leave Meredith alone with this officer that she had been standing with all night, even though he was paralyzed, and Aaron knew he couldn't do anything to his girl; but on the other hand, he could have his way with another woman without Meredith's upset emotions hindering the sex. "I'd like her home by midnight." He stared at her while he said this. It was clearly a warning that she would heed or else. He didn't care that Meredith was hurt over his actions; that she knew exactly what was going to happen once he and this mystery woman go to their house. He didn't care that Meredith was allowed no freedoms - not even to attend school, but he was allowed to bring home rogue women and do things with them.

"Yes, sir. I will ensure she is home safe by midnight," David diplomatically replied.

"Thank you, Aaron." They walked together to the door. "Have a good night, and I'll see you soon." She hugged him, and he insisted on kissing her. It was possessive, wet, and unnecessary, but as soon as he was done, he looked to make sure David was looking. He was. Aaron gave a wicked grin and waved before turning to go. Moments later, the little blonde he had been dancing with followed him out the door, looking excited and a little scared at the same time. She glanced at Meredith before dropping her gaze and nearly running out the door.

Meredith returned to David's side and pulled up a chair. "I'm sorry." She couldn't meet his eyes. His hand went to her thigh, thumb absently rubbing it in an attempt at comfort.

"It's not your fault. I can see why you didn't want to stay home while on your suspension. I hope I'm not intruding too much, but why do you stay with him when he treats you so poorly? I'd like to make an offer, if I may?" he asked softly.

Meredith nodded, not trusting her words at the moment. She didn't answer his question about staying with Aaron. The only reason she could think of was that she loved him, and even that sounded hollow and not true anymore. She had been asking herself the same question for several years, and all she could think of was that she was too worried he wouldn't be able to do anything for himself and would wind up starving to death or homeless.

"I'm going to be stuck in the hospital for several weeks to several months. Not to mention months to years of rehab ahead of me. If you decide you need to get away, you're always welcome to stay at my place. It's private, and you'd be doing me the favor. If it looks like someone is living there, it won't get broken into, and you could collect my mail and all the boring stuff. I mean...only if you need a place to get away?" His eyes were warm and inviting. She almost agreed right then and there, but the situation was precarious.

"I'll have to think about it, but I'm sure I could get Tim to agree to head over there tomorrow on shift so we can get your mail and keep the place looking lived in - at least let people know it's being watched so you don't have to worry about it. I appreciate the offer, David, I really do. But it's not as simple as just packing my bags and leaving him," she said. Actually, it would be that easy, but she still struggled with the decision.

"I wasn't asking you to leave him. Just offering a place you can stay in if you need to get away, whether it's an hour, a week, or forever. The offer stands for whatever you need."

Meredith nodded and took his hand. "Thank you." She felt nothing but a warm gratitude, and was unable to say anything else.

The current song ended and another started. Lowfield sauntered up and offered a hand to Meredith. "Would you like to dance?" She looked up at him, and then to Price. Price grinned.

"Go. You're here to dance. Go have a good time. Lowfield...behave." He winked at his partner while smiling and shaking his head.

Meredith stood up and took Lowfield's offered hand. He led her out to the dance floor as a lively two-step started. Meredith was admittedly a horrible dancer, but she avoided stepping on his toes too many times.

Every time they passed, Meredith's eyes met David's. She definitely felt the spark every time, and began to seriously consider taking him up on his offer. To be free from Aaron would be the greatest gift she could ever ask for, but then again, she wasn't sure if she could accept such a thing from David, or anyone, for that matter. She was too afraid that he would come after her, and would truly kill her this time.

As soon as the song ended, Lowfield walked Meredith back to Price. "She's a lovely dancer, sir. Get off your ass and dance with her." Lowfield winked.

"If I have to get up out of this chair, Lowfield, I'm going to kick your ass." The two men chuckled and continued bantering for several more minutes before Paul went to find another dance partner. Meredith sat down beside Price again.

"I'm glad you're here, David. I'll do my best to come see you as often as I can." She paused, giving him another sad smile. "I'm sure it won't be as often as I'd like, but I'll do the best I can."

"Don't stress yourself over it. I'll be there for a while. Take care of your business first, and I'll be there when you're done." He grabbed her hand again. "Really. It's ok."

The rest of the evening passed faster than she wanted it to. Nearing midnight, she told Price that she had to get going home. He nodded and called Lowfield over. "Pauly. Can you give Meredith a ride home? I would, but I'm a little…tied up?" He looked down at his waist. The RN had seat-belted him in prior to leaving the hospital. Lowfield nodded and offered his arm to her.

"Shall we?"

Meredith nodded and before she could lose her nerve, ducked in and kissed David on the cheek. She quickly took Lowfield's arm and followed him out to his car, a hot flush on her face, and not for the first time.

"What was that about, girl? That's not how you kiss a man!" Lowfield picked on her as they climbed up into his truck. She blushed again, but the darkness hid it, thankfully.

"I dunno." She couldn't look him in the face through her embarrassment.

"I get it. If I were brave like you, I'd kiss him too." Meredith's head snapped up and stared at him with surprise. Was Lowfield suggesting he was gay? She had never heard of a gay officer before. She blinked several times before Lowfield gave a lopsided grin. "Yep. I hide it well when I have to, mostly at work. I think David's the only one who truly knows. The other guys have their suspicions, but they don't' mention it." He shrugged and turned onto the highway. "You'll have to give me directions. To your house, I mean. I know my way around a relationship." He chuckled again.

"I thought you had a girlfriend? What happened with that?" She asked, perplexed.

"I tried it. I liked her and we had our fun, but she wasn't the right one. I'd rather be alone for a while than with a person who doesn't understand me. I don't care if they're male or female - when they're not right, they're not right. And she was crazy possessive, remember?" He shrugged.

Meredith gave directions while she pondered what he'd said. He would rather be alone than with someone who didn't understand him. That was fair. She thought he was immensely brave to face the world on his own. She wished she could be like him in that way.

Once he pulled the truck into the driveway, Meredith thanked him and hopped out. "I'll see you next shift. Thank you."

Chapter 19

Meredith walked into the house to find Aaron was already in pajamas with a self-satisfied grin on his face. The girl he had brought home had left prior to her getting there. She knew the girl had been there without a doubt because the bed wasn't made anymore, and the bathroom smelled like soap and perfume. She had spent half the night here with Aaron, then used Meredith's soap and perfume before she left again. Meredith could feel a flame of anger rising up in her chest. It was one thing for Aaron to blatantly cheat on her ("babe, it's not cheating if you know about it," justified Aaron), but it was another entirely to allow her to make herself at home as if she belonged there.

"Took you long enough to get home." He looked up at her with a flat expression, as if she had been the one doing something wrong.

"It's before midnight, Aaron. Besides, you were busy with your new friend." Her tone was bordering on angry. She was about fed up after nearly twelve years of him sleeping with every woman he could bed. She wanted a relationship where it was just her with the man she loved; not her, the man she loved, and all of his extra conquests.

"What's that supposed to mean?" His dark eyes narrowed, a very real threat evident in them.

"I'm not stupid Aaron. I know why you brought her home. It's not like you can hide it now. When are you going to grow out of this? Can't you understand that I just want to be with you? Only you? I want a relationship where I don't have to worry who my love is looking at, or who he will bring home while I try to enjoy a night with my coworkers. I don't want to have to worry about going out with him for fear of who he will find to fuck that night. It's getting old, Aaron." Her tone had previously blazed with anger, but was now defeated and depressed.

"You knew I was into swinging when I got with you, Meredith. You can't pretend now that you're too good for it. You can't just go back and say all of a sudden you aren't interested anymore," he retorted with hot blood and raised voice.

Meredith couldn't help but wrinkle her nose and growl. "I told you hundreds of times I wasn't interested. I went along with it because I love you enough to let you do what you do in the hopes that maybe you'll get sick of it and want to be with just me. I see now that you'll never be happy with just one woman. I...I think...I'm going to be leaving tomorrow, Aaron, after work. You will never be happy with me, and I will no longer stand in your way, or be your doormat." She paused, taking a breath, trying to not raise her voice too high. "You are welcome to bring her back here, if you'd like. I just ask that you wait until I leave for work in the morning."

He stood up and walked menacingly toward her. "You can't leave me. Nobody will have you. You're a whore. Worthless. You will never amount to anything." His fingers clenched into a fist before relaxing, then clenching again. He was itching for a fight she didn't want, and it seemed it was too late to deescalate it now.

"I don't care what you say, Aaron. Your words don't hurt anymore. I'm going to bed. I'm tired and I work in the morning, then I'm leaving. You're free to fuck whatever you want," Meredith finished, her voice full of a combination of anger and defeat.

She didn't have time to react before he hit her across the face with a solid backhand. She cried out in surprise, taking a step back, hands raising to defend herself from any further blows. Tears stung her eyes as she felt hot, salty blood pour from her nose, down her chest, and staining her green dress. She stared at him, wanting nothing more than to make him pay for what he did, but she was smaller than he was, weaker, and didn't have any way to protect herself. She wasn't much of a fighter, especially against a man who was as enraged as Aaron was.

He stood there, breathing hard, fists clenching and relaxing. She could see the beginning of a bruise on his knuckles. He advanced on her, ready to hit her again should she say anything further, either in defense of herself, or against him.

Instead or saying anything at all, she went into the bathroom to clean up her face. She didn't try to hide the tears anymore, and let them flow down her cheeks as she staunched the flow of blood. Once her nose had stopped bleeding, she went into the bedroom and stripped the bloodied dress and set it on the bed. Meredith pulled on a pair of jeans and a t-shirt, socks and her boots, ready to flee if necessary. She pulled out a suitcase and packed it with as much as she could - clothes and important papers, including her commendation, jewelry and her extra uniform stuff, until it was close to overflowing. The things she needed for tomorrow, including her uniform and radio went into her backpack.

Once she had it packed, she navigated around Aaron, who had situated himself on the couch, and put it in her truck and went back inside for the rest of her things.

"What in the hell do you think you're doing?" Aaron's voice was low and dangerous.

"I'm getting my shit so I can leave." She walked past him again, back into the bedroom. She began throwing the rest of her things into whatever bags and boxes she had close. She had several books she wanted, a couple pictures off the walls, a couple blankets and her pillow. The rest of these things went into her truck. Everything else she could figure out as she went.

"If you walk out of this house, don't you dare come crawling back to me saying you want to come home again." He meant it as a threat, but Meredith laughed a mirthless laugh.

"Don't worry, Aaron. I won't." She walked out the door, paused a moment, and then shut the door behind her with a firm and final slam. Once in her truck, Meredith broke down again, shaking uncontrollably with a mixture of fear, adrenaline, and shame. She had never been struck like that before. What made him think he was a big man to hit her like that? He had hit her in the past, but it was always with the open palm of his hand, or punches to the shoulders that nobody would see. This was different. This wasn't just a bruise - he had very likely broken her nose.

Starting up her truck and putting it in reverse, she had no idea where she was going to go. She had no friends that would take her in. Tim was probably asleep by now, and she didn't want to wake him. She wasn't going to bother Lowfield. She decided she would go to the hospital and sit in Price's room until she could leave for work. The nurses had begun to see her as a fixture in the room, much like a lamp or a chair, and no longer questioned her. Especially since she frequently brought them treats.

She drove slowly to the hospital, unsure of what she would say to Price if he was awake. She didn't want to relive the fight, but it was playing over and over in her mind anyway. The biggest fear she had was that she didn't want him to worry about her, or to put Aaron in jail. She knew it wasn't something he meant to do - he was just angry and lost control. He would probably text her soon to apologize. She started to worry about what she would do when that happened. He would apologize, thinking that everything was better and that she would come home. He would be kind and gentle to her for a day or two and then would slip right back into his womanizing ways. But where else would she go?

It took her forever to pull into the parking lot at St. Victory, and when she did, she sat in her truck for several more minutes, trying to figure out exactly where her life had derailed. This was so far from the vision she had in her mind of what her life was supposed to be like. She took several more minutes and sobbed uncontrollably until she was able to slow her breathing and dab her face with a napkin, taking care to not disturb the clots her nose had created to stop the bleeding. She was sure it was broken, but was in no mood to deal with the ER or their questions. Domestic violence wasn't something you could just not report. It scared her. She was afraid that if it was reported, Aaron would come after her. He would hurt her much worse than a bruised shoulder or a broken nose. He wasn't stable.

Once she had herself back under control, Meredith grabbed her work bag with her uniform in it, and went inside. When she got up to the ICU, she sat in the waiting room for a minute, not quite ready to face David. The little old lady from several days ago was there, and she looked like she had been crying, too. Meredith took another minute to be able to look up at her and talk.

"Is it your husband?" Meredith's voice was gentle as she placed a small hand on the lady's shoulder. The lady looked up and nodded.

"After so many years together, I don't know how to live without him." She gave a weak smile and shook her head. "I know he's not suffering anymore, and I'm happy for that, but we have been together forever, it feels like. Fifty years is a lifetime. Through so many ups and downs." It was then that she noticed Meredith's face.

"Oh, my! What happened to you?" She reached a wrinkled hand up to turn Meredith's chin to take a look at both sides of her face. She had bruising on the right side, swelling on both, and eyes puffy from crying.

"My boyfriend and I got into a fight. I lost," she said softly, eyes downcast again. She felt overwhelmed by shame and fear, and couldn't help the shaking once it started again.

The old lady clucked her tongue and shook her head. "I'm sorry to hear that. Is there no reconciliation? What about the police, dear? Are you going to call them? It looks pretty bad."

Meredith shook her head. "No reconciliation after this. He has been getting worse, doing things that he knows aren't good that hurt me emotionally. And tonight, he hit me. I don't want him to go to jail...I haven't told anyone but you." The words stung almost as bad as the hand that Aaron put across her face. She had never thought of herself as a weak woman, but saying those words made her want to break down again.

"Sometimes, dear, when you drop a plate, it breaks into so many pieces that if you tried to put them back together again, all you would do is cut your fingers. You have to decide if your plate is worth fixing, or if you need to find a new one." The old lady's faded blue eyes had a slight twinkle to them. "My husband and I had many broken plates, and together, we decided to put them together, but the difference is - he was willing to help me, and the pieces weren't so small." She patted

Meredith's arm in the most grandmotherly way. "Either way, that is something you'll have to decide for yourself."

Meredith nodded and sniffled, tasting blood again. "Thank you. I wish you the best too. Is there anything I can do to help?"

The old lady shook her head. "No, dear. Unless you feel like saying a prayer for my dear old Charlie's soul. Other than that, my children should be here soon, and from there, we will make all the decisions we need. You should go and see your friend."

Meredith thanked the old lady again and slowly crept into Price's room. He was snoring softly when she walked in, so she settled down in the armchair and closed her eyes. She was certain the night's outing was too much for him, and had worn him out. She worried that it had undone the healing he had accomplished. The room was dark and comforting. Even the machines seemed to be quieter, and she slowly drifted into a light sleep. Before she knew it, she was having nightmares about Aaron hitting her again. She woke with a start and could see the reflection of David's eyes with the faint light of the monitors.

"You were talking in your sleep," he commented softly. "Sounded like a pretty rough dream."

Meredith nodded, not trusting her voice to remain steady. David patted the bed next to him and shifted over, wincing as the pain in his back flared up. Meredith rose and sat next to him, not looking at him. A strong hand carefully reached up to turn her chin toward him, the same as the old lady had done.

"Aaron." It wasn't a question, and the anger he felt flared up in his eyes. They seemed to glow with fury. "Just wait until I get out of here. I'll make him regret ever touching you…"

Meredith shook her head. "It's ok, David. Really. Just get better and we'll figure everything else out later."

David's anger was still on the rise, far from the crescendo, but he was unable to do much about it. He was on another round of antibiotics to ensure there was no more infection in his back, and he had gotten another dose of steroids that hadn't kicked in yet. He had some feeling in his legs, but the movement wasn't back yet.

David reached for his phone and punched in Lowfield's number. "I need you to come back to the hospital, and bring a victim's statement with you. You're not gonna like it." They talked another minute or two before he hung up the phone, trying to force himself to be calm. His hands were shaking in anger, and Meredith put one of her delicate hands on top of his.

"We're going to press charges. He won't lay a hand on you again." He paused. "I'll have one of my guys get him booked in tonight, and he'll be looking at anywhere from one to twenty years after he goes to trial with this. I'm sure he won't want to plea and make things easy."

Meredith shook her head, terrified. "He'll kill me if you do this. He'll get out and he'll kill me. I won't ever be safe. Please don't do this!" She was trembling, tears welling up in her eyes and spilling down her cheeks again. David pulled her down next to him and wrapped his right arm around her.

"We will protect you. He won't lay a hand on you ever again," he promised.

He let Meredith rest against him until Lowfield arrived. He gently woke her and told her to go with Lowfield down to the ER, and to fill out the statement while she was waiting for test results. Her eyes were wide, rimmed with fear, but he assured her that Aaron wouldn't hurt her again. Lowfield led her to the elevator where he was able to get a good look at her. He swore softly, his own hands clenching into fists. He wanted to pummel Aaron for what he had done. Exiting the elevator, he led her down to the ER where he told the nurses to get her checked in. While Meredith was filling out paperwork, Paul Lowfield was getting a Victim's Advocate who would be able to walk her through the rest of the procedures.

While all of this was going on, another officer had gone to speak with Aaron, and arrested him on assault charges, taking him to jail for the night. He would be able to see the judge first thing Monday morning.

In the ER, Meredith had gotten checked in, and had been assessed by a nurse. She was waiting to be taken to X-ray to see if her nose, or anything else in her swollen, bruised face was broken. Lowfield remained sitting next to her while she filled out the statement in every excruciating detail. Just knowing he was there was a comfort to her, though she wasn't able to relax.

Some time passed before the tech was able to get her into a wheelchair and take her down to radiology. The lady was friendly and cordial, explaining everything they were going to be doing before it was done. They were treating her like a battered housewife, and she hated that thought. She was a strong, independent woman, and while she was terrified that Aaron was going to kill her, she didn't need to be treated as though she were going to shatter.

"Ok, Miss Thomas. Let's get you back to your room, and the doctor will be in to see you once he gets the results."

Meredith nodded and sat back in the wheelchair. She thought it was silly, since she had no problems walking, but the tech had insisted it was protocol, so she agreed. Once back in her room, she finished the statement for Lowfield and handed it to him.

"I'm sorry, Meredith. Had I known it was going to go this way, I wouldn't have taken you home." His tone was soft, apologetic, guilty.

"It's not your fault. Really. Had I known, I would have left him years ago." She shrugged. "Live and learn, I guess."

Another hour passed and the doctor finally came into her room. He was an older man, stoic, with a hooked nose and crooked smile. He sat down beside her and spoke to her as if they were equals. It impressed her enough that she found herself pleased to have him as a physician.

"It looks like your nose is broken. I'm concerned about the bruising you have as well, though I don't think it will leave any lasting effects. You're not going to like it, but I'm going to have to set your nose back in place."

She winced, knowing it was going to hurt. It didn't feel out of place. She couldn't help feeling it with her hand. It was swollen and tender, and no doubt looked frightening. She steeled herself and sighed, nodding reluctantly. "Whatever you have to do."

Without warning, the doctor reached up and snapped her nose back into place. She squealed and pulled back, but by then, it was done. She glared at him, wanting to tell him exactly what was on her mind, but held back.

"You would have been tense if I would have counted to three. Now, it's done, and you don't have to worry about it. We'll do one last x-ray to make sure it's in perfect alignment, then I'll have your nurse get you an ice pack, and you're free to go. No restrictions as far as work. Don't blow your nose for the rest of the night, if possible. Let's make sure everything has clotted appropriately before we start doing too much. You should be fine mid-to-late afternoon." He shook her hand and left the room. Meredith's hand went back to her nose. It didn't feel any different, and the swelling hadn't magically gone away. Too bad.

Lowfield chuckled softly. "He's good, but he's a little…rough around the edges."

"That wasn't quite the word I had in mind, but I guess I can't complain. It's done." A minute passed and the tech took her back to x-ray. After that, she was given an ice pack for her face.

"Looks like you're all set. I think Doctor Xavier gave you some basic instructions, but here is the full set. No blowing your nose for at least twelve hours. You will probably have some bruising remain for a few more days. If you have an increase in pain, inability to breathe, or anything abnormal, you need to come back in for evaluation. Take an over the counter NSAID for pain, but be cautious that it may be harder to stop any bleeding if it starts again. Do you have any questions?"

Meredith shook her head and got out of bed. She was ready to spend the last hour or two before her shift with David. She hated switching from night shift to day shift. She never felt like she had rested enough. Even when she was able to sleep all night in her own bed, it wasn't enough. With

Lowfield beside her, they returned to David's room. He was awake and waiting for her to return.

Meredith didn't have time to talk, because Paul jumped in to give the report. "It's broken, but the doc reset it. I'll make sure to list SBI in the report, and we'll see if we can't get him several years. Oliver text me and said Aaron is booked into jail, and he won't be able to see the judge until Monday morning, so the weekend, at least, is clear." David nodded, still thinking.

"How are you feeling?" His voice was now tender, the angry look on his face abated to a gentle concern. She sat down next to him again, and his hand went to her thigh. It was large, warm, and all the comfort she needed.

"I'm fine. The doc reset my nose. It hurts, but it'll heal." She changed the subject. "How about you? It was a pretty long night. How are you feeling?"

"I'm fine." His speech was clipped. He was still angry, even though it wasn't directed at Meredith. He truly wanted to get up and beat Aaron senseless. How dare he lay a hand on that woman! "Why don't you get some rest? You said you work tomorrow?"

Meredith nodded. "Yeah. Day shift. I'm sure I'll be able to convince Tim to stop by your place tomorrow if you want us to get your mail and make it look like someone is watching your house. Just need the address and we'll take care of it." She was trying hard to be nonchalant, and to make it seem like she hadn't just been through one hell of an ordeal.

"I'm at Thirty-Nine Bugle Way. You don't have to go by if you don't want. I can send Pauly." Lowfield nodded. "I don't really want to put anything else on you right now." Meredith shook her head.

"I don't mind that - it'll keep my mind busy for a bit. Now, if you're going to have me landscaping and cleaning your pool and all that stuff, then it may need to wait a little bit, but just checking the mail and all the easy stuff...I think I can handle it." She grinned.

"I wish I had a pool or a personal landscaper. That would be nice," David mused.

A few more minutes passed and Meredith settled in on the chair. Lowfield found a nurse and brought her a blanket. The two men were still talking in hushed whispers long after she fell asleep.

"She'll need somewhere safe to stay, Pauly. You know I'd rather have her at my house - it's got a spare room, and everything she'll need to get her through this, and I doubt her piece of shit man knows where I live. But no matter what she decides, can I trust you to keep an eye on her?"

"Of course. I'll see if I can convince her to stay at your place until you're up and moving again. But no matter what, I'll watch over her until you can." Paul Lowfield winked at his buddy. "I'll help her put whatever boxes and things she has in your spare room for now, that way she doesn't have to haul her entire life around to and from work."

Price nodded. "Thank you."

The decision was made then to wrap it up for the night. It had been a long night for everyone, and it was time for them to all get some sleep. Lowfield left for home, while Meredith whimpered in her sleep and Price stayed awake to watch over her, just the way she had watched over him not too long ago.

Chapter 20

Morning broke early, and Meredith got up to change into her work uniform. Splashing cold water on her face was painful, but she had to try to get some of the swelling down. She took her time buttoning her uniform and brushing her hair and teeth. She wasn't looking forward to seeing everyone and having to explain what happened. Once she felt presentable, she left the bathroom and smiled when she saw David was watching her.

"After your shift, I'd like you to go to my place. You can shower and get some good sleep. Pauly will take you over there and get you settled." There was little room for argument, though he wasn't demanding. Meredith couldn't do much but nod in agreement. Even though Aaron was in jail for the weekend and wasn't home, she didn't want to be there. She had everything important to her. And a good, refreshing sleep sounded like something she would really appreciate.

"We'll still get your mail and get things figured out for you after I get on shift, and if we can, we'll stop by and give you your mail. Unless there's a winning letter from Publisher's Clearing House. I'm keeping that." At his bedside, she grinned and placed her hand on his again. She knew he was trying to heal, but leaning on his strength was the only thing getting her through this ordeal. She let her fingers trail over David's hand as she left the room on her way to work.

Getting to the station, Meredith sat in the parking lot for a minute. She wasn't ready to go in and face everyone. Her right eye was nearly swollen shut and bruised, her nose was bruised, and she looked like hell. With a resigned feeling, she stepped out of her truck and locked it, heading inside.

"Damn, girl!" Tim exclaimed, having no idea what happened. "You lose a fight with a gorilla? You look awful!" He figured she had an explanation that wasn't the one she gave him.

She shook her head, eyes downcast. "Aaron." The word was soft, embarrassed.

"Holy shit! Are you ok? I mean, obviously you aren't...but wow."

"Yeah. I'm fine. He's in jail right now, and I'm pressing charges." She waited a moment. "We need to make a run over to Bugle Way and the hospital sometime this morning."

Tim nodded. "Let's get our rig check done and we'll go."

They got into the ambulance and went through their equipment, restocking what was missing and ensuring they were set for whatever calls they would get for the day. It was a Saturday, and traditionally, they were slow until late afternoon. Once they were ready, Tim hopped in the driver's seat and told Meredith he'd chauffer her for the day. His driving was frightening at best, but she was too upset to even want to argue with him.

On the way over to Price's house, they were both silent. Meredith was lost in thought, and Tim was trying to respect her privacy. He wanted to ask her what happened, why it happened, and how he could help. He wanted to offer her a place to stay with guaranteed safety until she could find a place of her own, but he figured he would have plenty of time to do that later.

Meredith's phone rang, and with some worry about the unknown number, she answered it with a shaking, small voice.

"Miss Thomas...my name is Tiffany Adamson. I'm with the Victim's Advocate's office. I was asked to give you a call and introduce myself. Can we go over a few things over the phone?"

"Sure..." She was confused. What did she need a Victim's Advocate?

"It sounds like your boyfriend, Aaron was arrested last night. What happens now is that he will see the Judge and District Attorney on Monday. The DA has been busy lately, so I'm guessing they'll offer him a plea deal. Now because you're the victim, you have the right to disagree with the sentence passed down, or to make a suggestion of your own. Does that make sense?" she asked. She was speaking fast, and Meredith wasn't sure what to think.

Meredith nodded, and then realized the woman on the phone couldn't see her. "Yeah, I understand. I don't know what he deserves. I mean...he's never done this before. I just...don't think I can go back to him."

She could feel the advocate smiling. "I imagine not. The normal suggestion for punishment for something like this, especially if he's a first offender, is a year in jail with several years of probation. You can request more time, or a harsher sentence."

"No...I don't think anything more than that...I just want him to leave me alone. I need some time to think...some space. I need to figure out what I really want. I just don't want him to end up in jail for years and years."

"Sounds fair. I'll make that recommendation to the judge and to the DA, and I'll let you know if they make any counter offers," Tiffany explained.

They said their goodbyes as Tim was pulling into David's driveway. Meredith jumped down to check the mail. There was only a small stack of it. She checked the front door, and as she suspected; it was locked. She peered in the windows, and looked around the general area and found no signs that anyone had been around or tampering with anything. She took one last look around the house and then jumped back into the ambulance.

"Do you mind stopping by St. Victory for a minute?"

"Sure. Hey...what uniform do you have on today?" Tim had a goofy grin on his face. Meredith panicked and looked down, afraid that she had put on the wrong shirt, or worse, that there was blood all over her top.

"It's my normal work shirt...what are you talking about?"

He chuckled. "I didn't realize our job description read "postmaster" too."

She tried to roll her eyes, but with the swelling she had in her right eye, was unsuccessful. She groaned. "I hope you never quit this job. You wouldn't make it as a comedian."

"Ramen noodles are cheap. I'd be fine. Besides...just one night with my jokes, and I'd have thousands of adoring fans; women to swoon when I walked into the room, and maybe one who could cook for me!"

They playfully bantered during the ride to the hospital, and parked the rig in the ambulance bay. They weren't planning on being there long. Meredith led the way up to the ICU. A nurse caught her before she went into the room, stared at her face for a moment, and then launched into her speech.

"Good morning. David said you'd be by. He's being moved to a step-down room this morning. He'll be just down the hall, and then he can start his therapy. I think he's having a rough day today. He looks upset. Try to reassure him that the doctors are optimistic he'll make a good recovery, will you?" Meredith nodded, but knew that Price wasn't upset just over his situation.

They entered his room and found him sleeping. Meredith crept in and set his mail on the bedside table before creeping out to return to work. She wanted to stay there and watch him. It relaxed her to see his even breathing, the expression of serenity on his face. She liked knowing that while he was dreaming, nothing was bothering him. But unfortunately, she was unable to stay there with him while she was on duty. There was too much going on, and if they got called out, she would hate for her pager to wake him.

The rest of the shift passed with only a couple minor calls. There was nothing major that required serious Paramedic intervention, and so Tim offered to take the calls as well, so she wouldn't be scrutinized by their patients for her appearance. It shouldn't matter, but people were so judgmental. She was grateful that she had a partner who was so understanding. She had several partners in the past who wouldn't give a single care in the world about what she had been through.

As soon as shift change was over, Meredith stepped outside and her eyes fell upon the waiting Lowfield. She waved and grinned.

"Are you ready to head to your home away from home?" She nodded. She wanted to go to the hospital to check on Price, but with the stress of the past several hours, she was ready to shower and crash out. She would stop by and see him tomorrow after shift. She knew where she was going, having been there this morning, but was grateful for the company anyway. She followed Lowfield in her own truck and they both pulled into the driveway.

"Here's your key. I'll give you the quick tour and then you can explore more after I leave."

They went inside and Lowfield showed her where to find everything. Kitchen, bathroom, how the shower worked, and the spare bedroom where she was going to stay. He showed her the security system and gave her the code.

"If it goes off, an alarm will go straight to dispatch, and you'll have several officers surrounding the house in no time. So if you accidentally set it off, shut it down as soon as you can, and call dispatch to advise them it was you who set it off." He grinned. "Not that I've ever set off the alarm before."

Meredith laughed. "You'll have to tell me about this one day. I'm curious to know more."

Lowfield shook his head emphatically. "Nope. That is a story that I don't think I will ever tell anyone. It's not my brightest shining moment of dancing naked in the living room while a group of my coworkers burst through the door." Meredith laughed a hearty laugh, imagining the scene he described. She would hear the full story one day, but for now, that was enough of a mental image. She really didn't need more.

With the tour concluded, Lowfield reminded Meredith to call him if she needed anything, and he would periodically check in on her to make sure she was doing ok. She thanked him, hugged him, and then he left. After the door shut, she locked it, still scared to death that Aaron would burst through the door. She knew he was in jail, and he wasn't just going to walk in, but the fear was still there.

She looked around and walked slowly through the house, taking in little pieces of David. A thin blue line flag on the wall, pictures of who she imagined were his parents (the man had the same blue eyes, and the woman had the same nose). There were other pictures that she guessed were from his younger days. Shirtless with a stringer of fish; on a horse; two young boys standing side by side, matching grins on their faces. They looked like they were brothers. She moved on. The living room was well decorated, but simple. Against one wall was an electric fireplace with a TV mounted on the wall above it. On the opposite wall was a large beige sectional couch, and on another wall still was a tan recliner. He had a coffee table with several magazines - Men's Health, Guns & Ammo, and an assortment of hunting articles. There was a clock on the wall that showed the time was 7:09 pm.

She continued walking through the house. A hallway had no photos in it, but it led to the master bedroom. She hesitated before opening the door. The room was large and airy, the walls off-white. The king-size bed was made with a dark blue comforter over the top. Across from the bed was a TV mounted to the wall. It seemed the man enjoyed watching movies. There was also a bookshelf that was filled top to bottom with various books. She hadn't imagined David as a reader, but it seemed he was. Dean Koontz and Stephen King seemed to be his favorites, but there were several law enforcement books as well. There was a book toward the bottom that she picked up. It didn't have a dust jacket or any sort of markings on it. When she opened it, it looked like a woman's diary. She opened it to a random page and couldn't help but get pulled in.

I've secretly been seeing Eric for six months now. He's the most sensitive, gentle man I've ever met. He doesn't work weekends, and he doesn't work late. He buys me things when I point them out. I don't have to put up with his obnoxious work friends always coming over. I hate that David is always with his work friends. I wish he would pay more attention to me, but I guess that doesn't matter now. I also just found out I'm pregnant. I know it's not David's. We haven't had sex in a while. I don't know how to tell him I'm leaving him. I know I don't have a choice - it's either tell him, or let him raise Eric's baby, and Eric wants this baby more than anything. I think I'll tell him tonight after dinner. I'll be moved into Eric's house by this weekend. I can't wait.

Meredith closed the book and stared at it in disgust. She didn't want to read it, but her curiosity got the best of her, and now she can understand why David is so hesitant to get into a relationship. That woman hurt him badly over his friends and not buying her enough "stuff?" She shook her head and put the book back. What an awful, evil woman. She was still angry when she left the bedroom for the master bathroom.

It was modestly decorated with several towels hanging on hooks, a few more magazines, and in the corner, a Jacuzzi tub. Meredith nearly shrieked with glee when she found it. Turning the hot water on, she put the drain plug in, and adjusted the water to the right temperature. Searching through several cabinets, she finally found a towel and went to the spare room to retrieve her backpack. In it, she dug out her travel shampoo and a razor. As long as she had a minute to do so, she was going to take advantage of a hot bath and freshly-shaved legs. There was almost no better feeling in the world than to have fresh-shaved legs in clean, soft sheets.

Being a man's house, there was no bubble bath or bath bombs. That did little to dampen her spirits as she stripped her work uniform off, put on her favorite 90's playlist on her phone, and stepped into the hot water to the sweet tones of Ginuwine's "Pony". She slid down into the hot water until it was up to her shoulders and felt the heat working to relax the tension she had been feeling for far too long.

They had the pool to themselves. It was some 'deal' that Aaron had worked out with the hotel. She didn't know how he was able to pull it off, but she wasn't going to question it, either. The speakers were pumping the same "Pony" into the room, and the hot tub was gurgling in anticipation of two bodies to comfort. She had a large, fluffy towel wrapped tightly around herself, self-conscious and feeling fat. She hadn't been swimming in years, and she was especially nervous as they were still new to each other. What if he thought she was hideous or fat and didn't want to be with her anymore? What if he decided he just didn't find her attractive after all?

She walked into the pool room with him, and he gently tugged on her towel. There was curiosity in his eyes, but something else, too. Lust, definitely, but a desire to see what she was hiding. It would seem that men are no good at being patient. She let the towel fall to the floor, and Aaron couldn't help but stare at her. She was a solid "B" cup with a narrow waist, and full hips. She was perfect in his eyes, and he made no attempt to hide the appreciation of her body from her. He had a few extra pounds around the middle, but was far from fat. He took her hand and they slipped into the hot tub.

The water was intoxicating, and the force from the jets was enough to relax her sore muscles. It had been a rather long week at work, and she had been looking forward to this since Aaron first suggested it. He repositioned himself in front of a jet, and moved her so she was sitting in front of him. His hands were warm from the water, and when he began to rub her sore shoulders, it was heaven. He also made no attempt to hide his excitement from her.

As the night progressed, Aaron grew bold and slowly slid down her swim suit bottom, and pulled his down just enough to expose himself to her. He wasted little time in getting what he wanted from her; but he was still gentle. She felt dirty, especially since this was a public hot tub. Who knows how many other people had been in here…but he seemed to enjoy it, so she decided it wasn't so bad.

The night progressed slowly, and before long, they were up in their room getting ready for bed. Aaron had pulled out his phone camera and urged her to lie seductively on the bed, "Like a Playboy model," he said. She had, as of yet, never seen a Playboy, so she guessed at how she was supposed to be lying. He adjusted her just the way he wanted her, and snapped several photos as she moved to his commands.

He continued to take pictures and once he felt he had enough, put his phone to charge and crawled under the covers, pulling her close to him in a possessive embrace. She fell asleep feeling protected and warm.

Chapter 21

Meredith stretched out in the tub, feeling the heat reach deep into her muscles. After she was sufficiently relaxed, she ducked her head under the water so she could shampoo her hair. After that, she shaved everything so she was smooth and ready for bed. She pulled the drain plug and stood up, feeling a little weak from the heat. Wrapping the towel around herself, she grabbed her bag and headed to her room. Finishing drying, she pulled on some pajamas and crawled into the queen-sized bed. It didn't take her more than three minutes to fall asleep, surrounded by true warmth and comfort. She didn't suffer any nightmares, nor did she remember dreaming at all. It was the most refreshing night she could remember having in quite a while. Maybe this was exactly what she needed - to be away from Aaron and the house of lies he had built around her.

The rest of the weekend passed much the same. She visited David in his room at the hospital and was updated on his prognosis. It seemed he was doing well, and they wanted to start him in therapy within two weeks. Meredith had several bad ambulance calls, including a suicidal teenager who had taken a bunch of pills. Meredith was able to get an IV started, and give some Narcan, but the medications weren't narcotic. There was little she could do except give fluids and advise the hospital to be ready. Despite the rough calls, there was nothing that could pull her down. Until Monday came.

She knew Aaron would be meeting with the judge and the District Attorney, and she feared what would happen. She was certain he would ask for a plea deal, and he would be free in no time. She wanted to be there to see what he would get, but was too afraid that he would hurt her again, despite court security. She stayed away from the courthouse and tried desperately to push the thought of it from her mind, unsuccessfully.

Toward the middle of her shift, in between several transfers and 911 calls that didn't really need an ambulance, while she and Tim were enjoying greasy burgers and chocolate shakes, her phone rang. Her heart went wild, hoping it was David, but she didn't recognize the number. She was apprehensive as she answered it.

"Hello?"

"Yes, is this Meredith Thomas?" a voice asked her.

"Yes, it is…" she replied, even more nervous than she had been a moment ago. Who was calling her that knew her name?

"This is Tiffany Adamson, your Victim's Advocate. How are you?" She sounded friendly, and far too happy with herself. Did that mean Aaron was getting a harsher sentence than the one they had discussed? Had the judge been in a bad mood? What was going to happen?

"Good…how are you?" she responded slowly.

"Good. The reason I'm calling you today is to advise you that Aaron was able to see the judge today. He was given a plea deal that he accepted. The DA took some of our recommendation, and made their own deal. He will be in jail for thirty days, minus three for time served, and he will have three years of probation, during which, he is not to have any contact with you whatsoever. This was the best deal we could get without you being there and putting him on trial," the Victim's Advocate said, a hint of sadness in her voice. It would seem she wanted to see Aaron get several years.

Meredith was stunned. Thirty days? And three years of probation? He could easily walk through a "leave her alone" command. It's not like someone telling him what to do ever worked for him. She stammered a quick, "thank you," and hung up. She had lost her appetite. She hadn't wanted him to go to jail to begin with, but she didn't want to have to fear for her safety, either.

Tim looked concerned as he stared at her, eyes full of worry. "What's wrong?"

"Aaron got thirty days in jail. He'll be out in a month, Tim. He's going to kill me. I mean, he got probation too, but that isn't going to stop him. He's going to kill me when he gets out." She didn't realize she had started rocking back and forth with her anxiety.

"I think there are enough of us around that we've got your back, Mer. We won't let him hurt you." He was trying hard to reassure her, but she was too far gone for that. She was trying to decide if she had enough vacation time to cash out and move somewhere else, where he would never find her again. She could change her name, change careers, and live an anonymous life. That was extremely tempting, but one thing kept holding her back - David. She couldn't leave him behind, and with him needing rehab and specialists, she couldn't just drag him away from his entire life, either.

They finished out their shift with Tim still trying to reassure Meredith that she would be as safe as they could all keep her. That she wouldn't have to be alone ever, if she didn't want to be. She had enough of a support system that Aaron wouldn't be able to get through to her anymore.

Meredith left the station that night and headed straight to the hospital. Once there, she went into David's room and sat down. The frustration and fear was clear on her features, and he beckoned her over to his bed. He picked up her hand.

"What's wrong? You look terrible," David asked, the concern evident in his tone. He struggled to sit a little higher to give her a little more room to sit comfortably.

"Aaron got thirty days, then probation. Thirty days, David. He's going to kill me. I didn't want this!" her voice was high, strained, and about to crack with fear.

"No. No, he won't. I should be out of here in a month. They want me to stay here for two more weeks to make sure everything is healing well. They're starting to do some minor therapy, and then, I'll have two more weeks of just in-house therapy. After that, they'll consider letting me go home, as long as I am able to make my therapy appointments so I can keep getting stronger. You can stay with me, and I'll keep you safe," he promised her, hand tightening around hers.

She was upset, scared, and didn't know what to say. She wanted to ask how he could keep her safe while he was still in a wheelchair, but she didn't. She didn't want to pass her black mood on to him when he had done nothing wrong. Instead, they spent several hours talking about other things - their favorite flavor of ice cream, favorite breed of dog, whether they were a dog or cat person. In that, Meredith had learned that he was a typical cop. He liked vanilla ice cream, black coffee with one sugar and no cream, he was a dog person and had always loved Rin Tin Tin, and once he was back out of the hospital, was going to apply to become a K9 officer. His favorite home-made meal was lasagna, and if he was going to a restaurant, he wanted a good, thick steak with a cold beer.

It was getting late when David finally looked at the clock. "Meredith, you should go and get some rest. You've got what...one day left for the week? Get some rest and come see me tomorrow." He smiled and pulled himself up in bed again so he could hug her. She didn't want to let go, and so he held onto her until she was ready. "It'll be ok. Really," he whispered to her as his hands stroked her hair.

She wanted to believe him. She really did. But she just didn't see how it could work out when Aaron would be free in so short a time. He was going to be furious that she had put him in jail. She hadn't wanted to even press charges, but David hadn't left her much choice. She took some comfort in knowing that David would be home soon, but it made her sad that she would have to find somewhere else to live. She assumed he wouldn't want her hiding out at his place forever.

Two weeks passed quickly with Meredith visiting after her shifts. Every day, she watched David growing stronger, little by little. By the end of the two weeks, they were no longer worried about rogue infections, or the fusion of his spine having massive issues like breakage. He had some minor movement back in his feet, but he was far from walking again. During that time, Tim and Paul had worked together with her to install a ramp for David's wheelchair at his front door, and re-worked the shower in the master bathroom to a walk-in shower with a seat in it for easier bathing. They had also brought in a Hoyer lift so he could get from his bed to his wheelchair without struggling. They had worked hard to make sure David's home was ready for him until he was able to get back on his feet.

Chapter 22

One day after her shift, Meredith was back in David's hospital room. They had been talking about what the future could possibly hold, and how long it would take to get back onto the police force. That was his main goal after he was able to walk again - to get back to work. He hated being sedentary, and was itching to be back on the job.

"I think once we have you walking again, it won't take long. We'll build you up slowly now so you're stronger than you were before. You'll have your K9 before you know it," she told him with excitement in her voice. She could see it - him back in uniform with a gorgeous dog at his side, ready to take on the world again.

David grinned. "I can't wait. And it sounds like they are going to release me home next week - a whole week early. As long as I can get back and forth to therapy appointments," he said with an eye roll. He would move hell or high water to get to where he needed to be as long as it meant he could be at home again. He was sick of the cafeteria food, and the nurses poking and prodding him all night. He wanted a good night's sleep.

Meredith nodded. "I can take you on the days I'm off, and maybe Lowfield can take you on the days he's off. We'll make sure you get where you need to go. I'm sure you'll be more comfortable at home, anyway."

"Have you given any thought to staying after I'm home? I wouldn't mind a live-in nurse." He winked. "I'm not sure how much I can pay you...but you can stay there rent-free...if you want?" There was the smallest hint of hope in his voice. He wanted her around, even though he wasn't ready for a full relationship. He liked the way things were going - they were easy. He could talk to her just like one of the guys, and she understood. She was solid and really *there* for him. He could see them being in a relationship, just not today.

Meredith had been saving up enough money to give to him as a rent payment when he got home. She knew between the workman's comp and

119

his insurance, it would cover the medical bills, but that wouldn't cover his other bills. She wanted to help out, on top of keeping his house stocked with bubble bath and food. She had thought about staying, but wasn't sure if he would really want her there.

"If you want me to stay, I would be happy to stay...I just don't want to smother you. I know you're not ready for any sort of relationship, and I don't want you to think I'm trying to push anything," she explained softly. The thought of staying with him was in her wildest dreams - one she didn't think she would ever achieve, but here he was asking her!

He chuckled softly. "I'm inviting you to stay. As you know, I have a guest bedroom and nobody else living with me. I assure you, I will let you know if you're getting to be too much."

The remaining days passed quickly and before they knew it, David was released home with specific orders that he would have home health checking on him every couple days. He had assured the doctor that he had a highly skilled Paramedic who was going to be staying with him as well, and if there were any issues, he would be immediately transported to the ER for evaluation. Meredith spoke with the physician at his request and took several notes on what to look for, just in case there was a random medical ailment that didn't present as it should, she would know what to do. They had a good conversation about pain levels and what was acceptable, and what could indicate a return infection, even though the likelihood was low. At the end of the discussion, David was cleared to return home.

Lowfield had arrived to assist with getting David in and out of the car, as he had not yet regained full function of his legs. He was getting stronger, day by day, but still had a long road ahead of him. Together, they wheeled him into the elevator, and then to the parking lot.

"Oh man, it's amazing, feeling the sunlight again! And fresh air! I thought I was going to be stuck in that damn place forever! Do you know how awful it is when all you can smell is old piss and bleach? And a god-awful mix of perfumes that the nurses bathe in? Ugh! And listen to the birds! Man, this beats hearing the daily news of which nurse is sleeping with what doctor. Birds are less dramatic, but I missed it so much!" David closed his eyes and raised his face to the sun, a wide smile spread across his face. He couldn't be happier.

"Glad we were able to bust you out, buddy. Let's get you home and settled, and then you can have all the fresh air you want." Lowfield was especially happy today, excited to see his friend's expression when he saw the ramp and the shower at home. He even whistled as they pulled the wheelchair up to the side of his car.

He and Meredith stared a moment, trying to decide the best way to get him in. In the end, they decided that Lowfield would help him stand and turn, and Meredith would guide him down into the seat from the inside. The two of them worked slowly as to not agitate any injury or soreness he had, or to hit his head on the frame of the car. Once he was inside, Price was beyond thrilled, proclaiming his joy at every little thought.

"I can't believe I'm going home. I was so sick of that place, and I absolutely cannot wait for a good steak. Lowfield, you can stop me by a good restaurant, right? Like an expensive steakhouse. I don't want any thin, shitty steak, or a flat beer that's all foam and no beer."

Lowfield shook his head. "No can do, boss. Meredith already has everything you need to get you started." He grinned as Price's expression turned stunned.

"Really?" David asked.

"Yeah...I know you've been asking for steak for a while now. Doc said no beer for a little longer because of all the pain medications they gave you, and the new ones you'll be on for a while, but he didn't say anything about steak." Meredith was pleased that he seemed so excited about dinner. It was the least she could do, especially when he trusted her enough to let her live there for a month without charging her rent.

She had ridden with Paul from the house to the hospital, and so, she climbed in the back seat and buckled in. She could hardly contain herself. She was hoping that David wouldn't be too upset that she and Lowfield had made changes to his house - a ramp to get in and out, a shower chair and addition of a walk-in shower, and the lift. She had tried to think of things that would make his life easier, and take the stress and worry from him.

Once they got to David's house, they helped him get from the car back to the wheelchair. He was itching to be independent again, and insisted he be allowed to wheel himself into the house. He smiled as he saw the ramp, the apprehension gone of trying to figure out how he'd get up the stairs. "You two are amazing. Thank you." His voice was full of gratitude and wonder.

Lowfield held the door open for him, and he wheeled himself inside. Right off the bat, he didn't see anything different. He had expected to see his house altered by the woman living there. He was almost disappointed that she had kept everything the way he had it. No flowers on every flat surface, no ballerina pictures or random oil diffusers; not even a scented wax cube diffuser. Did this girl not know how to decorate a house? Or was she that shy? Part of him was, admittedly, relieved to see his house hadn't been turned into a woman's paradise that he would have to convert back into his bachelor pad. He hoped that she, at the very least, had changed the guest room enough to make it her own space. She had been there long enough, she deserved to have it be a comfort to her.

"Let's go show you what we did to the bathroom," Lowfield told him. He was acting like a young child at Christmas, waiting to be allowed to open a present. He had to force himself to not push David into the room.

"Sure." He wheeled himself into the bathroom. "You changed my...shower?" It was still a standing shower, but they had modified it into a larger walk-in shower that would allow the wheelchair in so he could get to the seat. David's eyes were wide with surprise. "I can't believe you did this." He pushed himself into the shower and was astounded to realize he could reach everything important. He would have to figure out how to get into the shower seat, but everything else was easy for him.

"Now...go to bed!" Lowfield was practically bouncing now. Meredith rolled her eyes and giggled. She hadn't seen this side of him before; this child-like, it's-almost-Christmas excitement. It was endearing. She imagined he was great with children on the calls he went on, and probably a hit with the ladies, too. He might not be sure what he was looking for, but Meredith could easily see him as a kind and nurturing partner who would go above and beyond to ensure whomever he was with was as happy as possible.

David raised an eyebrow and complied, slowly working his way out of the bathroom and into his bedroom. The lift was there waiting for him. He grinned as he moved his wheelchair under it and picked up the control. He lowered the lift and put the straps under himself and lifted up. It had just enough control that he could easily get himself into and out of bed. "You guys are the greatest! Please let me know what I owe you for all the upgrades, and as soon as I'm back on my feet," he paused, chuckling at the pun he had inadvertently made, "...I will get you paid back."

Meredith and Paul shook their heads. "I figure this is fair compensation for letting me live here for the past several weeks." She had also saved up money in a jar for rent that she hadn't told him about. If he wouldn't accept it as it was, she would just pay her part of the month's bills with it. Or help him down the line with any further improvements, or medical expenses. She didn't want to be a burden on him.

"You've put up with me for years, bro. I owe you more than a shower." Lowfield shrugged.

"You two go ahead and get your bonding out of the way, I'm going to start dinner," Meredith chortled as the guys continued their conversation.

Meredith left the room with a smile on her face, heading straight for the kitchen. She pulled out the steaks and set them to rest while she worked on getting her marinade together. After that, she put the meat in the marinade and began boiling water for a pasta salad, while she put together dough for biscuits. She couldn't help but hum happily as she worked, feeling every bit part of a family again. It had been too long since she had one man truly care for her, let alone two. It was the best feeling she could think of.

The two men came out of the bedroom and situated themselves on the couch. Meredith shook her head and laughed as they were still talking about the Hoyer lift while turning on the TV to find a rerun of a cop show. David had been itching to get back to work, despite the injuries sustained. He wanted nothing more than to get back to the physical training, the mental challenges, and the application for K9 officer. She was happy to see that he wasn't afraid to get back on the street, but was still wary that maybe he would have some PTSD from it. They would have to work through it, if he started having issues.

Meredith worked on dinner until everything was at a point it just had to cook and she could step away. She sat on the couch by the guys. "You two are something else. Where did you meet?"

"Police academy. We battled the whole way to be the best. One week, it was me, and the next week it was him. Drove both of us crazy to have such a close challenger." David gave Lowfield a grumpy look, but then laughed. "I was sorely tempted to break his leg so I could win, but I guess it worked since we were the top of the class with nobody anywhere near either of us."

They discussed the ins and outs of police academy for a while, sharing stories of being pepper-sprayed, tased, and using handcuffs for the first time, until the timer beeped for dinner. Meredith went back into the kitchen and got everything plated and set out and ready. She called the boys who sat at the table in record time. Both of them stared at the plates before them - steak, pasta salad, rolls, and green salad. She was anxious for them to dig in, afraid that everything wouldn't be perfect. This was David's first meal home after nearly a month in the hospital, and the first time she had cooked for anyone other than Aaron in over a decade, with the exception of his family, of course.

The boys wasted no time cutting into their steaks and stuffing their mouths full with rolls and butter. The lack of talking and the noises they were making led her to believe that her meal was satisfactory. Once they had finished, Lowfield looked like he needed to be rolled back into the living room more than David did.

"That was possibly the best homemade steak I have ever had," he said. "This is absolutely better than steakhouse quality."

"I agree. Meredith, this is amazing!" David was just as stuffed as Lowfield.

The three of them sat around for a little longer after Meredith finished the dishes until Lowfield decided he needed to get home. "I'll be back in a couple days to get you to your appointment. Meredith said she's working that day." He hugged Meredith and shook David's hand and left for home, walking a little slower than he did when he came in. Meredith attributed it to the fact he was full of steak.

"That was the best homecoming ever. I don't know how to thank you." David's voice was soft and gentle, still full of wonder and gratitude.

"You gave me a place to stay when I needed it. Truly, I owe you more than a few dinners and a ride to an appointment. Really."

They sat in silence for a while on the couch while several commercials for random medications blared. David reached over to take Meredith's hand.

"Meredith…you really mean a lot to me, and truly… I can't thank you and Pauly enough for what you've done here. I spent a lot of time worrying about how I was going to be able to be home and make my appointments, and make sure nobody broke into my house. I was worried about how I'd be able to get in and out of my house, and the shower, and bed, and be able to cook for myself, and everything else. You have given me a gift that I will never, in a million years, be able to repay."

She blushed, head low, unsure of what to say, what to think. She had never been in a situation like this - where something she did was good enough for someone. Aaron had always found fault in everything she did, no matter how perfect it was. She remained quiet without knowing what to say. Her eyes were downcast, but they were full of love and admiration.

He pulled her closer, his hand reaching up to her cheek, tilting her head back up to him, thumb caressing her cheekbone. She closed her eyes and leaned her head into her his hand. It was comforting to feel such a gentle touch. Part of her missed Aaron, and the times when he was gentle like this, when the relationship was new, and he was trying hard to impress her. When he wanted to win her over.

Before she knew what was happening, David had leaned in and his lips met hers. It was surprising, but not unpleasant. It was absolutely how she had imagined it - soft, sweet, gentle, and she felt an explosion of fireworks in her stomach and time slowed to a standstill. Had she not been sitting, she would have lost all ability to stand due to the weakness in her knees. One of her hands was supporting her on the couch, and the other went to rest in his chest. A moment passed; the fireworks dimmed in her head and she slowly pulled away from him. Her brow was furrowed. He told her he didn't want a relationship...but then he kissed her? What was going on?

"Why...what...I thought..." Meredith could only stammer, trying to understand how she should feel. Part of her felt guilty. She still cared somewhere deep down for Aaron (not that she wanted to be abused by him anymore, but that doesn't mean the "care" wasn't there); but he had hurt her so many times, for so many years in so many ways, so she left. He was serving a jail term for what he did to her. She wasn't supposed to care about him anymore. Part of her also loved David, even though she hadn't told him when he was conscious and could hear it. She was conflicted, and sat there, waiting for an explanation of what just happened.

"I'm sorry...I shouldn't have..." David apologized with hushed tones. "It just...it felt right."

"But you don't want a relationship?" Meredith was confused.

"I don't think I'm ready to define what we are, but I do care for you, and I'd like to see where things progress. But if you're uncomfortable with it...I'm ok with that too. Just say the word and I won't be out of line again."

Meredith sat there, stunned. Her entire life had taken a complete 180 from where she thought it was headed. Slowly, she shook her head. "No, I don't think you're out of line. I'm just a little surprised, that's all. I think we should take things slow and see what happens, even though I want this more than anything." She was even more confused now, and was fighting feelings for David and Aaron. She knew she shouldn't have feelings for Aaron anymore, but after being with him for so long, it was hard to just turn it off.

"Understood." He grinned, and most of the tension melted away.

She was glad there wasn't an awkwardness between them, or an air of regret. She wasn't unhappy, but she needed some time to sort out her emotions. She wasn't expecting Aaron to still be a factor, especially after he had hit her, and then spent a month in jail. She wasn't supposed to still care about him or his feelings! She wasn't supposed to worry about whether he was fed, or had paid his rent; or if he was sleeping well at night; but there was something that wouldn't let her just shut him out of her mind completely.

Chapter 23

The kiss remained on Meredith's mind even after she returned to work. Between calls, she and Tim had talked about the case against Aaron, the time he was serving, and the probation he would have when he got out of jail. They had talked at length about David, and how she was feeling about him, and what to do about it. Meredith wanted to be with him, though he said he wasn't ready to call it a relationship. She had told Tim about the days they spent together when she wasn't working and he wasn't in any appointments. She told him how she and David would talk about everything under the sun, and how there was no topic off-limits, and that was something she had never had with anyone else. She and Tim had discussed many things in the past weeks, and Meredith was comfortable with him.

"He kissed me, Tim. He just up and kissed me. What am I supposed to do about that? I mean...I still care for Aaron, but I don't think I could ever get back with him...but David just got out of a bad divorce and isn't ready for a real relationship, but then he up and kissed me. I don't know what to think about it or what to do." She rambled on for minutes until she was able to get herself back under control.

"I think you should explore whatever is going to make your heart happiest. You've been through a lot with Aaron, both good and bad, and if you feel getting back with him is going to be best for you, then do that. I, however, think that's a mistake because he is a monumental asshole with no regard for you. But, if you feel like staying with David is going to make you happiest...do that. It's your life, and you gotta do what's best for you sometimes."

"That's the thing. I don't know what I want right now." She was frustrated again.

"Then don't decide right now. Just ride things out and see where they go. There are no timelines for love," he explained. There was just something about the way he would tell her things that made sense to her confused heart.

Meredith nodded again. That was a good idea, but it still didn't solve the worry she had. Aaron would be out of jail in about a week, give or take a few days, and what would happen to her then? Of course, he had a 'no contact' order, but that didn't mean much. He could walk right through it and kill her and that piece of paper wouldn't mean a damn thing. She guessed she would have to take it a day at a time.

After her shift, she went straight to her truck, fumbling with her keys in her excitement to be leaving work for the first time in years. The truck roared to life, as if it, too, were as excited to be going home to someone who would care for it.

Meredith's heart was full and racing with exhilaration as she pulled into the driveway. She could hardly contain herself as she climbed out of the truck and turned the knob to the front door. It squeaked softly as it swung open, allowing Meredith inside. She expected to find David on the couch relaxing, and was surprised when he wasn't there.

"David?" she called out, not wanting to startle him with her abrupt appearance. There was no answer from him. She began to worry, looking for him first in the kitchen, then the bedroom, and finally the bathroom. She was surprised when she found him sitting on the tile floor. He was furious and refused to look at her, cursing softly as she rushed to his side. She knelt beside him, a gentle hand going to his shoulder. "Are you ok?" She didn't try to lift him or coddle him, and didn't pity him. It was an adjustment that he was going to have to learn until he could walk again.

"No. I'm on the fucking floor. My stupid legs aren't working like they're supposed to, and I can't pick myself up. How am I going to get back into law enforcement if I can't pick myself up?" His fist hit the tile floor in frustration. "I'm fucking useless right now."

Meredith gave him a minute to finish before she replied. "You aren't useless, David. You're just having a rough day. Let me help you. We'll get you up and walking again. One fall isn't the end of the world. You don't have any new pain or anything, right?" She rested her hand on his shoulder and then slowly felt down his spine, waiting to see if he winced at any point.

David shook his head. "No."

"Good. We're going to move you so your knees are underneath you, and then you're going to help me so I can get you back up. Are you ready?"

He pursed his lips, wanting to fight and argue and be independent, but he realized there was no point. He'd be stuck on the floor forever if he didn't humble himself to accept some help. He nodded. With that, Meredith had him lean forward so she could help him get his knees under him. After that, he grabbed around her neck and she lifted. He was weak, but his legs held him just long enough to get him back in his wheelchair.

"No pain, tingling, or anything unusual? Your back isn't hurting?" she asked, using the "paramedic voice" on him. She wasn't going to tolerate him being a sullen child and not tell her if something was wrong that warranted him being seen by a physician.

David wanted to be a smart ass in his sour mood and tell her that he had no feeling in his legs, but he didn't. He shook his head and simply left the room quietly. Meredith figured he was going to need some time alone, and so, went into the kitchen. She had found a new cookie recipe she wanted to try, and so, spent some time whipping up a batch to let David cool down on his own. She was still hurt by his emotions, but she knew they weren't aimed at her. He was upset with his situation and didn't have an outlet. She didn't know what she could do to help him except let him vent when he needed to vent and to be there when he needed her to be.

It wasn't long before he rolled in. His voice was still surly, but she knew it wasn't directed toward her. "Thank you." She turned and offered him a warm smile.

"You're welcome. I know you're upset, but I promise you, somehow, we will get you walking again. I know the doctors were optimistic it would be a year before you'll regain full function, but research shows it could be as early as six months. Let's focus on physical therapy, and take it a day at a time. I'm here for you, whatever you need." It was nice that she was able to stay with him and be there when he needed something. She would hate to be away and he fall, or something worse happen and nobody know about it until he swallowed his pride and asked for help.

"I know. And I appreciate it. Now…when are those cookies going to be done?"

Time progressed slowly, as Meredith had suggested - a day at a time. They grew closer to each other, despite their turbulent pasts and their current worries, and learned that it was acceptable to depend on one another to get through their challenges. Meredith leaned on David to help her stay calm the day Aaron got out of jail, and he leaned on her when it came to appointments and working on physical therapy at home. They challenged each other, and in that, found a relationship that they had been searching for. They became an inseparable pair, each forcing the other to be better, stronger, more determined.

It had gotten to the point where Meredith felt comfortable asking him about his past, a little at a time. They had been relaxing together after a round of therapy when she stood up and went to the pictures he had on the wall. She pointed to the picture of the two boys. "Is this you?"

David nodded and looked at the picture. A sad smile came to his face. "Yeah. It was just after my parents died. That's my cousin, Gavin. We spent a lot of time together with my grandmother. We would go out and raise hell together, chasing the other neighborhood boys, throwing rocks at cars, exploring all the abandoned buildings that clearly said "do not enter." He was as close as any brother."

"What happened?"

David paused, recalling the memory in his mind before he could put it to words. It was clear he didn't want to think about it. "We were exploring an old abandoned shack in the woods. It was weak in the structure from years of just sitting there with no one to care for it. We went inside and a wall caved in. Gavin was in the way and it fell on him. I had to leave him to run and get his parents. They called an ambulance and we returned to the scene. We were able to pull him out with the adults. I just wasn't strong enough to do it alone. He suffered a broken arm and some pretty good cuts, but nothing worse. His parents wouldn't let us play together anymore after that day. They said I was a bad influence on him."

Meredith shook her head. "That's pretty shitty, I'm sorry. Were you able to keep in touch, at least? School and after?"

"Yeah. We didn't have many classes together, and he fell into the wrong crowd. Got into drugs and alcohol. The last I heard, he was in jail on charges for attempting to sell drugs."

"I'm really sorry to hear that. It must have been hard for you," Meredith reasoned.

David shrugged. "I guess it wasn't me who was the bad influence after all." He gently changed the subject, and Meredith let it go.

Chapter 24

A few days after Aaron got out of jail, Meredith received an email from him. She read and reread the "no contact order," but it seems the judge left out the part about "all" contact, and he was simply limited to no "physical" contact.

Hi Babe. I thought long and hard about what I would say to you when I got out of jail. I spent a lot of time being angry, wanting you to hurt for what you did to me, and then I realized…I hurt you first. I know you, and I know that this probably wasn't even your idea. That doesn't mean I'm not still hurt over it, but maybe I can understand a little bit. I would like you to come home so we can start over. I will listen to your needs better, and if you don't want to swing with other couples anymore, I can learn to live with that. I just don't think I can live without you, Meredith. Please think about it. I want you home with me. I want to marry you, Meredith, to be with you forever. You can have your white dress and fairy-tale wedding. I have it all planned out and everything. We can have a kid if that's what you really want. I just need you back. I love you.

Meredith read the email several times. There was a feeling of uncertainty deep in her chest. He had never done anything like this before, could he possibly be sincere about it? Could he really change? Did jail do that much to fix him and his demeaning nature? Did he mean it…that he would listen to her needs? A thousand thoughts swirled around her mind at a million miles an hour. She felt nauseated and dizzy.

"David…?"

He yelled from the living room, "Yeah?"

Meredith left her bed and walked slowly into the living room and sat on the couch. David set down the weights he was working with. He had told her there was no point in letting his upper body go to hell because his lower body was struggling.

"I got an email from Aaron." Her voice was uncertain, expecting him to blow up at her. It's what Aaron would have done. Instead, he turned his wheelchair toward her, eyebrows raised, giving her his full attention.

"And? Was it bad?" he asked.

"…No. He was apologizing for what happened, and wants me back." She was slow to meet his eyes, expecting him to have a fiery rage, expecting him to tell her to leave. That's what Aaron would have done, in his shoes, but David was calm about it. He knew she didn't ask Aaron to email her.

"How do you feel about that? Do you want to go back to him?" His voice was even, though his emotions were in turmoil just below the surface. He would let her go if she wanted to go, but he was certain Aaron would just hurt her again. A man who has a history of violence doesn't just turn it off. Maybe for a short time, until his victim feels safe again, but then the behavior will start again, and often, it will be worse.

"Honestly? I don't know. I mean, we were together forever, and it wasn't all bad. He had his moments, but he also had his flaws. Just the past few years has gone downhill pretty steadily. And he's never hit me before. Not like this, anyway. I want to believe he could change, I really do…but with that being said, I'm scared that he won't change, and it'll be even worse. Besides…I'm still waiting to see where this is going with you." She gave him a half smile. She was just as conflicted now as she was about hearing Aaron's sentence. She wanted the familiarity, but she loved David, too. She was starting to realize she always had, even though she had never acted on it. "I want to give us a good chance before I make any big decisions. That's not bad…is it?"

David shook his head. "I don't think so. It sounds fair. But I do think that if you're with me, you're with me. If you're with him, you're with him. I don't think it's fair to either of us to go back and forth." He shrugged. "That's all I can tell you. The jealous side of me wants to keep you here for myself, but I know that's what he would do, and I want you to have your freedom to make whatever decision you feel is best. I'll give you your space to work it out, however much space that may be. I'll be here no matter what you decide." He didn't want to crowd her and have her feel obligated to stay with him. Meredith nodded, leaned in to kiss him on the cheek, and went back into her room, settling on the bed, legs crossed beneath her.

She stared at the email with a frown. Why would he do that to her? Was he so desperate to control her that he would send her cyanide lies? Or was it a goodwill gesture that he honestly meant? He hadn't wanted to get married before - what changed? Deep down, she knew he was only telling her the sugared lies she wanted to hear. He truly believed that if he told her he would give in to all her fantasies - marriage and a family that she would run back to him. Meredith sighed heavily and closed the email. She was not in the right frame of mind to respond to anything.

Leaving her phone behind, she returned to the kitchen to plan dinner. She decided that it had been too long since they had eaten lasagna, and set to work preparing a pan of it. David wheeled himself in, curious as to what she was making due to the sounds of clanking pans, and rattling bowls as she set everything out, and pulled his wheelchair up to the table.

He watched her for a while, wondering what sort of a sadistic man would play with her heart in such a way. He could tell she was still upset by the jerky way she was moving, and by the way her breathing was erratic. She wasn't calm or collected anymore. Aaron was the lowest form of narcissist he could have imagined. The poor girl was frantic over what choice was right for her. David knew the right choice for her, but he wasn't the one who could make that decision. He wanted to wrap her up and hide her until Aaron faded away into nothingness. It was all he wanted; to keep her safe from his clutches and his abuse for the rest of her life. She deserved every benefit and joy the world had to offer, and Aaron was not the one to give it to her.

She was beautiful in every sense of the word. From her red hair to her green eyes to her body. He wasn't just interested in that, but loved her for her personality and the way she cared with every ounce of her being. She was a godsend to a man who would have otherwise died. She had a stubborn streak and a desire to heal the world of all its ills, at every cost to herself. She had become his reason to keep fighting, to struggle every day with physical therapy, to struggle until he could stand on his own two feet again. He would then ensure she never had to take care of him again, because he would be taking care of her. That was his greatest wish. Why couldn't Aaron appreciate what he had before he lost it? Why did he have to wait until she was trying to move on and was happy before he pulled this crap?

Oh, yeah. He was a narcissist. His only goal in life was to make himself feel good, and what made him feel good was putting her down. David wanted to destroy him. Not physically - he wasn't up for murder; but emotionally. He wanted to make Aaron regret every day he ever said a cross word or raised a hand against this angel that was in his kitchen.

He couldn't stop himself. He wheeled himself behind her and gently pulled her down onto his lap. She gave a surprised squeak when he wrapped his arms around her waist and just held her. He wasn't trying to influence her, but the feeling of a deep love had overcome him, and he felt endeared to her. He remained there for a minute, just holding her with his head pressed against her back, hearing her heart beating faster, before she began to struggle to stand.

"If I don't pull the garlic bread out of the oven, it's going to be garlic charcoal," she chided. She giggled as he still didn't let her up, and held her close while she continued to play-fight. He reached up to kiss the back of her neck before he let her go, blue eyes smoldering in their intensity. She looked at him and grinned while rolling her eyes. She grabbed a hot pad and pulled the perfectly-cooked garlic bread out of the oven before pulling out the bubbling lasagna. The entire kitchen smelled delicious.

"Get your ass to the table so I can feed you," she demanded with a grin.

David didn't need to be told twice, and quickly found himself at the table waiting for a square of the lasagna that now had the whole house smelling like an Italian restaurant. He whistled as a steaming plate of dinner was placed in front of him with some homemade garlic bread and a salad. He was afraid she was going to make him too fat to go back to work, no matter how strong he got. He had also decided he was at the point that he didn't care, as long as she kept cooking. He had never tasted anything so good, and it didn't matter what it was she cooked - it was perfect every time.

They carefully avoided talking about Aaron or anything that might trigger a conversation about him. David wanted to make it clear that he wasn't going to try and influence Meredith either way, despite how he felt about the entire situation.

"Do you have any of those bath bomb things that don't smell like a girl? I think I'd like to try to drown myself in the hot tub tonight, but I don't want anyone to come rescue me if I'm smelling like flower petals, or whatever."

"Why not? It may be a new trend." She chuckled as David wrinkled his nose. "I think I have a couple that are more manly scented - charcoal and dirt, or something like that. It's not pink, sparkly, or full of flowers. Will you need help getting in?"

"I think, if you can move the lift into the bathroom, I should be able to handle it. If you hear me drowning, do come in, though," he told her with a smile and a playful wink.

Meredith cleaned up after dinner and dragged the lift into the bathroom and unwrapped the bath bomb for David. It smelled like coconut and pine needles, so she hoped he would enjoy it. It was certainly not feminine in the least, though it wasn't displeasing. He wheeled himself in with a clean towel and pajamas and turned on the hot water.

"You're too good to me," he marveled. "What did I do to deserve you?"

"I always had a crush on you. And seeing you hurt made me think about what I wanted in life. After Aaron's stunt, I decided I wanted and deserved better, and you saved me. If you hadn't offered me a place to stay, I would probably still be there now. I know it sounds stupid that his email hit me like it did, but I can't help it. He wasn't always such an asshole. He was kind once; loving, and gentle. I don't know what changed. Or why," she finished softly. She was upset at herself for still caring about Aaron. She knew she would never go back to him, but she couldn't just stop caring all at once, either.

She remembered what Tim had told her - he changed when he knew she couldn't leave him. Was that really how it was? Was he really so manipulative that he read her like a book and made her believe she couldn't leave him? He had told her for years that she would never make it without him, that she couldn't afford to have a place of her own. He had told her that nobody else would understand her work schedule and the way she came home emotional after a shift with bad calls. He had convinced her that nobody else would love her, and she believed him.

"I don't think you would still be with him. You would have found the strength to leave him if that's what you had really wanted to do. Even if I wasn't here, you wouldn't stay with someone you don't want to be with. You're a strong, amazing woman. All I want for you is happiness. Even if it isn't with me," he told her, warmth in his voice.

It sounded cliché and cheesy-romance-novel, but he meant it. He didn't want her to be miserable. He didn't want her to be stuck with someone who didn't treat her like the damn princess she was. She was the best thing that ever happened to him, and he firmly believed she deserved the best the world had to offer. Even if that meant she would leave him to go out and find it.

"Would you maybe like to join me? There's enough room for both of us…?"

Meredith looked at the steaming water and thought about it for only a moment. "Sure. Are you ok with that? I don't have a swim suit or anything…"

"This is a private hot tub…you don't need a swim suit unless you're uncomfortable." Meredith blushed but shook her head. "Then you don't need one. You're free to hop in when you're ready. I'm going to be just a second." Meredith turned away and shyly removed her shirt, tossing it into the corner. Her bra came next, and, after a long day of wearing it, couldn't stop the moan of pure pleasure at having it gone as she rubbed her aching breasts. Slowly, she unbuttoned and slid off her pants and underwear, tossing them into the pile with her shirt. Once she was blissfully naked, she stepped into the tub and sank down until the water was up to her neck. It took David a minute to get his pants and shirt off; he had been lost in the moment of watching her, but trying to respect her privacy at the same time. He had turned away from her, trying desperately to not watch her undress, though he had failed miserably. It was then Meredith's turn to watch him, and she could see the scars where the doctors had gone in to fix his spine. The skin was tight and shiny, but there was no sign of infection or anything wrong. She reached out to touch it, as he was just close enough to reach, letting her finger trail down the line. David stiffened, but didn't try to pull away.

As soon as Meredith moved her hand, he lowered the lift so he could work on getting himself picked up and into the tub. It only took a minute of maneuvering before he was in the hot water. He sighed with complete and utter relaxation. "It's not quite the same as if I were able to just step in, but I'll take it." The soreness in his body slowly melted away as the scent of pine and coconut rose up in the steam. It was the strangest combination Meredith had found, yet, it worked. It was soothing and manly, and still left her skin silky smooth.

They spent far too long in the hot water. When they were ready to get out, they both had prunes for fingers. Meredith hopped out and wrapped a towel around herself, while David used the lift to get back into his wheelchair. He wasn't as concerned as hiding his body as she was, but still covered himself as soon as he was in the chair. He could feel Meredith's shy eyes on him, and turned to look at her. She quickly averted her gaze, and he chuckled.

"It's ok to look if you want. It won't hurt me one bit." She couldn't hide the blush in her cheeks and quickly pulled her t-shirt and shorts on. David stuck his tongue out at her and wheeled himself to the bedroom as Meredith dragged the lift behind her.

Using the lift, David was able to get himself into bed. He grinned and patted the spot next to him. "You're welcome to grab a bottle of wine and join me for a movie marathon, if you'd like. The doctor said no beer…he didn't say no wine." Meredith was struck speechless. She wanted nothing more than to be in the bed next to a naked David, but was that allowed? What if he wanted something more from her…was he…able? Was she? Could she face herself in the morning for doing this? Was she taking advantage of him?

She decided it was absolutely something she could do, and ran to the kitchen for a bottle of wine and a cork. She wasn't sure how well popcorn went with red wine, but she popped a bag and brought that, too.

Carefully, Meredith crawled into bed, atop the covers, as David was underneath them, and put the popcorn between them. She had brought two wine glasses so they wouldn't have to drink from the bottle. Handing one to David, she half-filled it, and then did the same for her own glass. The bottle was set on the bedside table so it wouldn't spill on the blankets.

David put on a movie she hadn't seen before and sipped the wine between bites of popcorn. It was a unique combination of fruity and salty, but it wasn't a bad one. The movie turned sappy toward the end of their first glass of wine, and by the end of the refill, they were both feeling warm and fuzzy. David had reached over to place a hand on Meredith's hip, his thumb caressing the skin around it.

She moved closer to him, and then crawled under the covers at his silent request. Nestling against him with his arm around her, she felt safe. There was no place on earth she would rather be. She was surprised to feel his hand on her breast, gently teasing her. He paused and looked down at her, making sure she wasn't uncomfortable. When she arched toward him, he continued, knowing he had the green light.

He slowly pulled her on top of him. Seeing as he was still literally weak in the legs, there wasn't too much else he could do - that, and it would give her the control to stop if she was uneasy about any part of it. She straddled him, feeling that despite having an injury to his spinal cord, he was still very much a fully functional man.

As of just prior to the hot tub, they had not seen each other naked. Even in the ambulance, she had kept his underwear on him to preserve some of his dignity, even though he was unconscious and wouldn't have known the difference anyway. That being said, his hands were delicate in their exploration of her velvet skin. He took his time, teasing every inch of her, starting at her breasts and then slipping down to her ribcage. His fingers dug into her flesh, massaging the tense muscles at her lower back, and then his hands were on her hips, reaching around to squeeze her ass. Her eyes rolled back and she moaned softly.

She leaned down, chest to chest with him, her red hair a veil that covered them both, and kissed him deeply. He tasted like red wine and lust, yet there was no urgency in this kiss. It was tender, curious, and passionate. It didn't take her long to feel the heat of need deep within her. She lifted her hips and with excruciating slowness (judged by the hot desire in David's eyes), slid him inside of her. He held his breath, blue eyes closed, afraid that if he breathed or blinked, the dream would come to an end, and he would wake up in the hospital, alone.

As she moved against him, he decided that this was not a dream. Even in his wildest fantasies, he couldn't create something this real; this sensual. Her hands caressed his chest, his stomach, and reached around to caress other things as she continued to slowly rock her hips. She could see the raw emotion in his eyes and grinned at him, shaking her head. She didn't want it to be easy. Not yet. She hadn't felt this connected to someone in longer than she could remember, and it was better because she was free to make this choice. She was free to make any decision she wanted; any man, any woman, both, or none. She hadn't had that option in over ten years.

His hands gripped her hips again, gently urging her on, and she knew she couldn't deny him. She moved with him, deep and slow, moving faster in his earnestness, until the building climax crashed over them both, their names echoing across the walls, on each other's lips, and they were both left breathless in a heap under the blankets. Several ticks of the clock passed before Meredith moved, untangling them and curling up against David's chest. He was trying to move his legs, readjust himself to be more comfortable, and he almost succeeded. He allowed himself that small victory and simply held Meredith until their breathing slowed to normal.

"Meredith?"

She sleepily murmured something along the lines of "Yes?"

"I think now is a good time to ask...are you on the pill?" He may be slightly intoxicated, but the thought of having children right now was frightening to him. He wasn't opposed to the idea, but trying to run after a kid when you're mostly paralyzed was a daunting thought, indeed.

"Mm-hmm." She rolled over and pressed her ass into his side. He groaned softly and rolled over as well, wrapping an arm protectively around her waist. She completely relaxed immediately and her breathing slowed to a deep, even breath. He quickly let the remaining alcohol in his system lull him into a similar state.

When morning broke, Meredith was up early to shower and get ready for work. She kept replaying the scene from last night, and felt a twinge of embarrassment. She had only had a couple glasses of wine...but she had acted like she was completely drunk. Had it been that long since she'd had a drink that she couldn't tolerate it? Or was there something more going on? Did she really love him? She knew she did, and firmly believed that her heart had made the decision of who she should be with.

Aaron had been the love of her life for so long, but it had also gone downhill quickly the past few years. Especially with the way he had to have his way or else. She couldn't see David being that way, even if he did change eventually. She could see herself growing with him, and that was what she wanted more than anything else - to grow with someone who wouldn't outgrow her.

She spent the day at work trying to avoid the topic of David, but Tim knew something had changed. She was jumpy, worried, and not acting like herself. She was avoiding eye contact and seemed to blush at the drop of a hat.

"What's up, Mer? Did you finally let him see you naked? I mean, it's only fair since you had him naked in the back of the rig." He was joking with her, but she was worried he knew something - had David told him? Who else knew? It was Lowfield, wasn't it? David told him, and now he was telling all the guys about it. She wouldn't be able to face any of them ever again!

"I did not have him naked! He still had his underwear on! Besides, when I'm undressing a trauma patient, I'm not looking at them from a "how sexy is this guy" standpoint. It's completely medical so I can assess for injuries! You can't let sex or something stupid like that play in when you're with a patient. That's completely unacceptable."

"Holy shit! You *did* sleep with him!" Tim laughed a hearty laugh. "There's no need to be sensitive about it. Everyone has sex. Well...except monks. Nuns. And those weird dudes who have their balls cut off for some strange and unknown reason like on the movie "Year One"." He paused. "Everyone *normal* has sex, Mer." He couldn't help but laugh again at how deeply she blushed again. They had talked about every topic known to man, had eaten lunch right after dealing with a GI bleed, and had seen several "sex send me to the ER" stories live in the back of their ambulance. It was adorable that she was so sensitive about the topic.

"But everyone isn't with a paralyzed cop! What would they say if they knew? That I'm taking advantage of him? That I left a "perfectly good" man for this one? That there's something mentally wrong with me for wanting to be with a guy who can't walk? I don't need their scrutiny! I'm still dealing with Aaron and all of his bullshit!" she exclaimed, a little touchier than she meant. All of her worries and concerns came out in that moment. She had fallen irrevocably in love with David, but she was terrified that the general masses would judge her; that they would shun her.

"Fuck what they think, Mer. People will judge you no matter what you do, or don't do. They will judge you for what you wear, what you think, how you vote, how you drink your coffee. It doesn't matter. All that matters is you're happy. To hell with the haters," he told her, a hand playfully on her shoulder.

She grinned. Tim was always blunt enough to make her feel better about things. Of course, he was right. Why did the opinion of strangers matter? Probably for the same reason people post things on Facebook - the validation is nice, but their criticism is not necessary. She nodded thoughtfully.

"So what's up with Aaron? Is he still in the picture?" Tim asked gently.

"He emailed me saying he wants me back. I still love him, but I don't want to be with him anymore. I can't take any more of his abuse, of the mind games and the punishments. I think I'm finally finding my happiness. I don't want to hurt Aaron, even though he's hurt me for years, but I know he's not the best thing for me anymore. I just...how do I tell him? I'm afraid that after all that's happened, he's going to kill me. He's out of jail now, and I'm worried he won't take it well," Meredith said, obviously stressed about it.

Tim pondered this for some time. "You could tell him you've found a guy with a huge dick and he's no longer sufficient?" They both laughed. Meredith rolled her eyes as she shook her head.

"Yeah. That would go over so well. Why didn't I think of that?" she joked.

"Honestly, though. Just tell him how you feel. Tell him that you care for him, but you can't be with him anymore. Tell him that he hurt you, and you're moving on. I would avoid telling him you still "love" him, though. I think that might not go over real well. But other than that, be honest with him. Be firm in letting him know you are not coming back."

Meredith nodded thoughtfully. Honesty was always good. But what if Aaron took it the wrong way? He wasn't known for being understanding. He would probably misread her email and decide he should try harder to get her back, but at least then, she would have said her piece. She would have told him that she wasn't interested. That could work. The chances of a backfire were great, and she was definitely worried about it, but leaving the subject open was even worse. If she closed the door, he would understand that there wasn't hope left.

On the way home after work, Meredith stopped and picked up some Chinese. She wanted to get the email to Aaron knocked out as soon as possible, and her mind wasn't right for cooking. She walked in the door and set the food on the table, and found David watching TV and working on stretches. He was getting stronger and able to move his legs more, and he was insistent on keeping his upper body as strong as possible. He was filling out his shirts better, she'd noticed.

"Hey there. I brought home Chinese. I hope that's ok." She couldn't help but blush a little while looking at him, remembering every vivid detail of the night before. She didn't understand why she was so shy now, why it was a big deal. Tim was right - everyone had sex. Why should she be worried about it? David didn't seem concerned. He turned to look at her and smiled, turning off the TV and wheeling himself into the kitchen.

"Chinese sounds perfect! How was work?" he asked, a genuine curiosity in his voice.

Had he just asked her how work was? Aaron hadn't done that in well over five years. She wanted to cry from the thought of it. This guy was absolutely perfect, no matter what anyone else thought. He was caring, sensitive, and interested in her life. What more could a girl ask for?

"Good. Only a couple bullshit runs and the normal paperwork. Looking forward to a few days off again," she replied. Her days off were something she now looked forward to - she could spend them with David, and not having to worry about whether or not she'd get hit, or emotionally abused.

They sat down to dinner and discussed the calls she had been on and how David had filled his day. Lowfield had taken him to his therapy appointment, and the physician was pleased with his progress.

"Sounds like I may be standing by the next appointment. They want to see how well I do and what my body can handle. I'm ready. I'm so done being in this chair. I'm serious - once I'm back to normal, I'm never going to sit again."

Meredith giggled. "I'm sure you'll get sick of standing, too. But I'm glad they're going to get you moving sooner than planned. Just don't push too hard and hurt yourself," she warned.

It was David's turn to roll his eyes. "I'm a boy. We're born hurting ourselves. I was a walking bruise as a child. The only thing that's changed is the bruises are bigger and more creative now." He shrugged and took a bite of his sesame chicken.

"Before I lose my nerve...I need to email Aaron back and let him know that I'm not going back to him. I don't want to say anything to him at all, but I know if I don't, he'll take it as a hint, and keep going. He'll keep pestering until I break down. He isn't supposed to be anywhere near me, but apparently he thinks that means he can still email me. So I'm going to shut it down now so we can focus on what we have going on... Is that ok?" she questioned, scared to look up at him, afraid she would see anger, or worse; disappointment.

David chewed and swallowed before answering, his tone and his gaze level. "You know I don't like it, but I think you're right. This might be what stops his crazy thoughts and gives him closure. I'll let you do what you have to do, and we can talk about it when you're done if you need to," he told her. Meredith leaned over and kissed him on the cheek in gratitude. They finished eating their meal with only minor conversation, and Meredith threw away the empty boxes.

She retreated to the guest bedroom and sat on the queen-sized bed, opening her laptop. The email was still open, waiting for her to acknowledge it. What was she supposed to say? Why did nobody teach you these things? She could tell you all about how the mitochondria is the powerhouse of the cell, but couldn't tell you the first thing about breaking up with someone. Especially someone as unstable as Aaron.

Aaron, I never wanted to hurt you. I hope you know that. And I hope you know this letter isn't easy for me to write. She paused, fingers poised over the keys. How could she gently, yet firmly tell him she wasn't coming back? *I loved you for a long time. I loved you enough to turn a blind eye when you changed. You became mean and stopped caring about my feelings. I felt obligated to please you, to go out and sleep with other couples because you asked me to, even though my morals told me it's wrong. I even told myself that you would change when you started hitting me. I believed that you truly felt guilty for hurting me. I tried so hard to*

140

change for you, and in the end, it was you who changed, and not for the better. All I ever wanted was for you to be happy. And as time went on, you needed more and more anger, painful sex, and other women before you were satisfied. Being away from you has given me time to think about what I really want, and what I really want is to be happy for a change. She paused, taking in a deep breath, trying to get her hands to stop shaking. I'm not coming back to you, Aaron. I wish you the best in life, and I know you'll find someone who will make you happier than I ever could. Please, find a way to be happy and move on without me.

She reread it again and again, editing small spelling errors, or grammatical errors before reluctantly hitting the "send" button. The screen flashed and then showed her a confirmation that the message had been sent. She stared at the screen with unfocused, watery eyes before she began to cramp up. Standing and stretching, Meredith left the room and sat on the couch next to David. He had been able to transfer himself from his wheelchair to the couch, and to other chairs. He was so proud of himself, and she was just as proud of him. Every little thing was a big accomplishment.

"It's sent." she leaned her head against his shoulder, seeking comfort. It was one of the hardest things she had ever done, and that includes all of her Paramedic testing. She stared at the TV. It was playing a commercial about OxyClean or something like it.

"How do you feel?" David gently placed a hand on her knee, knowing she needed to feel a sense of comfort and full acceptance. He figured she had a hard time sending that email to Aaron. His eyes were a soft blue now, like a child's wading pool: inviting and warm. She knew she could stare into those eyes forever and not ever get tired of them.

"Like shit. I mean, I'm glad it's done and over with, but I still feel bad. Does that even make sense? I don't want to hurt him, but I can't let him control me anymore. I don't want to sound like an asshole, but I do wish things would have been different. For everyone. That way, nobody would have to be hurt," she said. She hated that no matter what path she chose, someone was going to get hurt. But she also knew that she was done being the one always getting hurt.

"I understand what you're saying. It's going to be hard for a while, I'm sure." He moved enough to wrap his arm around her shoulders. She leaned into him and nodded, unsure of what else she could say. "I went through the same thing with my ex. The only difference was that she didn't try to hit me. The hardest thing I had ever done was let her go and to tell her I wished her the best. No matter who she was with," he finished softly. The hurt was thick in his voice and in his eyes, which had turned a slightly darker shade of blue. He didn't want to recall the bad memories, but knew that it would help Meredith.

She remembered the diary passage she had read, and knew that her situation sucked, but his was definitely worse. "Thank you." Her voice was a whisper, and he was almost questioning whether or not he heard her.

"For what? I didn't do anything."

"You did. You've been understanding and amazing," she told him.

He simply held her close and remained silent. Sometimes, no words are necessary to express what you're feeling.

Chapter 25

The following days progressed with no word from Aaron. Meredith believed that he had gotten the message, and so, she was happy to move on. Things with David had their ups and downs, too. Mostly, the "downs" consisted of a bad day at therapy, or pain that was worse than normal at home. They didn't spend much time arguing or bickering, and for that, Meredith was thankful. It felt like things were really starting to look up for her until one early morning after a night shift, she opened her laptop to find an email from Aaron.

You selfish bitch. I can't believe you won't give me a second chance. Do you know how many second chances I gave you, and every time you fucked those up, I gave you more? Everything I ever did was for you! I just wanted you to experience life and not have any regrets when we grew old together. I never wanted you to say that you wished you would have done something. Do you really think your cripple can love you like I can? Do you really think he can give you the same life? You really are a dumb bitch if you think he's half the man I am. You'll see. You're going to burn in hell for what you did to me. And when your cripple can't fuck you like I did, you'll be running back to me like the stupid bitch you always were. You're going to pay.

A shiver of fear ran through her. What did he mean, "you'll see?" and "you're going to pay"? She set her laptop on the kitchen table and began making some breakfast with shaking hands that wouldn't steady. She didn't want to wake David over it, but would let him know as soon as he got up. Luckily for her, he was usually awake shortly after she got home in the morning.

He wheeled himself into the kitchen and transferred himself to a chair. He yawned and stretched and then smiled at her. "Good morning."

"Good morning." Her tone was clipped and worried, unsure how to break this newest development to him.

"What's wrong? You don't sound like yourself. Bad night?"

"No. Yes. Well, I don't know. Aaron emailed me again." She was afraid to look at him, and instead, turned the laptop toward him so he could read it. She returned to the stove and cracked a couple eggs and began to scramble them for omelets.

"I think we should go to the courthouse and have a new restraining order put against him. If he thinks it's ok to make threats, he has another thing coming," his voice was dark, and low; hardly above a growl. He wanted to make threats of his own, and more: he wanted to carry them out, but that wasn't going to make Meredith feel any better about her situation. He sighed softly and forced the rage back down so he could speak with her calmly. "There is no need to tolerate this behavior, but I'll leave it up to you."

Meredith scrambled the eggs and thought about it before slowly nodding, biting her lip. "I think we should do that. Let's eat first, then I'll shower, and we can go. If you want to go, that is?" she asked him, apprehensive.

He rolled his eyes. "No, I have so much going on here, that I would rather leave you to face this on your own. Could you bring me back a shake after you deal with your crazy ex all by yourself while I sit in the house and watch TV?" He shook his head and then grinned. "Of course I'm going with you."

They ate breakfast in silence, Meredith's mind working overtime trying to understand again where things went wrong. Her email had not been mean, crass, or rude. It was honest and simple, the way she had been told to write it. Why had he reacted so poorly? Why was he so angry? He was certain to have numerous other contacts he could call to start a relationship, or just for a one night stand. She had seen him text and call these women several times. Maybe he enjoyed the control - if that was the case, he could easily find himself a submissive woman that would obey his every command and not be in danger of getting hit or worse. She took in a deep breath, exhaling it with as much stress as she could get rid of. No sense in panicking. They would just file a new order and be done with it.

The ride to the courthouse was tense. Meredith was struggling within herself to understand why Aaron had turned so ugly so fast. She couldn't understand that he was a narcissist who had lost his greatest treasure - a woman he could keep under his thumb to make himself feel good.

Once they had arrived at the courthouse, Meredith walked beside David as he insisted that he didn't want her to push his wheelchair for him. He did allow her to get the door for him, but he told her he didn't want her to be a servant. She always objected to that, but let him have his way. They worked their way to the clerk's desk where she requested a restraining order form. The clerk handed her a blank copy and asked if she knew how to fill one out. David sat up and nodded.

"Yeah. Thank you!"

The clerk grinned when she saw David. "It's been a while! I'm glad to see you out and about. How's the healing going?" she asked, a little flirtation in her soprano voice.

"Oh, you know. Some days are better than others. The doctors tell me I'll be up and kicking ass again in no time." He winked and the clerk laughed a high, fake laugh. It was clear she had a crush on David. Meredith didn't like it, but she couldn't blame the woman, either. Who wouldn't be in love with him? He was handsome and made everyone feel like they were the most important person in the room. Besides…the clerk wasn't going to actually do anything but flirt. David had assured her that no other woman in the world was going to take him away, unless Meredith told him it was ok. He meant it.

They moved to the bench where David parked his wheelchair, and Meredith sat beside him. She stared at the paperwork like it was written in Greek and scrunched up her nose.

"It's ok, Meredith. Take it one section at a time. You know your information and you know his. All you have to do is fill it out." David reached a hand up and squeezed her shoulder. "You can do this."

She steeled herself and nodded, each box coming a little easier as she filled out the required information. When it came to the narrative section, she stopped and stared at it. How could she write down what happened? It would be open record, and he would see it. He could easily walk through those doors and kill her, no matter how much she detailed.

Aaron was arrested after he hit me and broke my nose. He was sentenced to jail time, and after that, probation with a "no contact" order. He has since emailed me asking to get back together with me. I told him I wasn't interested, and the next email he threatened me. I'm afraid that this behavior will continue. I'm afraid to be alone because I worry he will try to hurt me again. I want to live my life in peace without having to look over my shoulder. He has a history of violence that I am afraid will continue.

She finished the paperwork and handed it back to the clerk. "We'll get you scheduled for a restraining order hearing in front of the judge. We'll call you to set it up." Meredith thanked the clerk, and she and David left the courthouse.

"It'll work out. What happens now is the judge reviews your request, and sets a court date if he feels it isn't a bullshit request, which yours is not. You and Aaron will both be there," Meredith's head snapped over to look at him, her eyes wide with fear. "…I'll be there too, don't worry…and the judge will hear your side and his. He'll then make a decision whether or not to give you the restraining order with the changed wording. I don't see why he wouldn't. All you have to do is tell him what happened and why you're afraid."

They got into David's car and headed toward home. Meredith asked, "Are you hungry? What do you think about stopping for some pizza? I could use a carb load." She gave a weak smile.

"Anything you want," he told her with a wide grin.

They enjoyed their pizza and talked about everything except Aaron, much to Meredith's relief. It was nice to be out with David. He didn't hit on other women, didn't suggest they take them home, didn't threaten her to comply with his orders "or else." She had truly found a gem and intended on keeping him forever.

Chapter 26

Tension continued to mount to an almost unbearable level before Meredith received a phone call from the court. She was a bundle of nerves as she listened to what the clerk had to say, though the words felt foggy, as if she were in a dream. They were going to schedule the restraining order hearing for that Friday morning. Meredith agreed, knowing she was off work that day. After she hung up, her anxiety ran through the roof. She didn't want to face Aaron. Not after he had hit her, gone to jail, and then she had left him for good. He was going to be furious to have to go back to court now. She hoped it wouldn't hurt his probation. She then chided herself for that thought. She wasn't the one who was hurting his probation - he was, by acting like this. He knew better than to act like a possessive child with a new toy. If his probation mattered to him, he would absolutely change his ways.

David had gone with Lowfield to his therapy appointment, trying to give Meredith a Tuesday off. She had spent the day cleaning, catching up on laundry, and grocery shopping. She had a pie in the oven and a roast in the crock pot. The house smelled great, and was clean. Meredith was happy to have a day to herself to catch up on things, and to just veg out.

After the cleaning was finished, she threw on some pajama pants and sat down to a Netflix series she had recently found to be fascinating. It was time for a binge with a bowl of popcorn.

The boys got home more than an hour late. Apparently, they took a detour to pick up a couple of movies and some beer. Meredith rolled her eyes as they came in laughing and joking. She didn't mind movies, though violent horror films weren't her favorite. They were excited because one of the scenes showed a rather attractive actress without a shirt. As if neither of them had seen a pair of breasts before.

"Boys. Come eat," she called from the kitchen. The roast had come out perfectly tender, the rice without crunching, and the gravy was thick. All in

147

all, she was pleased with how it came out. Roast wasn't always her strong suit.

She didn't have to ask them twice to come to the table, and before she had turned around with the first plate, they were there waiting, like a couple of cartoon children with their forks in their hands, noses in the air, drooling over the tantalizing scent.

"That smells amazing. David, feel free to send her over to my house any time." Lowfield chuckled and took the offered plate, hardly waiting to dig into the food that teased his sense of smell.

"How about not? You just come over and eat. Besides…if I send her with you, I won't have anything to eat. You can't do that to a friend!" David joked.

Lowfield put on a mock offended face. "I would never do that to you! How dare you suggest such a thing! You would just have to come over to my house for dinner," Paul retorted.

David laughed a deep, hearty laugh. "I think it's easier for you to come here. You're not stuck in a wheelchair. Besides…I have a ramp. You don't."

"Well…you've got me there."

Dinner went by with the three of them bantering about who was going to do dishes. They decided they could wait until after the movie, since they just couldn't wait to see it. Meredith put the dishes in the sink and sat down between the two men on the couch. David wrapped his arm around her, and play-punched Lowfield in the shoulder for trying the same thing.

"She's mine…and besides…I thought you weren't into women?" David asked, a mock-angry look on his face.

"At this point…I'll settle for a monkey as long as it can cook better than me. I'm getting tired of take-out and ramen. And, for the right woman, I'll settle down and swear off hunks like Chris Hemsworth." Paul raised his right hand as if he were on trial.

They laughed and then hushed as the previews started. Although it was a DVD and they could easily fast forward past them, they watched all the previews to see what other movies they could watch for a night. There were several that made the cut, and they decided they would have to watch them another night since nobody wanted to go back to the store or sit for an all-night movie marathon.

Once it started, nobody talked. They all grimaced at the violent scenes, and cheered when the intended victim got away. They knew what was going to happen - all scary movies are the same. The guys cheered even louder at the half naked actress and Meredith rolled her eyes, a grin on her face. Guys, like cheesy movies, were all the same. Even the gay ones, she decided. It didn't make sense to her why

Lowfield would want to see a half-naked woman if he wasn't interested in women, but then, maybe he was only half interested in men. That would make sense to her, but then again, it really didn't matter. She loved him all the same.

As the movie ended, Lowfield stood up and stretched, telling the two he was headed for home. He said something about wanting to sprawl out across his bed and be comatose until morning.

"Are you working Friday?" asked David.

"I think so, why?"

"Meredith has court for another restraining order against her ex. I'd like a good show of force so this guy knows to leave her alone. Restraining orders are great, but I'd like him to see what stands behind that order," David explained. He knew that right now, he wasn't very intimidating. But several of his friends all suited up for battle would be. Even if they didn't say a word... it would get the message across.

Lowfield grinned and winked. "You got it."

The days passed quickly. Meredith was off until Saturday, and enjoyed the days in between with David. She helped him with his therapy and he helped her with the problems with her ex. They made a great team when he wasn't upset about a minor setback with his recovery. On those days, Meredith knew to leave him alone so he could calm down, and then help him once he was in the right frame of mind again. He wasn't violent or mean, but he was surly and bitter, depressed in thinking he would never walk again. Those were the days she spent baking, or grocery shopping. She tried to not go places alone, as Aaron could be anywhere, she reminded herself, but there were times it was unavoidable.

Friday finally came. Meredith and David got into his car and headed for the courthouse.

"How are you holding up?" David asked.

"I'm nervous. Terrified. About to throw up," Meredith said, a little dramatically.

"You'll be fine. Remember - all you have to do is be honest. Show those emotions. Let the judge know how much this is upsetting you, and that you deserve to live your life like anyone else. You shouldn't have to be scared to just live. That's not right."

"I know...I just...I don't want to be scared. I want to be able to go places alone, like when you're in therapy. I want to be able to go for a walk and not worry about the next car that passes me. I'm scared to death, and I'm so tired of being scared," she explained.

"That's what you tell the judge. He'll listen. All you have to do is be honest and real."

Meredith nodded. They parked the car and went inside. They met Lowfield in the hallway and he walked with them. He gave David a sidelong glance and grinned. Meredith missed it, looking around in terror, waiting for Aaron to jump out of a hallway to hit her again.

Once they entered the courtroom, she stopped short and her jaw fell open. There must have been twenty other uniformed officers there between the city, county, and state agencies. Lowfield's grin turned into a full proud smile and a puffed-out chest as David shook his head. "Damn, son. Remind me to let you plan a surprise party, ok?"

"They're all here for official business. It just happened to fall on the same day as this hearing." He winked. The officers had all sat in the same row - the second row filling up all the bench space, so Meredith and David went to sit in front of them. She felt better knowing she had a small army at her back, and felt a rush of gratitude toward Lowfield for arranging such a thing. He was really one of the best friends she'd ever had. Tim had showed up as well, and was sitting amongst the officers. He grinned and waved as she saw him. Meredith waved back and then turned toward the front as the bailiff asked them to rise for the judge's entrance into the courtroom.

The judge ran through numerous other cases that seemed easy to her. Several traffic tickets, several "check-ins" from probation officers and their clients, and several minor cases. None of them seemed to last more than five or ten minutes each, though it still felt like forever to her. She was anxious, afraid that the judge would forget about her case with so many others coming first.

Before long, Meredith was up. She stood in front of the microphone, trembling, as the judge addressed her.

"Miss Thomas. I see you're here for a restraining order against a Mr. Aaron White. I also see that you have a court-mandated order in place. Normally, we would not have the defendant here until there was just cause to issue a restraining order, but in this case, I felt the need to have him here as well so we can work this out. What has changed that you feel you need to return to court for an amendment?" the judge asked with his deep voice.

Meredith tried to speak, but her throat felt like it was closed. She coughed and glanced up, expecting the judge to have an angry look on his face. Instead, he reminded her of a grandfather. He was older, but not unkind. He patiently waited for her to get herself under control.

"I understand the first order is to prevent him from physically contacting me. But it doesn't have any wording about him contacting me by other means, including email. Shortly after he was released from jail, he emailed me asking to get back together. I replied and told him I wasn't interested. I thought it was clear that I had no intention of ever going back to him. I had hoped that would be the closure he needed to move on. I assumed it had worked since he didn't contact me for several more days, but his next email was full of vulgarity and threats. I'm afraid that if this continues, it will only escalate. When I'm on duty, I need my mind focused on the job, not on what sort of threats I will have in my email that day." Her voice started out soft and weak, but grew stronger toward the end. She didn't want to be a victim anymore. "I have a copy of this email, if you would like it, your honor."

The judge nodded and the bailiff took the paper from Meredith, placing it in the judge's waiting hand. He read through it, and spoke again. "I understand. Mr. White, do you have anything to add?"

"Your honor, if Meredith saw my email as a threat, I apologize. I was distraught when I wrote it. I shouldn't have been so foolish. I don't want to hurt her. I miss her. I love her. I'm hurt and the thought of losing her scares me to no end. She's all I've ever known." He had the acting ability to even let tears build up in his eyes. Meredith was astounded. Her eyes desperately flew to the judge. He couldn't possibly believe this load of shit, could he?

"Miss Thomas? How do you feel about that?" he asked.

"I…I don't know. I'm afraid that it will continue. I just want to live my life without fear and worry. I'm also afraid of his violent streak and I don't want to be afraid anymore. His last outburst sent me to the emergency room with a broken nose. I want to live my life without fear."

The judge thought about it for a minute, flipping through some paperwork he had in front of him. "I think the court shall issue a temporary restraining order to include no contact of any kind, including email, text message, social media, and whatever else you can think of. I feel that will give you both enough time to finish separating and move on. I will have that dated to expire in one year from today's date. You can pick up those orders from the clerk as soon as she has them typed. Give her a few minutes," the judge finished.

Meredith nodded and thanked the judge. She felt a little let down that he had been so lenient, but maybe he was right. Maybe they just needed that time for Aaron to find someone new and move on. She hoped that was the case. She walked out with David and the entourage of other officers following closely behind; a wall of protection.

Once outside, they all spent a few more minutes around Meredith, talking amongst each other. Aaron walked out and looked like he wanted to approach her, but thought better of it, especially with twenty-something officers all in a defensive huddle around her. He shot her a look that was a combination of arrogance at his "win", and sorrow that he couldn't have her. He moved along quickly as several of the officers moved as if to speak with him.

"Thank you all. Really. It means a lot to have your support," Meredith addressed the officers with a soft voice.

Each one nodded, shook hers and David's hand, and made jokes with Lowfield about how he owed them something.

"We'll throw a barbecue soon. Meredith will cook. She is an amazing cook." Meredith's eyes widened and she stammered a few words before Lowfield jumped back in. "I'm kidding, Meredith. I'll make burgers, but you have to make cookies or something." She nodded. The officers all shared a chuckle and trickled back to work or home.

Chapter 27

On the next sunny Saturday, they did throw a barbecue for the officers. David was progressing very well with his therapy, though he still wasn't able to stand for longer than a fast transfer, or move his legs with any confidence. He was getting stronger still, but he felt he wasn't making enough progress. Today was a bad day, despite being surrounded by many of his work brothers. He sat amongst them, surly and quiet, speaking only when necessary to not offend the crowd.

Lowfield was manning the grill, and Meredith, true to her word, had made several batches of cookies to feed the hungry mob before dinner was ready. There were numerous comments about how delicious they were, and a few asked for recipes for their wives to make them again at home. Meredith grinned and wrote it down for them with the officers expressing their gratitude. The event passed without a hitch.

Time continued to pass with no word from Aaron. Meredith and David continued to grow closer. One night, he asked to take her on a fancy dinner date.

"I'll take you on a date, but you gotta drive." He winked. "I'm pretty tight with some of the cops, but I don't think they'll let a paralyzed guy behind the wheel. Not sure how that would slide in court." He grinned. He was still the most handsome man she had ever met with his soft eyes, messy hair, and charming smile.

She agreed, and they drove to the steakhouse they had both fallen in love with, at his request. They ordered the surf and turf, and a nice bottle of wine to go with the meal. David seemed preoccupied, and Meredith worried that he'd had another rough day at therapy, but didn't want to upset him, if that was the case. She let the silence span between them, though it was not uncomfortable.

They enjoyed appetizers and their meal, and once they had finished eating, David directed her toward the movie theater. They sat and watched a chick-flick that still had some manly action so that neither of them was cheated out of their favorite kind of movie. They shared popcorn even though they were full to bursting with steak and shrimp. Meredith happily rested her head against his shoulder until he wrapped his arm around her, kissing her forehead before letting his head rest against hers.

Once the movie finished, David asked her to drive to the town's Lookout Point up in the mountains so they could enjoy the stars and the view of the city. She agreed that it would be the perfect end to their date night. She was excited to see the city from the Lookout Point, as it had been quite a long time since she had been there. It was such a beautiful sight.

David was able to get himself out of the car and back into his wheelchair and had Meredith help him onto a blanket on the ground. They spent some time pointing out constellations and watching for shooting stars. They talked about their childhoods and what drove them to get into law enforcement and EMS. In the dark, it wasn't scary to bare their souls and reveal their deepest secrets. It was the best night either of them had ever had.

"My dad died when I was pretty young. Mom said he was an alcoholic and was into drugs, and he got into a bad deal. He overdosed on some bad shit. She's been ridiculously protective of me since. I decided to get into EMS because I didn't want another little girl to miss her daddy. He might have been a bad guy, but he always treated me well. We did things together, like go to the park, and played catch. What I don't understand though, is why my mom wouldn't take my side in the arguments with Aaron. I have never lied to her. Ever. I was always a good kid." Meredith shrugged. It was a helpless gesture.

"Sometimes, parents just don't make sense." David paused. He wasn't sure if he was ready to tell her about his mom and dad, but he figured it was only fair. She had to be curious by now. "My parents were both detectives. That's why I got into law enforcement. They were good at what they did. They solved a few cold cases, and were highly sought after for their expertise both in the field and for testimony. They were surprised when I came along, but they were good parents. They spent time with me and worked hard to balance work and family. We would go to the movies, and carnivals, and things, but often, work interrupted us. It sucked, but I knew they had to work to catch bad guys to keep us all safe." He paused, taking a couple breaths. "One night, they were investigating a murder case. The suspects had fled, but had returned to the building across the street. They had opened fire on the scene, and wound up killing both of my parents, another officer, and wounding two others. After that, I was raised by my grandmother. It wasn't the same as they couldn't take me places to do things like my parents, but she tried her best. She loved me and encouraged me to follow my dreams."

Meredith rested her hand on his knee. "I'm sorry to hear about your parents. That must have been hard for you. How old were you?" Meredith softly asked.

"I was thirteen when they died," David responded.

Before they were ready to go, David grabbed Meredith's hand and held it tightly, his trembling fingers running over hers.

"When I think of the future, it still scares me, but I think it's not so frightening knowing you're beside me. I haven't ever thanked you properly for standing by me through everything - all the therapy, the bad days, the household chores and things, and most importantly, for saving my life. I don't think I will ever have the words for you for what you've done for me," David started, his voice quaking, soft, and full of emotion.

Meredith blushed, and fidgeted around, trying to avoid his intense gaze.

"I know we've only been together for a couple months, but I feel like I have known you for my whole life, and I can't imagine being without you. It would be the greatest honor I could think of if you would be my wife." David pulled a small box out of his pocket and opened it. Inside was the most beautiful ring she had ever seen. "Meredith…will you marry me?"

Meredith's heart stopped. Had he really just…proposed? She stared at him with her mouth agape, struggling to breathe. It felt as if the entire world had closed in around them, so it was just the two of them left in the entire universe. Her heart finally started again, except it fluttered and floated and beat against her breast with such ferocity she was afraid it was going to come right out.

"I…of course! Yes!"

David broke out into a huge smile. He was glad she couldn't see how badly he was sweating or shaking. He had thought, for a moment, that she was going to tell him no. He carefully slid the ring onto her finger and watched as she stared at it with wonder. He could see that she had never been so happy, and he was pleased that he was the one to bring her that happiness.

Meredith leaned closer toward him and kissed him. It was a deep, passionate kiss. One that was no longer afraid of the invisible boundary of "take things slow". That line had vanished, and now, they were going to be together for always. It was a whirlwind of thoughts, feelings, and anxieties. She was happy to be moving forward with the man she loved, but worried that Aaron would walk past that restraining order now. She was overjoyed that she was finally getting married, and to a man that loved her just as much as she loved him; but what if Aaron showed up to hurt either of them? She was going to let the excitement outweigh the worries. There would be time for those later, she decided.

They stayed for a half hour or so longer watching the city lights and the stars before it started to get chilly. It had been a long night, and they were both ready to be home. Meredith helped David back into his wheelchair, and he climbed into the car from there.

"David...are you sure? You know I have a lot of baggage, and I'm difficult at times. My work schedule is crazy, and then there's my ex...are you sure?" she asked him, afraid that he would regret his decision, offering him a chance to back out before it was too late.

"You already said yes. You can't back out now." He looked at her with nothing but love and mirth in his eyes. He couldn't fight back a grin as he reached over to take hold of her hand, bringing it to his lips for a quick kiss.

"No! I wasn't backing out! I just want to make sure you know what you're getting into before you decide you want to back out," she replied.

"Meredith...I have thought long and hard about this. I didn't think I would ever want to be with another woman after what my ex did to me, but you changed my mind. I want nothing more than to be with you for the rest of my life. Baggage and ex-boyfriend and all."

She couldn't hide the joy she felt uplifting her heart. Everything she was going through with Aaron seemed to be less important, and this was everything that had ever needed. She smiled as she stared through the windshield, struggling to concentrate on the road through the starlight that seemed extra bright now.

"How in the world did you pull this off without me knowing?" she asked, very curious where he found the time to buy a ring when she had no idea.

"My last therapy appointment was less physical therapy, and more "retail therapy" with Pauly. That's why I had a couple drinks. I was so nervous about finding the right ring, and not blowing it with wanting to tell you about it. He helped me pick it out and then decided we needed to do something to cover up the excitement...that's why we decided a movie with a half-naked actress. That was enough to distract you from what I hoped wasn't odd behavior."

Meredith laughed. She should have known Lowfield was going to have a hand in it. He was a wily, feisty man. "I really should have known," she mused.

"I'm glad you didn't. It would have ruined the entire surprise."

They got home after taking their time down the mountain and enjoying the sights. They were too tired to have a celebratory soak in the hot tub, and so, they pulled on pajamas and crawled into bed. Meredith curled up against David and they softly murmured their ideas for the wedding until they fell asleep, dreaming of wedding bells and dresses.

Morning dawned and Meredith was sure it was a dream. Looking down at her hand, she saw the ring and realized it was not a dream. It had actually happened. David was already awake and watching her, and she grinned when she met his eyes.

"I thought it was a dream. I'm glad it wasn't."

David nodded in agreement, and worked himself into his wheelchair to head to the kitchen. They had decided to begin planning the wedding, and there was no time to waste.

They sat down and pulled out a calendar. They began discussing how soon they wanted to get married, and were in a debate about whether to have it in six months, or one year. Meredith argued that one year would give them enough time to plan and save up for the things they wanted, but David wanted six months so they could start their life together sooner.

"You realize nothing but my name will change...right? We have already started our lives together," she gently chided; but with a smile.

"Yeah...but I'm excited about it." It was cute how excited he was about getting married to her. Aaron never would have been so excited - even if he had proposed, he would have let her plan everything, and just showed up to save face. This was new to her, and she could not possibly be happier.

May eleventh was a fair compromise to them and was about nine months away. Meredith agreed that it would give them time to plan, prepare, and save, and David was willing to wait an extra of couple months if it meant the wedding was going to be better. Meredith hadn't yet called her mom, and so, once they had the date in mind, pulled out her phone.

She hadn't talked to her mom in a while; since she had taken Aaron's side in the arguments they frequently had. Her mom had bought all of Aaron's lies, and felt her daughter was dramatic and they should go to couple's therapy. Meredith checked in at least once a week, but they avoided all conversation about Aaron. She did tell her mom when he hit her, and what had happened after. Her mother was disapproving with the jail time, but it didn't matter to Meredith. He had been punished for a crime, the same that would have happened if she would have hit him.

"Mom?" Meredith was apprehensive, worried that her mom wouldn't approve, and worse - would reject the idea of her getting married.

"Meredith! I was hoping you would call soon. I hadn't heard from you in a while." Her mom sounded genuinely pleased to have gotten a phone call.

"I have some good news..." Meredith started slowly.

Her mom rattled off several "good news" scenarios, and Meredith shook her head and told her mom "no" with each one.

"I'm getting married!" she exclaimed.

"To Aaron?" Her mom had a hint of excitement behind her voice. She truly believed that Aaron was a good man who could take care of her daughter, despite the fact that he hadn't had a steady job in years, and he was abusive.

"No, mom. To David. The cop?"

"The paralyzed one? Are you sure that's for the best, dear? What if he never regains his ability to walk?" her mother asked.

Meredith visibly deflated, and David knew the conversation wasn't going well. They had only briefly spoken about her mother, but he had gathered it was a sensitive subject. Now, just seeing the look on Meredith's face, he was starting to understand why.

"Then I will take care of him, Mom. Can't you just be happy for me?" Meredith's voice had a slight edge to it now. She didn't want to be belittled anymore. She had found a good man! Why couldn't her mother just be happy for once?

Her mother made a clucking noise. "Of course I'm happy for you, Meredith! I just worry that you'll be unhappy with him if he doesn't walk again. I only want you to enjoy the finer things in life."

Meredith sighed. "My happiness isn't dependent on whether or not he walks, Mom. He treats me good, and that's what I have always wanted in life. I just want a man who loves me for me, and I have found him. We're planning the wedding for May eleventh. Once we have details finalized, we'll send you an invitation, but I wanted you to be the first to know," she finished, her tone flat and unhappy. This was supposed to be the first joyous event in a young woman's life - the marriage proposal. Mothers were supposed to be ecstatic for their daughters!

They spoke another couple minutes before Meredith hung up and avoided looking at David. She was worried that he wouldn't want to be with her anymore due to the reaction of her mother.

"Hey...it's ok. Moms can be like that sometimes. Especially when they are worried for their children. I can understand. It will be just fine, you'll see." He placed a large hand over hers. "Don't fret, Meredith," he told her with gentleness.

They worked through time and place ideas, and as the wedding would be happening in an unpredictable month, they were half-inclined to just have it in a church. Meredith had always wanted an outdoor wedding, so they put the "place" on hold. They were both hoping for a mid-morning wedding so they would have time for the reception and maybe getting away for a short honeymoon, if they were able to save the money for it, of course.

Chapter 28

As each piece of the wedding seemed to fall into place, Meredith found she had a lack of female friends. She asked David if he knew anyone that would be a good fit to help her with dress shopping, and the other ins and outs of planning that she could use a hand with. He thought for a minute and suggested the dispatcher who was on the day he got shot. She had always been the calm voice of reason in his ear, and had checked in on him throughout his hospital stay. Meredith had met all the dispatchers here and there throughout her career, but wasn't close with any of them, but thought it was a great idea. They decided they would ask her together.

They worked through the reception, a DJ, caterer, and where they would like to go for the honeymoon. They decided a non-religious ceremony would suit them best, since neither of them regularly attended church, even though they both read their bibles. They were able to find a justice of the peace who was available that could marry them. They worked through wedding favors and gifts for the best man and maid of honor. They finished their invitations and worked on getting them sent out.

Weeks passed with Aaron obeying the restraining order. Meredith had not heard from him or seen him since their day in court. She was able to breathe a sigh of relief, though she still looked over her shoulder on occasion, certain he would be there, looming, ready to destroy her and everything she had worked so hard to build.

Therapy continued to progress with David able to stand for short periods of time. He was still frustrated that he was not able to walk yet. He didn't have the coordination back that he hoped he would have. The doctors told him that was normal, that it would probably take longer for his coordination to return. He was already ahead of schedule as far as his healing went, and the doctors were extremely pleased.

The day came to ask the dispatcher if she would be Meredith's maid of honor. They had selected a beautiful bracelet for her that wasn't over the top, but still showed their appreciation. Meredith and David entered the dispatch office and found where she was sitting.

"Good morning everyone! We have a question for Carmen, if someone can cover her channels for just a moment?" David announced loudly to the group.

One of the other ladies agreed and Carmen turned her chair with an eyebrow raised. What was so important that they were interrupting her job? Of course, she didn't know they had cleared this plan through her manager so she wouldn't get into trouble.

David spoke first. "Carmen. You've been here forever, and have always been the calm voice on the radio. You have always been there for everyone, making sure we were all ok, and sending help when we weren't." He couldn't hide the emotion that had made his voice waver. "I know if you wouldn't have sent me backup right away, and put the ambulance on standby, I wouldn't be here today." Carmen's eyes were full of tears. "Meredith and I have discussed this at length, and have a question we would like to ask you."

Meredith knelt down so she wasn't towering over the sitting dispatcher as she pulled the box out of her own pocket. "Will you be my maid of honor?" Carmen's hands flew to her face as the tears welled up in her eyes and then spilled down her cheeks. This was a first. The other dispatchers, who weren't currently answering the radio, clapped and cheered.

"I would be honored." Carmen was still emotional as she stood up with Meredith and they hugged. Meredith smiled, but couldn't hide the tears in her own eyes. It was nice to have a friend, and one who was so important to their lives, even if she wasn't a daily fixture.

"Thank you for doing what you do, and making sure David had the help he needed to live through that day," Meredith whispered, her voice thick with emotion and unshed tears.

"All I did was send help…you guys did the rest." Carmen was struggling to regain her composure so she could return to her desk and finish her shift. She had Meredith put the bracelet on her and admired it, showing the rest of her crew with an excited flip of her wrist.

The details were slowly falling into place, and they had decided to get married outside at the park in town. There was a gazebo they could use, and would be able to put up tents in case of bad weather. They had chosen the ballroom at the hotel for the reception, and were still finishing out details on their honeymoon. They were hoping to spend some time in Jamaica to enjoy a resort with beaches, food, wine, and sights.

A couple nights later, Lowfield was over for dinner. It seemed he was over at least once a week. Tonight's dinner was homemade teriyaki beef with all the sides. The guys were at the table, discussing the wedding and the plans that had already been made. He was even more excited than David was, and wanted to know every detail, and to know exactly how he could help.

"Who's your best man? And the maid of honor?" he asked, nearly bouncing out of his seat while waiting for the answer.

David grinned. "We decided Carmen would be the best maid of honor, since she's been there for us for years, and as far as best man...I'm not sure yet," David said slowly, still grinning.

"Not sure? Man! Your wedding is getting closer and closer, and you don't have one picked yet?"

Shaking his head, David pulled a box out from under the blanket on his lap and passed it to Lowfield. "I was hoping you'd round out our absolutely non-traditional, police and paramedic themed wedding party."

Lowfield opened the box. It was a nice, smooth whiskey with a glass, stone ice-cubes, and a cigar. Lowfield stared at it through a moment's confusion and then squealed like a child who had just gotten a pony for Christmas as it dawned on him. Him!

"Bro! For real!?" David and Meredith both nodded and laughed. "Hell yeah! Let's crack this open right now!"

Lowfield opened the bottle of whiskey as Meredith gathered another two glasses. She asked for only a shot, since she wasn't big into drinking, and the two boys enjoyed a little more. It was mellow and full, going down without the burn many alcohols have.

"Oh. Oh, that's good." Lowfield was impressed by the quality of the whiskey. "It's like you know me or something."

More time passed without any issues from Aaron, or work. Everything was lining up the way it was supposed to go. They had only faced some minor setbacks, like the DJ had double booked himself, and they had to find a new one, and the caterer wanted to charge more than they agreed on, but with some calm conversations, everything had leveled out.

Carmen and Meredith had gone dress shopping while David and Paul went tux shopping. The girls had a great time looking at options and styles, colors and materials. In the end, Meredith settled on a conservative strapless dress by Alfred Angelo. There was some beadwork on the chest portion and a little more toward the floor. The back had a color panel, and that was the next challenge the girls overcame - what color to choose. The woman at the store showed them all the options, trying hard to push a blush pink, and in the end, Meredith picked a dark blue - half because she was in EMS, and half because David was law enforcement. It only seemed fitting to represent the Thin Blue Line.

Carmen found a dress that was a similar color, but would not outshine the bride. Meredith sent a picture to David of just the accent color. She didn't want him to see the dress before the wedding. She'd heard it was bad luck, and wanted all the good luck she could save up. He sent her back a "thumbs up" emoji, and she knew they would find matching suits.

With dresses and tuxes on order, the four of them met up early that evening for dinner. They had decided on Chili's, as it was everyone's favorite "non-specific" restaurant. David and Lowfield both ordered the big steaks, while Meredith settled on fajitas, and Carmen wanted a burger. They discussed the day's events and whether they had been successful or not. The girls giggled and nodded.

"David...just wait until you see her!" Carmen was excited for the wedding, and wasn't afraid to show it. "She is going to be the most gorgeous bride ever!"

"Oh yeah... David too. Meredith, he's pretty when he dresses up." Lowfield batted his eyes in an exaggerated cartoon way and they all laughed. Meredith shook her head.

"Paul, you're biased. I can't trust a thing you say," she told him with a mouthful of chips and salsa and a giggle.

Their meals arrived, and they continued their chatter until they had finished eating. Everyone went home for the night, leaving Meredith and David to have an evening alone at home. They settled on a hot tub night with some of the not-so-feminine bath bombs. Those were always nice for unwinding after a long day. The night finished with a movie in bed and soft snores while being wrapped up in each other's arms.

The day of the wedding crept closer, day by day, hour by hour. Carmen kept up with Meredith to make sure everything was going as planned, and informed her they had a photo shoot that afternoon. Meredith was due to pick up her dress that morning, so it was perfect. She was excited to see the dress, and to have photos done as a keepsake for later.

Carmen picked her up and together, they drove into town to the dress shop. The dress had already been paid for, so all they had to do was try it on, ensure a proper fit, and leave. Meredith was pleased to find the dress fit impeccably, and the color panel on the back was exactly how she wanted it. The shade was perfect, and would match the vest that Lowfield had gotten with his tux. Everything was coming together as Meredith had imagined it was supposed to.

The girls left the shop and headed to the park to meet the photographer. They first went down by the river that flowed through and were able to shoot some pictures. After that, they walked closer to the trees for a more outdoorsy and rustic look. They spent quite a bit of time trying to get the right shots that Meredith and David would treasure for years to come.

After the photo shoot, the dress was safely put back in its plastic and left with Carmen to ensure David didn't see it. She would have it back to Meredith the morning of the wedding. David had arrived so they could do couple's photos as well. They spent more time out in the fresh air to make sure each shot was perfect. By the end, they were both exhausted from smiling so much, but had full hearts and the promise of keepsake photos that would last a lifetime.

Chapter 29

The days before the wedding drew to a close, and finally, the wedding was the following day. Invitations had been sent out and hotel rooms booked for the out-of-area guests, the caterer and DJ were early to the hotel to start setting up their part of the reception, photographer and her assistant were already at the park, following David and Meredith and snapping candid photos of guests. The tents were set up, the sun was shining warm in the clear blue sky, and there was not a trace of wind. Everything was perfect.

David was sitting in his wheelchair after being helped up the steps by Lowfield. They were patiently waiting for Meredith to be ready. They knew it would be a little bit, and refused to hurry her along. Besides, she still had a few minutes before the wedding was set to "officially" start, and David knew she wanted everything to be just right.

Carmen came out of the small tent they set up for Meredith to change in and took her place as the maid of honor and looked over at David. He was nervous, afraid she wasn't going to come out, and glanced at the dispatcher. She gave him a wide grin and nodded, telling him everything he needed to know. She was almost ready.

Minutes passed and once Meredith was visible to the small orchestra, they began playing Mendelssohn's Wedding March. All the guests stood up, and David struggled to see over the crowd, but the moment Meredith began her slow walk down the aisle, his jaw dropped. She was the most stunning woman he had ever seen. Her hair was in a brilliant updo; her makeup was tasteful and not overdone; the dress was flawless. She walked slowly and deliberately, forcing herself to slow down lest she ran down the aisle to her almost-husband. Beneath the bouquet of flowers, her hands trembled.

She consciously slowed her breath down, afraid she was going to pass out. This was now the scariest thing she had ever done. She wasn't afraid of David, or the thought of forever, but she was afraid of having such an intimate moment shared with so many people. What if she fell? How many cameras would catch the moment and live forever on Facebook and Instagram? What is she said the wrong thing, or worse - what if she vomited on David or the Justice of the Peace?

Before she knew it, she was standing under the gazebo with Carmen, David, Paul, and the Justice. She hadn't tripped, hadn't vomited, and hadn't made a fool of herself. The music came to a close and silence spanned for a moment, only interrupted by a few chirruping birds and coughing relatives.

"Dearly beloved, we are gathered here today to witness the joining of two families into one, and to share in the joy of this occasion, which should be their most memorable day as they begin their new life together.

"On this day of your marriage, you stand apart from everyone here. You stand in the circle of your love for one another, and that is as it is supposed to be. Love is not meant to be felt separately by two individuals, but rather as one. Your joys, your sorrows, your worries, and your triumphs should be shared between both of you, carried between you that neither of you feels the full burden. From this day forward, you should come closer together than ever before, that you love one another in sickness and in health, for better or for worse.

"Standing here before me with the full understanding of the meaning of this ceremony, do you, David Price take the woman before you to be your lawfully wedded wife, to love, honor, and cherish through sickness and health, through times of happiness and travail, until death do you part?"

David struggled to standing on his own two feet, and took the ring from Paul and slid it onto Meredith's finger. "I do." He grinned as he was able to remain on his feet for longer than he had yet, despite the slight swaying to remain upright. He had been working hard to regain some muscle control for this very day, and was pleased he had succeeded.

"And do you, Meredith Thomas, take this man before you to be your lawfully wedded husband, to love, honor, and cherish through sickness and health, through times of happiness and travail, until death do you part?"

Meredith took the ring from Carmen and slid it onto David's finger. "I do."

"Please join hands." Meredith and David did as they were asked. "By the act of joining hands, you acknowledge that you are becoming man and wife, and solemnly promise to love, cherish, and care for each other, forsaking all others, for so long as you both shall live. By the power vested in me by the laws of the state of Colorado, I do pronounce you man and wife. David, you may kiss your bride."

Cheers went up from the numerous law enforcement officers, EMS workers, friends, and family as David pulled Meredith close and kissed her deeply and without reserve. Meredith returned his passion, unconcerned about the thoughts of those who were witnessing this intimate moment. As soon as they separated, breathless and weak in the knees, David sat back down in his wheelchair, knowing he wasn't going to be able to stand much longer.

"Ladies and gentlemen, friends and family, I offer you for the first time, Mister and Missus David Price!"

The crowd cheered again as Meredith walked down the steps, and David was again assisted by Lowfield. They continued cheering and throwing flower petals as the newlyweds made their way to the waiting car that would take them to their reception.

Meredith and David were too busy basking in their love of each other to notice someone who didn't belong watching them from across the park. Aaron was standing at a distance, behind a dark-leaved tree in full bloom, the vile look of hatred painted upon his reddened face, fists clenched in rage.

The wedding had gone off without a hitch in front of all their family and friends. They had spent the rest of the night at the reception in the ballroom of the Elks Hotel, enjoying the finest hors d'oeuvres and dinner the caterer had to offer. The bar was mixing drinks like mad, and the DJ had the guests dancing and swaying to everything from the 80's to current music, as requested by the newlyweds. The guests couldn't have asked for a better evening.

Meredith and David stopped off at home to change into clothing that would better facilitate a long night of dancing and socializing with friends and family. Once that was done, they were taken by their closest friend, Paul Lowfield to the hotel. Once they arrived, there was an announcement made by the DJ, that the "newlyweds are in the house!" followed by cheering and clapping when they entered the ballroom. Meredith was blushing furiously, and was thankful that the room wasn't brightly lit.

The DJ asked if the happy couple was ready to enjoy their first dance as man and wife, and Meredith looked at David. He grinned and nodded, standing slowly and somewhat shakily. He had been working hard on getting the strength back in his legs so he could dance with her at their wedding. He was still uncoordinated, and unable to walk long distances on his own, but with her helping him, they made it through their first slow dance as man and wife.

It had been nearly a year since he had been shot and almost permanently paralyzed by a bullet that ricocheted of his patrol car and into his chest by just missing his bullet proof vest. Nearly a year since he had met Meredith; the fiery redhead who had defied all orders and common sense and blazed into the scene of a violent hostage situation, with bullets flying overhead; to pull him to safety. Nearly a year since he almost died. They had faced their share of trials and hardships, including his paralysis, and subsequent therapy; her dealing with her crazy ex-boyfriend, and learning the little things about each other; and they had grown stronger because of it.

Aaron hadn't been seen or heard from since they had gotten the restraining order modified by the judge to include no emails. It would seem that he fell off the face of the earth, and for that, they were thankful. Meredith still worried about him - she had been with him for twelve years, and it's hard to just "turn off" caring about someone, even when they are abusive and no good for you. She still worried whether or not he was ok, and whether or not he had what he needed; but she also realized it wasn't her concern anymore. Her concern was caring for David now, and that was a task she was glad to undertake.

The department had put him on administrative work until he was able to go back to active duty. David absolutely hated working a desk job, but at least he was back with his coworkers, and felt better about having a real income again. He hated that Meredith was covering so much of the bills. The guys had all pitched in, however, to donate PTO so he could go on his honeymoon. The donations also came with bawdy advice that he ignored, rolling his eyes and grinning.

Meredith and David made it through the rest of the reception and at the end of the night, were taken home by Paul. The three of them made it into the house, laughing and replaying the entire event, until David had to gently kick Paul out so he could have some alone time with his new wife. They would be leaving in the morning for their honeymoon. Paul reluctantly left with a grin on his face, and the order to "take pictures" for him so he could see Jamaica.

Chapter 30

The plane landed with a series of small bumps on the tarmac in Montego Bay, Jamaica. The sun was just beginning to set, and Meredith could hardly contain her excitement at finally arriving after a very long flight. Staring out the window, she could see lights, but was disoriented - these weren't the mountains she was used to. There was too much water, and she could feel the warmth and humidity already. She was excited to try an island drink and meet the locals, learning the best spots for tourists to travel to. She also wanted to see a dolphin in the wild, and bury her toes in the sandy beach.

They slowly made their way off the plane and into the heat. It didn't take long for them to find their shuttle to take them to their resort. It was probably a little cliché, but they had determined Beaches Resort would be a good place to have a honeymoon. It was all inclusive, and that meant their room, food, activities, and all the alcohol they could want was all covered with the fee they paid. Meredith was looking forward to sitting by the water and just enjoying the waves.

Getting into their room, Meredith's eyes widened as she looked at the king-sized bed, the ocean view, the gigantic bathroom, and the immaculate hardwood floors. There was not a single detail that was overlooked when this place was built. She felt as though she had died and gone to Heaven, it was so perfect.

"Wow! This is the most beautiful place I have ever seen!" Meredith exclaimed.

"I agree...I can't wait to see what's for dinner. What are you hungry for?" David asked, obviously getting hungry.

"How about we check out their steaks? I know you're probably craving one, since it's been, what...a whole day or two since you've eaten half a cow?" She winked.

"It wasn't half a cow. Maybe a quarter...but not half!" he retorted, laughing heartily.

The two of them made their way to one of the numerous restaurants at the resort and sat down. Before long, a waiter was asking them about drinks and handing them menus. Meredith looked over the menu while David ordered them some wine. Together, they discussed what they were going to order, and in the end, they both decided on a T-bone with all the sides. The picture in the menu made it look too good to resist.

Cutting into the thick, juicy, marbled meat, both were impressed. They had never seen a steak cooked to such perfection. The grill marks were deep, and the steak was perfectly seared on the outside, with just the right amount of pink inside. The flavors of butter, salt, and savory herbs they had not tasted before exploded in their mouths. They knew they would be coming back to Jamaica again and again, if only for the perfect steaks.

"What shall we do tomorrow? Maybe a catamaran cruise? We could see the fish and things from the boat's glass bottom. Maybe we can do some fishing? And pictures on the beach. Maybe a couple jet skis?" Meredith was excited at the opportunities they were looking at. "We could see a concert, or maybe check out the water park? Then we could do a massage!"

They spent the night wrapped up in silk sheets, drinking wine and making love like it was the first time. To be honest, every time was like the first time - every day, David was getting stronger, and had more ability to use his legs. He was getting steadier on his feet with less weakness. They took their time, exploring each other with feathered fingertips and probing kisses, listening to the distant sounds of the waves crashing against the shore with candles flickering around the room. There was no more romantic setting that Meredith could think of.

The moon rose high in the velvet sky, shining in on their bedroom. Meredith woke and looked out the window, smiling in the darkness. She nestled close against David, hearing his heartbeat, feeling his strong arms around her, his even breathing. There was nothing in this world more perfect in her mind. She snuggled under the blankets and let the ocean sounds lull her back to sleep.

Dawn broke slowly with no sign of clouds in the vast blue sky. The smell of salt-water and exotic flowers was strong, but the smell of breakfast was stronger. Meredith woke and stretched, yawning broadly, and sat up in bed. David was already up and had called for room service. She smiled when their eyes met.

"How did I get so lucky to find such a thoughtful man?" she asked him, yawning again.

"I feel like I kind of...fell into your lap?" They shared a laugh and a plate of food. There was bacon piled high, scrambled eggs, hash browns, fresh fruit, yogurt, and juice. It would seem that David must have been hungry when he ordered this - it was more than two people could eat, but she decided they could save it for a little later. The fruit would make a perfect snack for after several activities on the beach and the water.

"I scheduled us a catamaran cruise today. I think we board the boat in an hour or so," David said. He had always enjoyed smaller fishing boats when he was younger and his dad took him out on the water. He hadn't been on a boat in years, though. He was a little nervous about the thought, but was excited to see Meredith get to experience the world.

Meredith nodded. "Sounds good. Shall we shower first?" She finished her plate and set it down before heading to the bathroom to set the water temperature. David wheeled himself in and then stood, shuffling slowly toward her. He was getting better every day, but still had a ways to go before he would be cleared for "real" work again. He was still dreaming of becoming a K9 officer, and that made him push limits.

They took their time stripping each other of the few items of clothing they had on and stepped into the walk-in shower. They were not shy about soaping each other up, fingertips still probing every inch of exposed skin, lips tasting the water as it cascaded down necks and shoulders. They decided to postpone further "activities", as David was not yet strong enough to stand for them, and they didn't want to be late for their cruise.

Together, they dressed and headed out to the beach. Meredith was able to push David in his wheelchair on a walkway down to the dock. Overhead, seagulls screeched and wheeled around in the blue sky that still had not a single cloud in it, looking for an easy meal of snacks dropped by tourists. They knew that they would eat well wherever there were people. People dropped delicious snacks all the time.

They checked in and waited until the boat was ready and they were asked to board. Settling in, Meredith rested her head against David's shoulder as they looked at the water from the glass bottom. Several little fish swam by, and Meredith couldn't help but grin.

"This is going to be an awesome day." She looked up at David who looked slightly apprehensive. "What's wrong?"

"Mm? Nothing." Meredith looked at him and nudged his shoulder.

"Don't lie to me. What's going on?" she persisted.

"If we sink, I'll wind up swimming with the fish. That's a little too close to them for comfort. I doubt I can swim as well as I did a year ago." He gave a half-smile and then shrugged.

"I'll keep you floating. We'll pull a door off and float like Jack and Rose from the Titanic if we have to."

"I hope you'd let me on the door, too. I don't want to freeze and then be left at the bottom of the ocean!" He chuckled.

"Ladies and gentlemen, today we will be taking a cruise around some of our favorite reefs to allow you the chance to see the marine life we host in Jamaica. If we're lucky, we may see a sea turtle, or a manatee. The other marine life you can expect to see are nurse sharks, eels, barracudas, eagle rays, tuna, blue tang, puffer fish, amongst the rest of our 260 fish species. We hope you enjoy your trip."

With that, the boat began moving, and several of the other passengers clapped with glee as they stared out the glass bottom of the boat. Several fish they had never seen before passed and then circled as if they were there to provide a show for the passengers. Each one was announced by their tour guide with his thick Jamaican accent. Hours passed, and Meredith was mesmerized by the beauty beneath them. She had never seen such fish before. She pulled out her phone to take pictures, as they hadn't brought a camera.

They pulled back into the harbor and Meredith put her phone away. She had taken numerous pictures of the animals. Her favorite was the nurse shark that passed back and forth four or five times. She had stared at it, having never seen a more majestic animal that wasn't on TV. She was full of love and admiration, and even more, of wonder that they had been able to pull off this honeymoon.

The rest of their week went smoothly, enjoying the most magnificent painted sunsets either of them had ever seen, gourmet meals cooked by award-winning chefs, activities that neither of them ever thought they would be doing, including concerts on the beach and a water park in Jamaica, and most importantly, spending time with each other. They were sad to board the plane on their way home, but knew that no matter how amazing it was, they would have to return to the real world and work sooner or later.

Chapter 31

At the airport that morning, Lowfield was there waiting for them. His face broke into a wide grin when he saw them and waved frantically.

"Well aren't you two a sight for sore eyes! I've been dying of boredom without you." He was too happy, too excited, and David began to wonder what was up. Maybe he really was that dependent on them for his entertainment. Meredith didn't seem to mind, and hooked her arm through his with her other hand on David's shoulder as they made their way to the car.

The drive home was as expected. Traffic was ridiculous and backed up for miles, but it gave them ample time to discuss how their honeymoon went. Lowfield wanted every detail. Meredith promised to show him all the pictures when they got home, but took advantage of the stand-still to show him her favorites.

They made it home in the early afternoon and dragged their bags in the house. They would have to catch up on laundry and putting things away another day. For now, Meredith had a wedding surprise for David, confirmed by Paul with a striking grin and a nod.

"I got you a little something...a wedding gift that I hope you'll be able to use for a long time."

David raised an eyebrow. "If it's a cane, I swear I'll beat you both with it," he said with a fake threatening glare.

Meredith grinned and shook her head. "Not a cane. Paul, will you do the honors?"

Lowfield practically skipped to the bedroom and when he returned, he had a wiggling, whining ball of fur in his arms. He set it down and passed a leather leash to David.

"His name is Bullet. He just turned nine weeks old. His papers are in the bedroom." Paul and Meredith had matching ear-to-ear smiles on their face when they saw how David took immediately to the pup. He was a handsome black and red pup with alert eyes that followed everything at once.

"He's from some pretty impressive lines, as far as I could understand. All of his relatives have honors in protection and tracking, and his daddy was huge. His breeder said he should mature around eighty pounds or so." Lowfield paused. "And, because I know you'd want everything perfect, I fenced in your back yard for him so you can train him without fear he'll take off on puppy adventures, or to go prowling for bitches when he's older." He led David to the kitchen to look at the back yard. Sure enough, it was fenced in and there was already a dog house set up. "Meredith wanted you to start training him so when you're ready to get back to working the good stuff, he'll be right there and ready to work, too."

"How did you pull this off?" David was aptly surprised, staring at the pup with such wonder, it was as if he had never seen a dog before. Unconsciously, his fingers pet the puppy, scratching him behind the ears, and feeling his soft, downy fur. The pup flopped over so David could scratch his belly as his hind legs went nuts with pleasure.

"The same way you did - I had a "therapy" day with Paul. I had been researching breeders with the best records for a month or two, and found one who had a litter that was due to be ready when we were leaving for Jamaica. I arranged for Paul to pick him up after he dropped us off. He agreed to take care of him for a week, until we could get home and you could take over."

David gave the pup a final pat on the belly and stood up, shuffling his way to his new bride. He wrapped her up in his arms and kissed her. "You are the best wife a man could ask for." He then turned to look at Lowfield, taking a small step toward him.

"Hey man, this might be a dream come true, but I don't want you to kiss me. It might make your girl a little jealous." David and Meredith laughed deeply and heartily.

"No worries on that front…I like you and all, but I'm definitely not interested in kissing you." David hugged Paul. "You're a pretty damn good friend, though. Thank you."

They stayed talking for a little longer before Lowfield made an excuse to leave. "I'll be by for dinner in a few days. I want to see pictures of your trip and hear every other detail you've left out." He winked and left the house with a spring in his step.

"Shall we go play with Bullet?" Meredith was excited to see the pup in action. His parents had more titles than she could begin to remember, and he was pick of the litter. She was thankful she had been saving up money for a while now - he was the perfect pup for David.

Outside in the newly fenced back yard, David tossed a ball a few times. Bullet wasted no time in chasing it. Bringing it back was another story. He wanted to keep the ball and chew it to death, but eventually, he got the hang of playing fetch. He was also quick to begin learning commands, and by the end of the afternoon, had nearly mastered the "sit." David was beaming as they went inside to begin dinner.

"You are truly an amazing woman, Meredith. I really don't know what I did to deserve you," he marveled.

Chapter 32

Days progressed into weeks with David walking further and further each day. He had regained most of the feeling in his legs, now it was time to strengthen the muscles. The doctors were convinced he would be back to normal duty in another few months. To David, that was too long, and he spent the days he wasn't at a desk walking slowly around the yard with Bullet, teaching him basic commands. He was intelligent and happy to work with David.

David was still on desk duty, but his administration had cleared him to do several ride-along days. He was thrilled to be out of the office, and so was Bullet, who had been going to work with him every day, and had become the office mascot. Everyone who passed by David's desk had to stop and pet the pup, and on the days David wasn't at work, he received several messages asking when Bullet would be back in the office.

Bullet was happily nestled in the back seat, bouncing around and sticking his nose out of the prisoner bars as David climbed in the front and buckled in. They were going on several paper services, so nothing exciting, but at least they weren't stuck in the office doing paperwork.

At one residence, David slowly climbed out of the car and pulled Bullet out as well. He may not be an official member of the force yet, but there was no better time to continue his training than the present. They walked up to the door along with the other officer and knocked. Bullet was immediately at a "heel" and attentively watching David.

The door opened and a man answered the door.

"Are you Mr. Sandoval?"

"Yes…?"

"Sir, we have some papers to serve you." David handed the papers to the man. "It looks like it's a restraining order. There should be instructions and a court date in the paperwork. If you have any other questions, you're welcome to call the courthouse. They should be able to direct you better."

The man grunted in reply, his lips pursed. He muttered something about his "damn ex-wife" as he went inside and slammed the door unhappily. Bullet yapped a warning bark at the closed door, more startled than actually angry. David laughed and scratched the pup behind the ears.

"You're a good boy." The pup wagged his tail furiously as they shuffled slowly back to the car. David was doing great, but he was still unable to a full day's work while standing. He opened the back door and gave Bullet the command to "kennel in" and the pup jumped in, though he struggled with the height of the car briefly. David shook his head, astounded that of all the millions of dogs in the world, Meredith had picked one that was this ridiculously smart, and suited for this sort of work.

Getting home that night, David and Bullet were met at the door with the scent of pork chops baking in the oven, and a pie that was cooling on the counter. David took off Bullet's work harness and let him run around the house, sniffing around for treats and his favorite toy. He yipped playfully when he found it - a tug toy that David was using to teach him to bite and hold. Bullet picked up the toy and shook it ferociously, the ends batting him on the sides of his head with each vicious shake. He crinkled his little nose and growled, biting harder until the toy stopped fighting back.

"That smells amazing. How long until it's ready?" He walked up behind Meredith and wrapped his arms around her, kissing the back of her neck and peeking over her shoulder to see how much longer until he could eat. His eyes fell on the pie she had made - it looked like a cinnamon apple pie. He reached his hand out slowly toward it, itching to break off a piece of the crust, until Meredith batted his hand away.

"Five minutes till dinner and don't you dare touch that pie! Why don't you get Bullet fed and I'll get everything for us dished up. How was your day? How'd he do with the car ride?"

David was putting food in Bullet's dish so he could eat with his family and not stare at them, hoping for a scrap. He didn't want the pup to get in the habit of taking food from people, afraid that one day, somebody would try to poison him, especially if he got good at his job and was able to catch lots of bad guys and drugs.

"Good. Paper services today, but it got me out of the office. I really can't complain too much. He did great. He's learning to stay at my side and not want to play with everyone he meets. I think he's going to be an excellent dog when he's fully trained." David patted Bullet's shoulder and beamed at the pup, who wagged his tail happily.

As they sat down to eat dinner, Bullet looked up and began barking angrily, rushing to the living room window. He jumped and barked, trying desperately to alert his family to something amiss. Meredith got up and turned on the outside porch light, peering outside. She didn't see anything, and so, brought Bullet back into the kitchen where she pointed to his food dish. He groaned his frustrated puppy groan and laid down facing the window with a hrmph.

"Maybe he saw a squirrel in the tree or something. There's nothing out there," she told David.

David shook his head. "That's ok. He's still young at what, twelve weeks? At least we know he'll save us from any squirrels trying to break in." He chuckled softly. "You're still a good boy."

They finished dinner and Meredith began picking up while David took Bullet outside to use the bathroom and do a little more training. The pup was quick to learn new things, and David was thrilled to introduce him to the jute toy - a rough toy that taught young dogs how to bite and hold on. It would be a while before Bullet would know exactly what he was supposed to do, but if he could develop the desire to bite when directed early…he would make an excellent bite dog.

Curling up on the couch with a worn out puppy at their feet, Meredith and David put on a movie to end their night. On and off, Bullet growled at the living room window, against admonishments by David. Every time, Meredith looked, and saw nothing. She shrugged it off to him seeing movement of the trees in the wind, or squirrels, or people passing by on the street.

With Bullet secured in his kennel in their room, the newlyweds climbed under the covers. The night was dark, so Meredith had her bedside lamp on as they talked late into the night.

"So, we've been married a whole month. What do you think?" Meredith was curious. They hadn't had any major fights or disagreements. They had been able to work through most things without serious or angry discussion. When did the happiness end? For her last relationship, it ended as soon as Aaron knew he had gotten her. Now that they were married, David had her locked down. She loved him with all of her being, but that didn't mean she wasn't afraid he would change.

"I think we have a lot of months to go. Why? Is something wrong?" He pulled her close so she was laying on his chest. He reached his opposite hand over to brush the hair off her face. He still couldn't get over how beautiful and brave she was. He knew he had found his once-in-a-lifetime, perfect woman. He was in awe every day that he woke up with her, still wondering if the dream would end and he would wake up in the sterile environment of the ICU with machines beeping and nurses prodding.

"I don't know. I guess I'm afraid you'll change. Like, you'll stop holding me, and stop caring about how my day went, and we'll start fighting about stupid things. I don't want to lose this feeling right here," she admitted, softly.

He nodded thoughtfully. "I'm sure at some point we'll argue and fight. It's only natural. But I think as long as we still love each other, we can overcome it. It may take some time to cool down and have a rational discussion, but that's normal. The honeymoon phase doesn't last forever." He smiled warmly at her. He didn't want this feeling to end, either, but he knew it was unrealistic to believe it would stay like this for always. The honeymoon phase would end at some point, and the reality would set in. Bills, children, bad days at work, him getting back to work, her crazy ex...they would all take their toll on the relationship, but he was confident that they could work through it. Together.

"So can I ask you a question?" There was hesitation in her voice, mixed with a hint of fear.

"Of course."

"Do you think you'll ever want kids? I mean, I know we just got married, so I'm not saying today or tomorrow...but do you see kids in our future?" She took a minute before she adjusted herself to be able to look up at him. She was apprehensive, worried that he would lie to her and tell her that he wanted kids, and then refuse to talk about it again.

David remained silent for a short time, thinking about how he could answer her question honestly. After his ex-wife had gotten pregnant by another man and left him, he was sensitive about the topic. "I can, but I'm worried about the world and the way it is. I'd be scared to bring a child into this place where there is evil on every corner." His words were gentle, and even so, he could feel her heart breaking beneath his hands. "But that doesn't mean I'm against it. I think if we decide to have a baby, we'll have to work extra hard to protect it from the evils of the world." That seemed to soothe the ache in Meredith's heart.

She stayed silent, not sure what to say. It wasn't the answer she had been hoping for, but then, life always seemed to do that. Just when you thought you had it figured out, everything changed as it threw you a curveball. Meredith sighed softly and nodded. She was disappointed that he didn't give her a resounding "yes!", but that was to be expected. All she could do was work with it and see what the future had in store for them. Maybe he'd get excited about the idea of a kid once he was back to his old self and working the streets again.

Meredith rolled over and turned off her lamp and inched back toward David's broad chest. Even though she was turned away from him, she could see the grin on his face as his hands went around her waist and pulled her closer. He kissed the back of her neck and they both closed their eyes. In the stillness of the night, they could hear Bullet growling softly from the foot of their bed.

"Bullet, hush now. It's bedtime." David's voice was soft, but stern. The pup groaned and stood up in his kennel, his little hackles raised and teeth bared. Meredith flipped on her light and stared at the pup. He was glaring out their bedroom window, entire body tense. A shiver ran up Meredith's spine as she got out of bed to look, afraid she was going to see someone staring in at her. When she looked out the window, she saw nothing. No trace of movement, no sign that anyone or anything had been around. With a sigh, she crawled back into bed beside David.

"Nothing there?" David asked her, certain he already knew the answer.

"No. Not sure what he thinks he sees out there. Silly pup," she replied with a sleepy smile.

"It's ok. We'll keep working with him so he only barks when there is really something there. He's still young and dumb. He'll get there." David yawned and rolled over. Meredith shut off the light and did the same, curling up behind him, arms wrapped tight around his chest. Bullet occasionally growled softly as he stared at the window, confused why his people weren't doing anything.

Chapter 33

Morning broke later than expected, with both of them forgetting to set an alarm, and both Meredith and David had to work. In a mad dash to get ready, they skipped breakfast and took a short shower. Bullet was left outside in the fenced yard to use the bathroom while his people finished getting ready.

Meredith left first, having to be to work a little earlier than David did. She kissed him goodbye, grabbed her bag, and left for the station. David walked out to their back porch and called for Bullet, but the pup didn't come running like he normally did. David called again, thinking the pup was maybe intent on digging a hole, or sniffing out a new scent. Listening, he could hear the pup whining and struggling with something.

Walking carefully as to not trip and fall, David found him. He had been tied to the chain link fence by a large carabiner and was unable to get free. He had let him outside, and knew that Meredith wouldn't have done this to him, as it was cruel and pointless. David bent down and unclipped his dog from the fence. Bullet immediately shook himself and took off running, happy to be able to do so. He was no worse for the wear.

David looked around, but saw no sign of anyone around. There were no obvious footprints in the dirt, and only a small piece of meat as a lure on the opposite side of the fence. There weren't even any cars on the street passing by. Hot anger welled up inside him. He hoped it was only a stupid neighbor kid who was messing with Bullet. Maybe they just wanted to pet him, and used the treat to get him close, and for some reason only a child could understand, clipped his collar to the fence. If it was anyone else, they were in for a rude awakening when he found out who it was. He wasn't going to tolerate anyone trying to hurt his little family, and that included his dog.

Going back inside, David saw nothing amiss as searched all the rooms. Bullet followed, wagging his tail and zig-zagging around his person. He didn't alert to anything strange, or growl in any particular direction. David decided it must have just been a stupid neighbor kid messing around, and would keep a closer eye on his pup if he had to be outside alone, checking on him more frequently when possible.

Once his ride had arrived, David was pleased to see he was working with Lowfield for the day. "Bullet…do you want to go to work?" The pup yipped and bounced around as David grabbed his harness off the hook on the wall. "Sit down." The pup sat and fidgeted, dancing around from paw to paw until David had his harness secured on the pup and ready to go. Bullet nearly pulled him over to get outside to the car. "Heel!" The pup groaned in frustration, but returned to David's side, nosing his hand in an attempt to not only get scratches, but to find a treat. He found exactly what he was looking for once he calmed down enough to stay at the 'heel' position - a piece of hotdog…it was his favorite.

Once the pup was loaded and David was seat-belted, they were off. "What are we doing today, Paul? Chief has me out of the office more and more, and I'm ready to be out for good!"

"Just general patrol. Running traffic. Does your dog find drugs yet?" Paul asked, a gleam of excitement in his eye.

"No. He's only thirteen weeks. I've got him started on the bite toys. Drugs are next, if we have any synthetics that Chief will let me take home," David explained.

Lowfield thought about it for a minute. "We may. We'll ask Chief when we get into the office. If not, I'm sure we have enough in our budget that we can pay for some. How's the training in general going?"

"Good. He really likes to bite, and he's extremely attentive. He's been growling at my windows, though. Not sure what he thinks he's seeing." David shrugged. "I'm guessing just the trees swaying back and forth. That reminds me that I have to trim them before the winter snows make them heavy. I don't want to have a tree branch crash through my roof," David replied, slowly shaking his head, imagining a broken branch suddenly appearing in his bedroom.

"No problems with the crazy ex-boyfriend?" Paul asked.

"No. We haven't heard from, or seen him since the restraining order court date. But I think Bullet wouldn't mind getting a mouth full of him if he shows up." David chuckled. Bullet, hearing his name, yipped with excitement and wagged his entire butt. "Won't you? Who's my good boy?" The excited pup yipped again and bounced in uncontained exhilaration as they drove off in pursuit of tickets.

The day was going slowly when the call came out for a rollover with injuries. David and Paul began heading that direction and heard Meredith and Tim on the radio that they were also en route. David was pleased knowing it was Meredith's rig that was closest - the patients would have the best care they could possibly ask for, but he was also concerned. He didn't like her being on bad scenes. Perhaps it was just the protective nature he had toward her.

Pulling up, David saw a mess of a scene. There was debris scattered everywhere, and they had a patient on the ground. Unfortunately, his duty was to block traffic and keep bystanders away while EMS came in to do their job. He was unable to do anything more than directing traffic around the scene, urging drivers to keep moving and stop looking at the scene - they were bound to cause another accident.

Meredith and Tim arrived on scene to assess what they had. They found a male patient ejected from his vehicle and incoherent. He was combative, flailing his arms around and thrashing his body back and forth, which lead them to believe he had a head injury. His pupils were almost pinpoint, which went against the head injury theory. Maybe he had both a head injury, and was on drugs. That was a possibility. They were too close to a trauma center to call for a helicopter for faster transport, and so, with the help of the fire department, finally got his neck secured into a c-collar, and then strapped securely on a backboard, and safely loaded into the ambulance. They left the scene in nearly record time.

Meredith was able to get vitals and an IV with fluids going. The patient was getting more and more combative, and so Meredith had to restrain his hands so he wouldn't hurt himself or her. She was able to give him some pain medication to help with any pain, but was hesitant to sedate him due to concerns that his blood pressure would drop too far down. Instead, she tried to calmly talk to him while monitoring him and assessing for injuries. Aside from the head injury, she didn't find much other than some possibly broken ribs.

They pulled into St. Victory where Meredith and Tim got the patient unloaded and taken inside. She gave a report to a large room full of people who were all busy doing a large number of things at once, trying to ensure the patient was stable and had all of his injuries attended to as quickly as possible. The doctor yelled for radiology to get a head-to-toe CT scan, and for the nurses to get more pain medication on board. He yelled for someone to hang another liter of fluids, and for lab to draw blood and also do a type-and-cross in case he needed a blood transfusion. At this point, Meredith and Tim were rendered no longer needed and quietly left the room, gathered their equipment and paperwork, and headed back down to their rig.

Leaving the hospital, Meredith pointed out a truck that looked awfully familiar. "Tim...is that Aaron's truck?" Tim looked and shrugged. He couldn't be sure, as he hadn't really paid attention to Aaron's vehicles.

"I wasn't able to get a good look at it. Even if it was, I imagine it would just be a coincidence. There's only so many main roads that go places. But we'll keep an eye out, just in case." He didn't want to downplay the fear his partner was feeling, but he didn't want to get her hyped up, just in case it was a random person and not Aaron. He was trying hard to keep her level, to keep her grounded. He knew she was upset by the thought it was Aaron.

Meredith nodded, feeling mildly shaken. She wasn't sure if it was from the adrenaline with taking care of their patient or if it was the thought of seeing Aaron's truck in the same area they were in. She brushed it off as just a coincidence that it was just a similar truck.

The rest of the day was uneventful. Only a few minor calls for a kid with a cough, an elderly lady who pressed her Lifeline button (but was completely fine, having no idea she accidentally pressed the button), and a transfer from a smaller hospital to St. Victory. Meredith was happy to clock out after her shift and get home, and was happier when David and Paul pulled up with Bullet.

"Boys! Are you hungry?" She knew it was rhetorical. Men were always hungry. The true trick was feeding them enough so they stopped eating for five minutes.

"Yes, ma'am!" Pauly winked and Meredith shook her head, laughing. She knelt down as David let Bullet out of the car and he bounced around. She called him, and he ran to her, jumping up to give her kisses on every inch of her face and neck he could reach with his slobbery tongue.

"No, Bullet. Don't jump." She pushed him down off her, but that didn't stop him from trying to kiss her anyway. "Eew!" she laughed as she fell onto her butt and Bullet pounced on her, attacking her with slobbery kisses.

David was laughing too hard to call him off for a minute or two, but was finally able to wrangle the wayward pup back into a semblance of control. "Well…you don't need to shower anymore, I think he's got you pretty well clean." He couldn't stop laughing as Meredith wrinkled her nose, but then laughed, too.

Meredith wiped the puppy kisses off her face. "Ugh. Better that than him biting, but gross." She giggled and hugged David, reaching up to kiss him hello. "I'll throw us together some macaroni and cheese with bacon. Give me maybe forty-five minutes and we'll eat. You go clean up and I'll put something on for Paul to watch while you do that. Otherwise, he'll be hounding me in the kitchen, asking every three seconds when dinner will be done." She winked at Paul, who grinned while pretending to be offended by the accusation.

They put Bullet outside to run out some of his puppy energy, and for a while, Lowfield stayed outside with him, playing fetch. He was careful not to give too many commands - David didn't want the pup to obey everyone. That would make for a dangerous situation in the future if Bullet would obey every bad guy who told him to lay down and stay while he ran away.

Inside, David had put his belt in the closet, stripped off his uniform and gotten into the shower while Meredith started boiling water and shredding cheese. In a separate pot, she worked on getting a roux together, and then adding milk and cheese for the sauce. In the first pot, she threw in some noodles. In a small pan, she fried up some bacon to add into the mixture once it was ready. Preheating the oven, she put everything together, mixed it, and then put it all into a pan to bake in. Throwing some bread crumbs on top, she set the timer and then went into the bathroom to shower as David was getting out.

She quickly stripped and then teased her clean husband, who was still steaming from the hot water. His eyes were bright with lust for her, but he knew Lowfield was in the living room, or would be as soon as he finished playing with Bullet. "You just wait...you'll get yours." He winked and quickly dried and dressed, leaving Meredith with the hot water all to herself.

Meredith was quick to shower, wanting to make sure dinner was ready and not burning. Once she was clean and felt the calls of the day had washed off, she got out, dried, and dressed in her pajamas. She wasn't planning on going outside again if she could help it.

"Do you want me to feed Bullet yet?" she questioned, looking outside for the pup who was normally running past the door with sticks and leaves in his mouth, but was curiously absent for now.

David nodded. "Please. I think he's probably getting hungry. It's been a pretty long day."

Meredith went to let the pup in, as Paul left him out in the yard, but he didn't come when she called him. She called again, but he still didn't come. Meredith left the porch and walked around the yard, unsure where he could have gone, or what he could have gotten himself into. She was mildly concerned, as he always came running at the possibility of eating. She found him tied to the fence, growling and pulling at his collar, trying desperately to free himself.

Meredith untied him and looked around. There was no sign of anyone, but Bullet continued to growl toward the trees on the other side of the fence. His hackles stood up, and he sounded vicious when he barked, despite still being very young. So much so, that David and Paul came out, both with weapons held tight in their hands.

"What's going on?" David asked.

"Bullet was tied to the fence...did you do that?" Meredith looked up at Paul, wondering why he would possibly tie the pup when the back yard is fenced.

Paul grimly shook his head. "No. When I came in, he was chasing blowing leaves."

"I was hoping it was a neighbor kid, but I'm not so sure now." David walked to the fence, looking out, but seeing nothing. "Come out!" Nothing happened. "Meredith, go inside. Take Bullet and check him out, make sure he's ok," his voice was tight, with no room for argument.

Meredith was hesitant to leave the boys, but didn't fight it. Bullet was another story entirely. He didn't want to be taken in the house, and in the end, Meredith had to carry the violently squirming pup. He whined and whimpered, and barked at the door once they were inside, and she set him down. Bullet ran from Meredith to the door and barked, desperate to get back outside to his master.

"Bullet, calm down. He'll be right back in, buddy." Nothing calmed the pup. She held his collar and gave him a quick once-over, but found no injuries or soreness. It would seem that whoever tied him wasn't out to physically hurt him. At least not yet. The hairs on the back of Meredith's neck stood up. What if it was Aaron? Could he possibly be here, at her house?

Meredith forced the thoughts from her mind. All it was going to do was drive her crazy with worry. She sighed and pulled the macaroni out of the oven, setting it to cool on top of the stove. She opened the door and Bullet bolted out and Meredith followed. The two men were just returning to the porch with frustrated looks on their faces.

"We caught sight of a man hauling ass away from the house, through the trees. Not sure who he was, but if I catch him fucking with my dog again, I'm going to shoot him." David was furious, letting off some steam. "This is the second time this has happened." Meredith looked at him with alarm.

"Second?" Her voice was high-pitched with strain and uneasiness.

"Yeah. The first, he was tied with a carabiner. I thought it was a neighbor kid jacking with him, but twice is too much to be a coincidence," David said, still angry.

Meredith nodded, but didn't say anything. Was it a coincidence then, that she saw a truck that looked so much like Aaron's? "David...when we were getting into St. V's today with our rollover guy, I saw a truck that looked a lot like Aaron's. Tim and I thought it might be a coincidence - that it was just a similar truck. Do you think it could be him?"

"Without evidence, it's hard to say, but I wouldn't put it past him. He's been quiet for quite some time now." His brow furrowed. "We'll just have to pay attention and make sure he's not hanging around." David scooped some food into Bullet's bowl.

"Hey, speaking of paying attention…that macaroni is getting cold. Let's eat." Always the chow-hound, Paul pulled plates out of the cabinet and began to dish up dinner. "Go sit down!" He commanded as he placed a plate in front of Meredith, then David, and lastly, himself. They sat down to eat, discussing what to do about the mystery person.

Chapter 34

Several weeks passed with no further incidences, though they began taking Bullet's collar off if he absolutely had to be outside alone. They worked hard to make sure he wasn't alone, afraid that this person was going to escalate and hurt him for real. The pup was turning into a well-tuned K9 option, and the thought of losing him to Aaron or anyone's cruelty was too much to bear.

Bullet still occasionally growled at the windows, but every time David or Meredith got up to look, there was nothing there. David kept a loaded firearm in his bedside table and began to teach Meredith to shoot when they both had days off. They would spend hours at the range working on form, how to assert herself in the hopes she would never have to shoot, but in the event that loud verbal commands didn't work; how to shoot accurately and without hesitation.

Bullet stayed by their side during this, though he wasn't fond of gunshots. David had rigged him a pair of ear muffs so his hearing wouldn't be damaged during this training. He was becoming a fine dog, and was now nearing five months. He was big, bulky, and ready to work, even though he was too young. He had excellent drive and liked to bite the small bite toys, and was working up to the sleeve. David couldn't be happier.

One night, as they were crawling into bed with Bullet kenneled and content, David put on a random movie. They began to drift off to sleep when Bullet stood up and began to growl menacingly, staring at the window again. His teeth were bared and his hackles were up. Whatever was out there…he really didn't like it and was making sure his people knew it.

Meredith paled and tapped David several times. "David…it's Aaron. It's Aaron!" David picked up his firearm and let Bullet out of his kennel as he went around to the front door. He was still moving slow, but had regained the majority of his leg function back. Bullet was snapped on a leash, and fighting to get free. They rounded the house and saw a man fleeing.

"Aaron! We know it's you! Come back and I'll put a bullet through you if my dog doesn't get you first!" David yelled, knowing he wouldn't be able to catch up with him, and Aaron would likely have just enough sense to not willingly return when they were awake.

The man didn't slow down. Bullet was inconsolable, barking and growling, lunging at the retreating figure. He wanted nothing more than to "play" with the man. This was a new game, one he was determined to win. He remained in his high state of alert as they retreated back into the house. David was sad he couldn't let Bullet loose to bite Aaron, but doing that would classify his dog as a weapon, and he'd wind up getting charged with having a dangerous dog, and Bullet would be put down.

"I'm going to call this in. I'm done playing nice with this asshole." He sat on the bed as Bullet jumped up to stare out the window, growling softly as Meredith pet him, whispering softly to him.

"Hey Carmen; it's Price. I need to make a report of a protection order violation. Aaron White decided to put his face in my bedroom window and sniff around. Had he stayed just a minute longer, my pup would have taken a chunk out of his ass." There was muffled talking on the other end of the line. "Meredith saw him and confirmed. I would prefer Paul take the case if he's willing. I know he'll treat it like it should be treated," David calmly relayed into the phone. He still had an edge to his tone, and his heart was still rapidly beating in his chest, but he also knew that screaming at Dispatch wasn't going to get him anywhere.

He was angry that he couldn't jump in his patrol car and go arrest Aaron. Unfortunately, there was a conflict of interest, and he would be unable to remain neutral in this situation. He already wanted to violently remind Aaron who he was dealing with, and David knew he couldn't protect Meredith if he beat her ex and wound up in jail next to him.

David ended the conversation with Dispatch. "We'll go in and file a report tomorrow morning, and from there, Paul will take care of it. He'll find and interview your ex, and arrest him. Then we'll see the judge to decide what to do." He sighed heavily, rubbing his head with his hands. "I think I'm also going to send Bullet to a trainer who can finish him and have him certified as a K9, if you don't object. It won't be cheap, but he'll be fully trained and ready to go once Chief clears me for that sort of work. He's only just put be back on the street with a partner. I imagine it'll be another month or two before he clears me to be solo again."

Meredith nodded. "I think that's a good idea. How long will he be gone?"

David shrugged. "I'm guessing a few months, at least. The department has always looked at getting dogs that were already trained, and the officer would be gone for several weeks to train to the dog's level. This way…it's new to me. But I'll start calling around in the morning. Let's try to get some rest now." They crawled into bed after David shut the bedroom door. Bullet refused to get off the bed, adjusting so he had his front paws on Meredith's legs, and as soon as David was in bed, put his back legs on David's. His alert eyes watched the window, and then glanced at the door, ready to attack whatever threat they faced next. He growled softly throughout the night, but did not alert to anyone peering in their windows.

When morning dawned, Meredith got up and put Bullet outside to use the bathroom, removing his collar so he couldn't be easily caught by Aaron or any other stranger who decided it was a good idea to stick their hands through the fence. She walked around the yard, looking for any signs that Aaron had been around again, but found nothing. She was shaken and upset, worried that he would try to hurt her and her family. She fought back tears - she felt so violated in knowing that her home…her sanctuary…was no longer sacred. It had been invaded by a man who was ordered by the courts to leave her alone. All she wanted was to live her life in peace. Why couldn't he see that? Was he so desperate to punish her for leaving him that he was going to drive her insane with his little appearances? Would he actually hurt her, David, or Bullet? She wanted to think he wouldn't…but with this new development, she wasn't sure.

After a thorough search of the yard, Meredith and Bullet returned inside for breakfast. She was still upset and unsure of how to proceed with things, and nearly burned the bacon. David came into the room and wrapped his arms around her. She melted against him and shed a few tears of frustration.

"Why is he doing this? Can't he just move on? He has so many other women, or men, or whatever he's into now to call and be happy. Why won't he just do it?" she cried.

David hugged her tighter as she flipped the French toast. "Because you're the one who gave him his power. He feels weak without you to push around. I'm guessing nobody else has fallen for his shit, and now he's realizing he screwed up bad when he pushed you away." He shrugged. "That's his problem. And now, he'll likely face some jail time again. I'm hoping he'll learn his lesson and just move on. Is there anything holding him here, besides you?"

"Yeah. His parents," she said, sniffling and regaining control of her emotions.

His parents were his biggest enablers. They pushed him to believe he was a good man, that his refusal to work wasn't his fault - that the shops he applied to just couldn't see his value. They insisted that she was the problem; that she refused to bend to accept him as he was and help him become a better man. They refused to see that she had tried to help him be a better man, but he didn't want that. He wanted to be the same angry, hateful man he had always been.

David nodded thoughtfully. There was nothing they could do to make him leave. Not if he had ties here that were holding him. Too bad.

They finished their breakfast and Meredith quickly washed the dishes. David took Bullet outside to use the bathroom so they could go to the office without worry that he would mess up their truck, just in case they couldn't bring him inside, for whatever reason.

Meredith got dressed and glared at their bedroom window. There was no need for anyone to be looking in, invading their privacy and making her feel unsafe in her own home. She was beginning to feel angry now instead of victimized.

They had finished getting ready and got into the truck with Bullet in the back seat. He was all too happy to put his nose out the window and take in all the new smells that weren't new at all. He was young enough that everything was new to him. The same tree they passed every morning moved a branch in a different way, and it was new. He had to inspect it until he was satisfied it wasn't a threat to his people. It was unusual that he was so protective over them. With the right training, he would be even better, and not dangerous to anyone who was a friend.

The office wasn't too busy, and Bullet was allowed to come inside. He stayed attached to David's hip, even when strangers tried to pet him. People were upset that he didn't come running to play, but David politely explained he was a police dog in training, and he wasn't supposed to respond to everyone's command.

Together, they talked to a burly sergeant who took their complaint. David explained that Aaron should be contacted at some point today and would hopefully be served papers about a court date. The sergeant nodded and took their paperwork. "Here's your paperwork with the complaint, and the court date is here." His pudgy finger pointed to the date printed in bold. "If he hasn't been served by that date, we will reschedule it and let you know, but there is no reason he won't be arrested today."

They left his office and went down to talk to the chief. "Good morning, sir. I hope I haven't caught you at a bad time?" David's voice was fluid and warm. It was impossible to not drop what you were doing just to hear what he had to say.

"No, Price. Sit down. And you too. Meredith, is it? Have a seat." He glanced at the pup, who was intently staring at him, trying to figure out why he had the same uniform as his person, but didn't smell like his person.

"Sir, I want to send Bullet to training as a full K9. He is incredibly smart, and has his commands down. I just need your blessing in writing so I can send him to K9 School. I'll cover costs and things myself, so there is no burden on the department, but my end goal is to use him as a partner once he's fully trained and ready to go."

"Let me talk to the commissioners about that. I don't think we have a budget for it yet, but if you're covering costs, I don't think they will have a problem. I'll see what I can work out. Give me a few days and I'll get back with you." He paused. "In the meantime, I don't see why he can't go to training." He gave a cheeky grin and a wink and sat down at his computer, typing up a quick letter allowing Price to send his dog to K9 School with full police department blessing.

"Thank you, sir. As soon as I have found the right trainer, he'll be on his way. Hopefully the commissioners will allow him to remain on duty as my partner. We're saving thousands of dollars by doing it this way."

With lighter hearts than they had arrived with, David and Meredith left the station with Bullet in tow, tail wagging as if he knew what had just been accomplished. They decided to go to the park where he could play and stretch and they could practice commands in a new setting.

A couple days later, Meredith received papers about a court date in regards to the violation of protection order. They went to court where the judge found Aaron guilty and sentenced him to three months in jail. The judge admonished Aaron and told him that was unacceptable, but the sentence was lenient as it was a first offence. The judge warned that any subsequent offenses would be harsh and unwavering. Aaron nodded as they took him away in cuffs.

The look he gave Meredith sent a chill up her spine, and she cowered closer to David who wrapped an arm protectively around her, eyes darkening with a clear threat toward Aaron.

David and Meredith enjoyed their time free of Aaron while he was in jail, but that still didn't stop her from worrying about what would happen next. During that time, David installed several motion cameras with lights, and with Paul's help, they removed the chain link fence and replaced it with a wood fence so Bullet wouldn't be at risk of getting tied again. David had no doubt that he would bite anyone who tried to grab him, but he felt that prevention was the best cure.

Chapter 35

Three months later, they were able to find a decent K9 trainer with the full blessing of the commissioners. They even offered to pay for the training with a contract stating that Bullet would belong to David, but would be utilized by the department. He agreed without hesitation, and Bullet was off to the trainer. He would be gone four months, and would return when he was a year old. The trainer stated they don't usually like dogs so young because they can be unpredictable and easily distracted in their youth, but Bullet was so well-behaved, they couldn't turn him down.

Aaron had gotten out of jail about the time Bullet went into training, and Meredith was apprehensive. David occasionally worked nights, and without the pre-warning Bullet gave, she felt exposed and alone. She took to sleeping on David's side of the bed so she would have faster access to his handgun if Aaron broke in. She had also bought and put up privacy blinds. She enjoyed the light, gauzy blinds that let the sunlight filter through in the mornings, but with the risk of Aaron finding her alone, she couldn't afford herself the luxury.

Thankfully, Aaron wasn't foolish enough to get caught again. Meredith believed he stayed away, especially with David and Paul always around, and one of their coworkers passing by the house at random intervals during the day. Aaron wouldn't be able to predict their schedule. She still saw him occasionally in town, passing by the hospitals, or cruising past the station. She couldn't do much about that, as he wasn't technically harassing her, nor was he close enough to actually break the restraining order. The court had explained that unless he was directly harassing her, or causing her severe emotional harm, they couldn't prevent him from driving on city streets.

Meredith was upset with this, as she felt he was stalking her. But she conceded that maybe the court was right - the city streets were public, and she couldn't rightly prevent him from his freedoms until it got to the point of actual harassment.

This continued for months, and by then, Bullet was ready to come home. David had gone to the school to spend the last couple weeks with him to get used to their training methods, and ensure Bullet would obey his commands. There wasn't a single issue, as Bullet obeyed without falter. They practiced general obedience, some minor narcotic work, and bite work on the sleeve and the full suit. David was impressed that his pup had grown so much in just a couple months, and was a fine dog now. He had filled out and was well-muscled, looking every bit as intimidating as a Rottweiler with a spiked collar and a growl. He was going to make a great police dog, and the department would be lucky to have him.

Together, they went home to be put on the streets as a team. Meredith was just as excited to see Bullet as she was David. Bullet wagged his tail when he saw her and let her pet him, hugging him and telling him what a handsome boy he was. David rolled his eyes and patiently waited. "Oh, you're a good boy too, David." She teased him playfully, and then hugged him, kissing him deeply.

"I have steaks ready for the grill. Do you want to invite Paul over? I know he's been missing you," she told him, beaming.

David nodded and set Bullet loose in the backyard to stretch after their long car ride so he could change clothes and shower. While that was going on, Meredith started the grill and sent a text to Lowfield, inviting him over for dinner.

Bullet was barking and whining at something in the back yard, but it didn't sound like his alert bark, so Meredith took a minute to get back there. When she did, she found him barking at his ball that had been suspended just out of his reach by a rope in a tree branch. A slat in the wood fence had been broken, enough for a man to fit his arm through. Meredith quickly called him inside and let David know things were happening again. She put Bullet's leash on his collar and kept him with her in the front yard while she tended the grill until David was ready.

Lowfield showed up shortly after and took over the grill while Meredith went in the house to work on the side dishes. She'd decided mashed potatoes and roasted asparagus sounded amazing, along with an apple pie. It was nearing Thanksgiving now, but the weather was unseasonably warm. Apple pie just seemed fitting.

With the pie baking and the boys drinking a beer and arguing over the best cut and rarity of a steak, Meredith returned outside. Bullet's ball had been retrieved and the back yard deemed secure. They would look at the footage later, since it was all saved on a drive. David had already isolated the timeframe they were looking for, and didn't want to spoil dinner with being angry.

They retreated inside with their steaks and brought Bullet inside to enjoy his meal as well. His wasn't as tasty - just dry dog food with a can of wet food mixed in for a treat.

"How can we stop this guy from messing with you? It's getting out of hand."

"Shy of a life sentence or death...I'm not sure. He's relentless. I'm hoping he'll catch on sooner or later that Mer's not interested anymore, but he's pretty dense." David was trying to keep his emotions in check. He still wanted to beat the stupid out of Aaron for continuing to harass Meredith.

"We could always move?" Meredith's voice was soft. "I think we're both qualified enough to go wherever we want and start over." She didn't really want to leave, but seeing Aaron this frequently was too much for her. All she wanted was to be left alone to live her life without constant fear and anxiety.

"No. We aren't letting him chase us away. This is our house. Our town. Our life." David was firm on the matter.

"Besides," Paul chimed in. "If you leave...you're going to have to take me with you. I don't have many other friends here, and who knows if they'll take me on with David. I mean...they might just take me and he'll wind up staying at home getting fat." Paul laughed at the thought.

"Ok. We'll stay. I'm just so tired of him being like this. Following us around. Showing up at our house. What if it gets worse?" Her voice was rimmed with fear.

"Then we will take care of matters as they arise. Hopefully, he'll get the hint and go away before we have to go back to court. Or worse." David's thoughts held a thinly-veiled threat. They would take care of whatever problems Aaron caused, even though they didn't like the thought of violence.

Dinner ended with them changing topics to happier things. They decided to watch some reruns of cop shows in-between making s'mores over the coals of the grill. The wood chips Meredith had used for the steaks gave the s'mores a unique flavor that wasn't displeasing.

During their shows, Bullet stared at the window and growled again, head low, hackles high. Paul went to the window and peered out while David crept out the front door. Before he had a chance to tackle Aaron, he took off running again. David was still not quite completely normal, and didn't yet have the coordination for running. He also couldn't send Bullet after him as there was no immediate danger to himself or the general public, and that would lead anyone to believe Bullet was a "dangerous dog" and have him put to sleep. David yelled obscenities at Aaron, threatening that if he was caught again at his house, David was going to kill him.

194

He returned inside and called into the station, making a report of the continued stalking behavior. It was unacceptable, and he was getting tired of it, just as Meredith was. She was in the bedroom, softly crying with Bullet sitting in the room with her, soft eyes trying to console her, wagging his tail and trying to give her kisses. She loosely draped an arm around the dog's large shoulders.

David entered the room and sat down beside her on the floor. "I've requested another complaint be filed. There's no reason it shouldn't go to his probation officer. He could be looking at jail time - a significant amount. And with the footage I'm sure we have now, he should be arrested again very soon."

Meredith sniffled. "It doesn't matter. It'll stop while he's in jail, and as soon as he's out, it'll continue again. We know this. He's crazy, David. I don't know why I didn't see it sooner, and leave him before it ever got to this point. Now I'm stuck with him forever." She buried her face in his chest and cried softly.

"The doors and windows are all locked with no sign he was trying to get in." Lowfield peeked his head in to report this to David and then sat back on the couch. He knew everyone was upset, but there wasn't much he could do to console anyone, so he offered them some space without leaving. A short time later, David and Meredith rejoined him on the couch.

"We'll get it straightened out, Meredith. One way or another. Really." Paul reached over and patted her knee. He knew that nothing he could say was going to reassure her, but he still had to try something. Meredith looked at him with gratefulness in her swollen, red eyes. She stayed silent, her throat still tight from crying. She knew that she wouldn't be able to speak yet.

They watched the rest of their cop shows in near silence, only commenting about how they would do things differently, and inevitably, better than the guys on TV. Meredith was able to crack a smile a few times and every time they showed an ambulance crew, made the same comments that she could do it better. By the end of their evening, she was feeling better. Bullet showed no other signs that anyone had been around.

The night ended without further incident. It stayed that way for several days until one morning, as they were both getting ready for work, Meredith found a small box on the porch. She brought it inside and opened it, eyes widening and hand flying to her mouth in horror. Inside were numerous pictures of her and David throughout the house. There were pictures of the backyard and Bullet, and several of him tied to the fence. Meredith began to shake uncontrollably. David came to see what she had found, and his face darkened in rage. There was only one person who would be sick enough to photograph them in their own home; and the reason Bullet spent many nights growling at various windows.

Aaron.

It would seem that none of the pictures were recent - maybe a month old. David gingerly took the box from Meredith's hand and stored it in his bedside table. He was going to have to do something about it, but now wasn't the time.

"Bullet! Let's go to work." The dog bounded through the house and into the waiting harness. He wiggled with excitement. "Meredith...? Let's go. I'll drop you off at the station on my way in." She nodded and grabbed her bag. She looked defeated.

Their day went on with agonizing slowness until nearing the end of the shift. The ambulance had just gotten a call to standby for an armed male arguing with law enforcement. Meredith's mind flashed back to almost two years ago when David had been shot. Her anxiety flew through the roof, imagining then, that Aaron was the man with the gun.

"Oh God. Not again." Tim had the same feeling - he didn't think they would be commended again for disobeying orders if something bad happened. They got to the scene to find a man with a very large knife yelling at the officers. He wasn't advancing, and neither were they, though there were numerous officers with guns or tasers drawn. Bullet was there, barking his ferocious bark.

"That's my boy! Isn't he handsome?" Meredith couldn't help but feel some excitement seeing him at work. She had seen the suspect was not Aaron, and that David was not shot, so she was able to relax, however marginally.

"Yeah...a real heartthrob." Tim rolled his eyes. He wasn't much of a dog person, especially when that dog had the ability to bite and tear flesh. He was terrified of them, to be honest.

Several commands later, the suspect refused to put the knife down and continued to advance on officers. He was still too far away for the tasers to be effective, and they didn't want to shoot him, so David loosed Bullet who flew like a rocket and clamped onto the suspect's arm. The man dropped the knife and screamed in agony, trying to push the dog off. Bullet didn't let go.

The officers ran to him and took him down, and Bullet still didn't let go until David gave the command. He continued to bounce and bark at the suspect in his excitement over this game. The other officers were able to get him into handcuffs and walked him to the ambulance where Tim and Meredith were waiting.

They assisted the suspect into the back where they were able to clean the deep bite and wrap it. "He'll probably need stitches, but you are welcome to take him if you want, as he's in custody. He's wrapped and not bleeding from any arteries that we can see." Meredith looked up as

David approached, Bullet securely back in the car with a treat. "That's one hell of a bite he's got."

David proudly nodded. "We'll see you over at St. Victory."

Chapter 36

The end of the shift came quickly, and without further incidents. Meredith was still amped to have seen their pup in action, knowing he was a fine K9 officer with a bright future. David had arrived to pick her up, and that's all she could talk about - how deep his teeth went into the poor guy's arm, and the stitches he was going to need, and how it's so different from seeing dog bites on TV or YouTube.

"Yep. He got to play his favorite game, and he got a treat for being such a good boy." They could hear his tail thumping against the cage. He poked his nose out so he could see his people. Meredith gave his muzzle a scratch.

They didn't talk about the box of pictures, but instead, made sure to close all the blinds and made plans to replace them with others that would keep out prying eyes. Every little bit helped, and if they could keep Aaron from finding what he was looking for, that was all the better.

More quiet weeks passed with no sign of Aaron. Meredith wasn't even seeing him pass by the station anymore, and hoped that maybe...just maybe, he had moved on. She imagined he had found a young woman who was as dumb as she had once been, and could only hope that she would learn before things got bad. She would hate to see any other woman go through what she had been through.

She and David were relaxing in the hot tub one early evening when their luck ran out. They heard a thump at the front door and Bullet went crazy barking, running back and forth between the bedroom and the bathroom, trying to alert his people that something was wrong, even though they already knew it.

Meredith was quicker and jumped out, wrapping up in a towel and heading to the front door. Looking through the glass, nothing seemed amiss. She cracked the door open and found a brick with a paper tied to it sitting harmlessly on the porch. Meredith reached through the door and brought it inside as David was coming into the room. He calmed Bullet and took the brick from Meredith.

You will pay for what you've done. Hell has a special place for bitches like you. No place is safe anymore. You are going to bleed for your sins.

It would be hard to prove it was Aaron, but David called into Dispatch anyway. Everything they could report would help them later. Meredith and David quickly dressed in pajamas to avoid awkward stares when the officers showed up. Within ten minutes, a uniformed officer had arrived, and so had Paul, out of uniform. Both came into the house and looked over the letter. The rage was clearly etched on David's face as he finished reading the few words again.

"I want him in jail for stalking and threatening Meredith, and harassment. Not to mention this…" he got up and retrieved the box from his bedside table, setting it beside the officer. He looked up at David with a confused look on his face. David internally sighed and removed the lid from the box. *This kid must be new*, he thought.

The officer pulled photos out of the box, one by one. Concern outlined his young face as he figured out what was going on. The pieces all fit together in a nice package once he had them all in his hands. The guy who was taking the pictures and throwing bricks was downright crazy.

"I'll handle this, sir." He stood up and collected the paper in an evidence bag and the box of pictures. "I'll be in touch." He left without further instruction or promises. Paul stayed behind with his friends.

"Man, that's fucked up. I don't even know what to say." Lowfield looked up at David and then at Meredith, who was staring blankly at the table. She had faced so much stress lately that she felt on the verge of a complete break. She jumped when Paul reached across the table and put his hand over hers. "You know we won't let him hurt you. We may not be able to prove it's him right now, but if they collect fingerprints, I know they'll match his." Lowfield was confident that they could thwart Aaron, and David agreed.

"Besides, between the two of us and Bullet, do you really think anyone stands a chance?" Meredith was able to give a small grin. "That's my girl." David stood up and kissed the top of her head. She smelled like shampoo. "How about we go out tonight? All of us, if you want?" Bullet sat next to David, patiently waiting for them to make a decision. He had caught onto their tension, and was ready for whatever action they had planned.

Meredith nodded slowly. "That would be nice. We can take Bullet, right? I don't want to leave him alone here, knowing Aaron could come back and try to hurt him."

"Yes. He can come. He'll have to stay in the car, but at least he won't be home alone."

Meredith agreed and they retreated into the bedroom to change. Paul stayed with Bullet who was enjoying a good belly rub, wiggling happily on the carpeted floor. Once they were ready, they jumped into Paul's truck and headed for the Chinese place nearby.

They enjoyed dinner without worrying about Aaron, even though Meredith was still concerned that Bullet was outside in the car. David assured her that the windows were down, and the July heat was dissipated enough that it wouldn't hurt him. They finished eating and ordered desserts with a glass of wine. It had been so long since they had forgotten about Aaron, that for one night, they were in Heaven.

After dinner, there wasn't much to do but go home. When they got there, they went inside to find nothing had changed. Meredith felt her anxiety relax marginally. She was pleased that Aaron hadn't been back, but was still worried that would change any moment. She took Bullet outside to use the bathroom while the boys decided they were going to watch some boxing.

Bullet returned without any issues and laid by David's feet, rolling over for more belly rubs. He remained there until the guys got a little too excited about the boxing match and began yelling at their favored boxer. Bullet sat up and howled along with them. The noise was horrendous, and Meredith retreated into the bedroom for pajamas, a book, and a glass of wine.

The fight ended with Paul's fighter winning. The guys bantered for a short time before Paul headed home. "Morning shift comes early," he said with a wink. David walked him out.

Chapter 37

July faded into August without further incidents caused by Aaron. They were still on edge about everything, and waiting to see what he would do next. They hoped that he had gotten the hint, between the threats of jail time, and the threats of being shot. They went on a short vacation on their days off, just up to the hot springs to relax their tense muscles. Bullet stayed with Paul for those few days, undoubtedly eating junk food and running amok. Paul had a ridiculous soft spot for the dog, and refused to keep him in line.

September came in quietly as well. Meredith attended a conference with Tim for work, and was able to network with other Paramedics. There were some good ideas for equipment grants, and training funds that her department would greatly benefit from. She was excited at the possibilities for furthered training, new tools, and serious improvements for their department.

Meredith and David were both off to work on a brisk, but sunny September morning. David told her that he'd pick her up after her shift and dropped her off at the station. Meredith went inside and began her shift-change routine. David and Bullet went to his station to pick up his patrol unit and begin the day.

Before long, David stopped a vehicle that was speeding. The driver was acting suspicious by fidgeting, looking in his rearview mirror, and fumbling to provide his license. He came back with a warrant for drugs. David quickly called for backup and then arrested the driver, putting him in the backseat of his patrol car. Bullet was brought out to do a search for drugs. He alerted that there was something in the car.

David put Bullet back in the cage with a treat and once his backup arrived, they searched the car. They were able to recover 50 grams of heroin and numerous baggies of cocaine, ready to distribute. David took the driver to jail while the other officer had the car impounded and took the evidence to the station for safe-keeping. It was the largest bust they'd ever had in a single incident.

About a week later, Bullet was honored as a crime-fighting hero on the news and in the paper. He had his picture taken with David, who was beaming from ear to ear. He had never been a real celebrity, and was enjoying everyone's treats and scratches. David had never seen the dog so excited to go to work.

Several local schools then wanted to meet Bullet, and so, David set up a day to go to the elementary schools. One class of youngsters were all questions and stories about their dogs, and could their dogs find candy instead of drugs, and bite bad guys too?

"Bullet had to go to school for a long time before he could fight bad guys. He had to learn who was a bad guy and who was a good guy. I don't want him to hurt a good guy." He smiled as the kids solemnly nodded. He answered another hundred questions or more, or so it felt, before they were done.

He invited the kids, one at a time, to come pet Bullet. At the very end of his time there, he sat Bullet in the middle of the students and let the teacher take a picture. She was excited and promised that he would receive a copy as well. It would seem that he had become as big a celebrity as Bullet had.

"Thank you for coming into our school and teaching the kids about what your dog does. It sure is impressive." The teacher was flirting blatantly as they stepped into the hallway. "What else does he do?"

"He finds drugs, and he's also a bite dog. That means if someone is trying to hurt myself, another officer, or an innocent member of the public, and it's too dangerous for us to go in, I'll send Bullet and he'll take down the suspect so myself or another officer can go in and arrest him."

"That is so brave. I don't know how you do it." She placed a hand on his bicep. "Oh! You're so strong!" David grinned and took a step back, disguising it by reaching down to pat Bullet, who was looking up at his master with the same loving look in his eyes.

"My wife thinks so, too." His words were gentle, but to the point, and the teacher was visibly deflated. Apparently, she hadn't seen the ring he wore; or maybe she thought it was just a ruse. David almost felt bad that she was so hurt over it - he didn't feel he had done anything to lead her on.

"Yes, I'm sure she does. We hope to see you here again." She smiled, but this time, it wasn't as flirty. David shook her hand and walked out with Bullet and the promise to visit again one day.

"Women. Boy, you're lucky. All you have to do is breed and move on. No weird ladies trying to pick you up, no strangers wanting to break

up a marriage for a chance at you. Don't ever lose that. Just stay a dog."
Bullet wagged his tail and sneezed in response.

When his shift was over, David picked up Meredith and told her about the teacher. "The nerve! I hope you set her straight." Meredith had had a rough day with several bad calls and a transfer that didn't need an ambulance, and she was a little cranky.

"I sure did. I told her that my crazy wife would shank her if she even looked at me again. And then she would shank me in my sleep." He widened his eyes in mock fear. "I don't want to be shanked. I told her she'd better just find herself someone else."

Meredith laughed. "Good. I'd sure hate to shank a teacher in front of her kids."

When they got home, they found their front windows had been broken.

"God dammit." David was furious as he jerked his truck into park and let Bullet down. The dog set to sniffing around, looking for someone to bite. David called it in and another report was taken. There was no sign of who had been there, even though they knew who it was. Meredith stayed in the truck, trembling, while David searched the property and the house. He waved her inside after a thorough search.

"We'll board them up for the night, and fix them in a day or two when we can get the right size windows. Guess we'll make a day of it. Anything else we need to upgrade or remodel while we're at it?"

Meredith shook her head. "I don't think so?" She was too upset to really think about it.

A few days later was October first. They went into the city with window measurements and found nice replacements and a rug that matched the curtains for the living room. They ate lunch at Red Lobster, and in a spontaneous movement, went out for a massage. They got home feeling relaxed and calm, ready to repair the damage Aaron had caused to their home.

When they got there, Paul was on the couch and Bullet was snoring next to him. David slammed the front door, causing Bullet to jump on Paul on his way over the couch to see who the intruders were. He barked once and then happily yipped several times, wagging his butt as he recognized his family.

Paul, on the other hand, grumbled under his breath. "Damn dog caught me in the balls…why are you home so early?"

David laughed as Paul waddled over, hands cupping his sore testicles. "We got our business done, got lunch, and a massage. We didn't hurry by any means. Why is he sleeping on the couch by your junk anyway?"

"He wasn't on my junk 'til you scared him." He wrinkled his nose and waddled back to the couch, gingerly sitting down. "Let's get those windows installed. What's for dinner?"

It was Meredith's chance to laugh. "You sat here all day just waiting for dinner, didn't you? Get those windows in and I'll throw together some spaghetti, meatballs, and garlic bread."

With the windows back where they belonged and dinner eaten in record time, Meredith was ready for bed. It was early evening, but with the stress they had been feeling lately, coupled with the massage that had worked every knot out of her back and shoulders, she was done. Paul and David stayed talking in the living room for a while, but she crawled into bed, only to have nightmares about Aaron, broken glass, and dog bites.

Chapter 38

November provided nothing from Aaron, but Meredith had a bit of news. She and David went out for dinner at the fancy Brazilian steakhouse and enjoyed numerous cuts of meat they hadn't ever tried before. Everything was tender, and spiced to perfection, the salads crisp and green, and the bread crunchy outside, but soft inside. They ate until they were nearly bursting before Meredith broke the news.

"David...I know you wanted to wait for this for a while...but it would seem God has other plans for us." He quirked an eyebrow, placing his chin on his folded hands, waiting for her to finish the speech she had clearly rehearsed. He was apprehensive about what she had to say, but forced himself to be patient and calm.

"We're going to have a baby in a few months." She gave an uncertain smile. She was nervous that he would be angry with her, despite the fact that she was on the pill. He remained silent for a minute, processing what Meredith had just told him. Her anxiety exploded along with the butterflies in her stomach as he slowly stood up, all eyes in the restaurant turning to him.

"Ladies and gentlemen...it would seem I'm about to be a father!"

The diners, dressed to the nines, politely clapped, with a few whistles from bolder guests. "I would like everyone to raise their glasses, if you're so inclined, to my wife, and to the good health of her and my child!"

Glasses were raised and calls of "hear, hear!" were spread around the room. David sat down, a wide smile on his face. Meredith was red as a firetruck by the time he had finished.

"It didn't need to be such a spectacle! We don't even know these people!" she whispered angrily.

"Exactly. But it made their dinner something to remember, didn't it? When did you find out? Have you been to the doctor? Are you on prenatals? What do we need to do now?" David fired off all these questions on a single breath.

"I just found out I'm three months along. My doctor put me on medications, and I have an appointment in another four weeks to find out the gender. If you want to know, that is?" She wanted to know so they could plan accordingly. David thought about it, and then nodded.

"I think that's a great idea."

December crept in with a massive cold front and snow. Four weeks had passed quickly, leaving Meredith and David in the doctor's office. She asked Meredith questions about morning sickness, advising it should have passed by now, and if she had any other symptoms. Meredith shook her head, indicating that everything was going well. She had been reading everything she could find about babies and how to deal with pregnancy, wanting to be as prepared as possible. She'd even begun to buy baby items that were gender neutral - bottles, diapers, burp rags, bath toys.

The doctor chuckled. "This must be your first, then?" Meredith blushed and nodded. "Well, no shame in being prepared. The ultrasound tech should be with you shortly. If you have no other questions, you're free to leave after that, and we'll see you in another two to three weeks." Meredith nodded.

The tech came back to get Meredith and took her to a dimly lit room with a rolling computer in the corner. The tech introduced herself and had Meredith sit on the table and relax.

"Now, this is going to be cold." The tech squirted some ultrasound gel on Meredith's abdomen and placed the probe against it, looking around. There was a sound of a heartbeat as the ultrasound magnified the sound. Meredith's own heart fluttered as she reached out for David's hand. The tech moved around a little bit and did a few other things Meredith didn't understand.

"Are you wanting to know the gender of your baby?"

Meredith nodded in anticipation. She had always hoped for a daughter. The tech pointed to the screen. "I know it's not much, but that right there makes your baby a little boy."

Meredith and David both grinned broadly. David, like the average man, wanted a son to carry on his name. A son to work on cars with, and play football and baseball with. A son to take hunting and fishing and camping. He envisioned teaching his boy to drive and offering dating advice when he was old enough for that.

Meredith's dreams of dressing her daughter in all the bows and frills had vanished in that instant, but she wasn't upset. Rather, now she would focus on raising her son to be the gentleman that another mother's little girl needed. He would open doors for her, pull out chairs for her, and protect her just like his daddy did for his mommy. He would also know how to cook and clean, so when his wife was having a bad day, he would know how to help, instead of feeling like he couldn't do anything.

The tech wiped the jelly off Meredith's stomach and hit the "print" button on the monitor. It showed the gender of their baby and Meredith kept staring at it in disbelief. They were really going to have a baby. This was a dream come true.

They left the office with full hearts, Meredith's hand resting on her stomach, still feeling butterflies.

"How about some ice cream?" She had a hopeful tone to her voice, sounding every bit like an excited child. She even bounced on her toes a time or two.

David couldn't tell her no, and agreed, heading toward Dairy Queen. He knew they had the best soft serve, and Meredith was a die-hard chocolate soft serve fan. She squealed in delight as they pulled into the parking lot.

"I guess I should call my mother, shouldn't I?" She didn't want to, especially after the way her mother had been displeased she was marrying the "crippled" cop instead of the "perfect" Aaron. David nodded.

"Yeah. You probably should." He reached up and gave her shoulder an affectionate squeeze.

Meredith received her ice cream and then sat down, staring at her phone. She decided she would call first, and devour the cone after as a reward for keeping her cool. The phone rang several times before her mom answered.

"Mom?"

"Meredith! How are you?" she asked, her tone pleased at the phone call.

"Good. Hey, I have some news for you," Meredith started slowly.

"What is it, dear? Is everything alright?"

"Yeah…mom, I'm pregnant." She couldn't hide the smile. Her mom was silent for a minute. "Mom?"

"Yeah, dear. Are you sure it's David's? Is he even…capable of fathering a child?"

There it was. The dissenting, condescending tone. Meredith clenched her fist and took a deep breath. "Yes, mother. He's been back to work for months and he's been doing very well for even longer. I have not been with anyone else." She wanted to be angry, to say things that would make her feel better, but she swore she would be nice.

"Oh, well, congratulations then, dear." Her mother sounded disinterested. "Do you know what gender it is yet?"

"It's a boy. We are due in late April or early May."

"A boy! How wonderful!" The tone was still disinterested. A granddaughter would have been better - a little girl to corrupt was just up her mother's alley. For a moment, Meredith was pleased to have disappointed her mother this way.

They spoke a little longer before her mother made more excuses to get off the phone. As soon as she hung up, Meredith attacked her ice cream cone.

"That good, huh?" David knew it was a bad conversation. It always was. For whatever reason, her mother couldn't stand him and was convinced that Aaron was the best man for her daughter. He brushed it off, refusing to let it get to him.

"She asked if I was sure you were the father. Maybe I should have told her it was Paul's. She'd really have a scandal if she knew my baby was fathered by a gay cop and the friend of my "crippled" husband." She wrinkled her nose in disgust. "I still can't believe she's like that!"

"Ignore it, Meredith. She'll be lonely until the day she dies. I'm happy enough for the both of us." He grinned.

Chapter 39

Time passed slowly. Much too slowly. Meredith was anxious to meet her son. Work didn't seem to slow down, however, and David had an inservice he was required to attend. It was on a snowy late-December day, and he was planning on being gone for the entire miserable day. He was especially sad that Bullet couldn't come with him, but was happy to leave him home with Meredith, hating to leave her alone, especially now.

Seeing as they were both working for Christmas, Meredith was in the kitchen since early in the morning, working on dinner for herself, David, Paul, Tim and his parents, and several of the other officers who didn't have a family to spend time with. She had a ham in the oven, and a turkey in the roaster. Potatoes were peeled and ready to be boiled for mashed potatoes, and several pies were ready to be put in for dessert after the ham was finished. Sides were stacked up, each one waiting for its turn to be cooked or warmed, and the cold sides were in the fridge. All she had to do now was wait for everyone to arrive. They had determined six was a fair time.

Meredith had the food spread out across the counter by the time everyone started arriving. They mingled and introduced themselves to each other while she opened a couple bottles of wine and set out glasses.

"You're all welcome to start serving as soon as you get hungry. Pies will be ready by the time you're done eating," Meredith announced happily.

Paul shook his head. "You don't know me very well, do you? Unless that pie is ready in two minutes flat…I'm going to make you a liar." He laughed and poured himself and her a glass of wine. She shook her head.

"I can't drink," she told him.

He looked at her. "What…are you pregnant or something?" She laughed and nodded. She hadn't told many people, wanting it to wait until after the holiday. Paul screeched his excitement, causing everyone else to stop talking simultaneously and stare at him. David had joined them, standing next to his wife with a grin on his face. He kissed her on the cheek.

"Meredith is pregnant! We have to have a baby shower!" The party-goers clapped and each congratulated her as they found an opening in the conversation.

"How about on Valentine's Day? We'll have your party early so you and David can still spend the night together? Can you all make it here on Valentine's Day? Say, eleven?" Everyone shrugged and agreed that Valentine's Day was perfect for a baby shower. "What is it, Meredith? Boy or girl?"

"Boy."

The partygoers with children took turns offering her advice on how to raise her child, and what to do if she had cravings, or how to know when she was ready for labor. She took it all in, but knew most of it was superstition.

Dinner was a noisy affair with everyone conversing amongst each other. For the first time in a long time, Meredith felt surrounded by her family. She felt nothing but love for this group of rag-tag strangers who filled her home. She was proud to be the place they could all go to when they needed somewhere to be.

People slowly started to trickle out after dessert, leaving Meredith, Paul, and David to tackle the dishes. They put the scraps together and let Bullet enjoy Christmas dinner, too, after freeing him from their bedroom. With so many people, David wasn't comfortable leaving him to roam the house. Too much risk for him getting antsy, and potentially biting. He was very well behaved, but David didn't want to risk anything.

The evening was a huge success, and once they were finished putting the leftovers away, the three of them collapsed on the couch to watch Christmas movies. Meredith closed her eyes and smiled, reveling in the new family she had surrounded herself with.

"We should do this again. But not real soon. I need time to recover," she said, still smiling broadly.

"I agree. I think the next big date we have planned is the baby shower. Are you up for it?" Paul asked.

Meredith giggled. "Yeah, there should be enough leftovers to last us until then." Paul shook his head.

"I don't think so. I'm taking at least half of that home. It'll feed me for a month!"

It was David's turn to argue. "What? You aren't going to be coming over for home-cooked meals for a whole month? Are you mad at us?" He winked.

"Oh, no. I'll still be over for dinner, but this will get me through lunches and my midnight snacks. Don't worry, bro, you'll still have me around for a long time."

Chapter 40

The day of the baby shower had arrived, and Meredith was busy baking treats to share. She had started a ham early in the morning, and it would be ready as the party started. The house smelled heavenly - a mix of glazed ham and sugary, baked goods. She was ready for a day of friends and family.

Guests began to arrive with bags, boxes, and gifts for the baby. They put everything on coffee table and gathered, talking amongst themselves. Paul, of course, was late to his own party. Meredith rolled her eyes as he texted David and let him know he'd be there "soon". She was certain he'd be late to his own funeral one day. He showed up nearly thirty minutes late.

With the food done, the guests piled into the kitchen, serving up lunch with gusto. They continued talking and discussing what the baby should be named, what things to look out for, and cures for the common ills. They discussed diaper rash, fevers, teething, and colic too.

After lunch was finished, they gathered and played several games that Paul had thought up. They devoured the desserts Meredith had baked, and began to pass out presents.

She received boxes of diapers, bottles, teething rings, blankets, clothes, and one of the officers gave her a car seat. Tim and the crews from her service put together a "baby wellness" package that included a thermometer and bulb syringe, tiny nail clippers, baby Tylenol, and some bedtime bubble bath and lotion.

Even Meredith's mother sent a gift along with a note. *Sorry we couldn't make it. Lionel and I are vacationing in Germany for the month.* Who the hell was Lionel? Meredith shrugged off the question, assuming it was one of her mother's many boyfriends. What mattered was that she cared enough to send a gift. It was a beautiful crib with bedding. Meredith smiled as she looked at the boxed crib. It was going to go perfectly in the guest bedroom, which they were slowly remodeling into a nursery for their new arrival.

Paul, however, topped the cake with a photo album full of pictures of himself and David, several of Meredith, and newspaper clippings of the "big" calls they had been on. It detailed David's career, with the help of "Uncle Paul." There were pictures of Bullet as a pup, and as a grown dog during trainings, and his big drug bust. The article where Meredith saved David was in its own page, with pictures of them holding their commendations. It also had pages of "helpful advice" and stories of Daddy and Paul for when the baby was older.

"I thought it would be different. Oh! And there's one other thing." Lowfield pulled out a small box and handed it to Meredith. She opened it and her jaw fell. Inside was the most adorable little suit she had ever seen.

"I wanted him to match when he goes for his baptism." Lowfield blushed. "I have the same suit, but, you know, a little bigger." He grinned a lopsided grin. Meredith hugged him tightly, tears in her eyes.

"You are amazing, Paul. Thank you," she told him.

Everyone was getting ready to leave, and they all got their hugs and handshakes and promises to be able to see the baby as soon as he was born and could go out to be seen. It would be a little bit, yet, as he wasn't ready to make his grand entrance. The advice was still coming as everyone was leaving, each person having the "best" advice on how to raise a child.

Days turned into weeks and the baby continued to grow, as did Meredith and David's excitement. Life continued on for them, as did training opportunities for David, who took them as often as he was able without leaving Meredith home alone too often.

A month after the baby shower, David and Paul were in a three-day conference and not expected home until after, and Meredith was home with Bullet. They were relaxing in the early evening hours after spending the day cleaning the house top to bottom. Bullet had been outside playing in the freshly fallen snow and was now curled up at her feet dreaming about chasing bad guys while she watched reruns of old favorite movies.

The tinkling of broken glass at the front door alerted her that something was wrong. She ran into the bedroom closet and hid in the corner while trying to call Bullet to her. The dog was growling with vicious intent while Meredith called 911. The alarm began to chirrup its angry tones as the front door was kicked open unceremoniously.

"911, what's the location of your emergency?" the Dispatcher asked.

"I'm at thirty-nine Bugle Way. Someone's breaking into my house."

"I see there is an alarm. Officers are on their way." The dispatcher kept Meredith on the line, trying to find out more information. "Ma'am…where are you right now? Are you safe?"

"I'm hiding in the closet. He forced the front door open. My husband's K9 is barking." Her voice was wavering. She wanted to scream for Bullet to get into the closet and hide with her, but instead, she heard Aaron's familiar voice screaming in pain, cursing and yelling. Bullet was growling ferociously. "My dog just bit him. I know it's a good bite."

Several tense moments passed as she heard Aaron struggling and Bullet growling louder and louder. A gunshot echoed through the house with a loud yelp in response and then everything was silent as her ears rang. The sounds of struggling were gone, and now, she could hear Aaron moving around, still cursing.

"Ma'am…are you there? What was that?" the Dispatcher's voice was insistent in Meredith's ear.

"A gunshot. I think he killed my dog." Tears welled up in Meredith's eyes and spilled over as she struggled to maintain her calm. Aaron had a gun. He wasn't just here for harassment. He was here for revenge. Was leaving him really worth her life? Was getting away from the abuse really going to lead to her dying? He was insane.

"The officers should be there in two minutes. Are you well hidden?" the Dispatcher kept asking questions, trying to keep Meredith calm and find out as much information as possible.

Meredith could hear Aaron cussing as he found his way into the spare bedroom, knocking things over as he searched for a towel to staunch the bleeding in his arm from Bullet's vicious bite. She was trying to maintain her calm, trying to steady her breathing. On the verge of panic, all she wanted was Bullet to come into the closet and be safe. She needed him to be ok.

"For now. He's in another room. I know he was bit hard. I can hear him yelling about it."

More tense minutes passed and Meredith had yet to hear the officers pull up. "Ma'am, the officers should be there now," the calm voice on the phone told her.

"I don't hear them. He's moving around. I know he's looking for me. Can you call David and tell him what happened? Tell him I love him, and I'm sorry about the baby. Tell him it's ok to find someone new when he's ready, and I didn't mean for this to happen."

"You're going to be ok. My officers are there now. They aren't using sirens because they don't want to alert the intruder. They want to catch him so he can't hurt you."

Aaron had just gotten into the master bedroom and slammed the door when Meredith heard the sounds of strangers outside her house. She could hear them outside, searching intently for signs of Aaron. Tense minutes passed and there were voices at the front door. She imagined they were looking in, waiting for any sign of either Aaron, or her.

"Come out with your hands up! We have the house surrounded!" They were bluffing, but Aaron didn't know that. In his mind, there were a hundred officers with guns pointed at him. He knew he was now in a desperate situation - he wasn't going to make it out alive at this rate, and he knew he wasn't going to leave until he killed Meredith for leaving him.

Aaron swore loudly and Meredith flinched. She didn't think he knew she was there - she had been quiet when she entered the room, and had buried herself underneath layers of discarded clothing. The dispatcher was still on the line.

"Ma'am...I can hear them. They're with you. Are you still alone where you're hiding?"

"No." Her voice was barely a whisper. The dispatcher spoke to the officers on the radio, her voice muffled as she updated them about Meredith's location and status.

"They know you're in danger. Just hang on, ok? They'll get to you," the Dispatcher promised.

Time seemed to slow to a crawl. Meredith could only think about the child she was carrying, that she wasn't going to live to see; the one who was going to die with her. She hoped David would be ok, and that he would move on without too much emotional trauma. She hoped he would find a new wife, and that they would have the little boy he was now excited to have, once he was ready to have a baby again. She was upset to be the second woman in his life to take a baby away from him. She never wanted this to happen. How could she have known Aaron was crazy?

Aaron was pacing the room, talking to himself. He was muttering about stupid plans, stupid Meredith, and having to make her pay! The officers were hesitant to just burst in and take him down, unsure of exactly where she was, and whether or not she was safe. What felt like hours later, she heard a familiar voice.

"That's my goddamn wife in there, and I'll be damned if you're going to stop me from getting to her!" David had arrived. She didn't know who called him, but he arrived in record time and she hoped he wouldn't be around when she got shot to death by her crazy ex-boyfriend.

There were sounds of arguments as David barreled his way into the house. He found Bullet lying in the living room, bleeding and whimpering softly. He knelt down beside his canine partner and gently pet him. Bullet wagged his tail once and tried to lick David's hand. "You're ok, boy. We'll take care of you." He stood and saw no sign of Meredith and asked the officer in charge, "You haven't found her yet? Are you even trying?"

The officer shook his head. "No, sir. We just arrived, and are waiting on back up so we can do a search of the house. There is a negotiator on the way, too, so maybe we can resolve this peacefully."

David was furious. There was no "peacefully" with Aaron anymore. One of them was going to die before the night was over, and David had a baby on the way - he knew at the end of the night, he'd be left standing. He was tired of the system telling him there wasn't enough evidence to convict the man who was stalking his wife. That they didn't have the proof to say he broke their windows and traumatized their little family. He was tired of the system failing not only him, but how many hundreds of other women with crazy stalkers?

"Aaron, get your ass out here and face me like a man you asshole chicken shit." David's voice was full of uncontained rage. "You shot my dog and I'm going to kill you for that. And so help me God, if you laid a hand on a single hair on Meredith's head, I'll rip you limb from limb." His face was nearly purple, frantic with fear, hatred, and helplessness. He wanted to rush into the room and save his wife the way she had saved him, but he knew it was suicide. And his dying wasn't going to do anything to protect her.

Paul had been outside talking with other officers, trying to see what they needed most. He was able to push his way inside as well, hearing David's raised voice, and saw Bullet lying on the floor. He pointed his finger at a rookie, who was shaking on the porch, trying his best to blend into the wall. He hadn't signed up for getting shot. He imagined the job was all glamor, little true risk. Especially in their little town!

"You! Get our K9 out of here. Immediately."

The rookie stared at Lowfield, dumbfounded. He was going to go into a hot scene to save a dog? Dogs were tools to be utilized to save the life of a human officer - not something he was prepared to lose his life for.

"Did I stutter, kid? Get this *officer* to the vet *now!*"

The rookie jumped and delicately picked up the dog, who was limp, and rushed out the door. Lowfield looked at the blood that had soaked the carpet and splattered against the wall and shook his head. This was not going to end well.

The rookie ran into the ambulance crew, who had arrived and looked lost and scared. They weren't all as bold as Meredith, running into gunfire.

"Help me. It's our K9. He needs to get to the vet, and I don't know what to do for him! Help me!"

The crew opened the back doors of the ambulance and helped him in. They laid Bullet on the cot. One of the EMTs called into dispatch, advising them of their unusual destination and to please dispatch a second ambulance to this location.

The medic in the back laid an oxygen mask near his face and turned it on. There was no way to properly secure it to his muzzle, so this would have to do. He looked at the wound on the dog's hip and sighed heavily. He wasn't a vet...what could he possibly do for him? Grabbing a stack of gauze pads, he placed it on the bullet hole, and then wrapped it tightly around both hips with coban. Bullet whimpered, but didn't fight. His breathing was heavy, and his gums were pale. It was a very bad sign, indeed. That was the extent of the medic's veterinary knowledge, and that he learned from watching random vet shows on TV. He was able to get an IV in the dog, and ran fluids at a very slow rate. He didn't know how much fluid a dog could have before they had too much and faced kidney and heart damage.

Back at the house, the two responding officers had retreated to the driveway to wait for their backup and make a plan. David was pacing back and forth, biting his nails and staring at the door. Paul had stayed inside after they took Bullet out, looking for another way into the master bedroom. He had quietly peeked into the rooms with open doors, but had found no sign of Meredith or Aaron. He found a blood trail and a bloodied towel leading to the guest bathroom, assuming it was Aaron's from where Bullet bit him. It was a pretty good injury, and Paul was proud of the dog.

"Aaron...we know you're in there. Come out and make it easy on yourself. You heard the other officer - the house is surrounded." Lowfield's voice was loud, but gentle.

Aaron stared at the door and then sat on the bed, rocking back and forth. "She did this. She deserves to die. She deserves to burn in hell!" His voice steadily grew louder until he was yelling through the door. "She broke my heart. She has to pay!"

"No, Aaron. She doesn't deserve to be hurt. Neither do you. Why don't you come out and we can talk about it?" Lowfield knew he was no negotiator, but he also knew that Aaron wasn't in a stable frame of mind, and Meredith and her baby were in grave danger. He knew he had to do something to try and buy Meredith some time before the other team arrived to pull her out of the room.

"Bitches should die. She broke my heart. She left me. She deserves to die for her sins." Aaron's words were disjointed, spoken with pure hatred. He was absolutely not in his sane mind.

"Come on out, Aaron. Put your gun down and come out to talk to me. Let's get your bite looked at. I'm sure it hurts. We can get you some medicine to make it feel better."

"Hurts. Damn dog. Shot him. Going to shoot her, too." He had apparently had a psychotic break. He wasn't in his right mind, and was even more dangerous.

"Come on out, Aaron. Let's get you patched up so you don't hurt anymore," Lowfield was practically pleading now, but his tone was that of one in command.

Aaron kept the gun in his hand, arm loosely at his side, but opened the bedroom door. The other officers had moved up to the porch and were peering in through the windows, waiting for their opportunity to take him down with as little risk as possible. They didn't know where Meredith was, and were concerned about having a clear shot where they wouldn't shoot Paul in the process.

"Put your gun down, Aaron. We don't want anyone to get hurt. Put it down and let's talk." Paul had his pistol on his hip, but was trying to appear non-threatening to the crazed Aaron. He didn't want to resort to having to shoot him if it was at all possible. David, on the other hand, was upset that Aaron was still talking, and that he hadn't been taken down. In his mind, Meredith was dead, and Aaron deserved a double-tap to the chest.

"Come on out and let's talk, ok? Put your gun down and let's talk like men." Paul ignored the angry shouts from David, who could see them through the front window and was being restrained by other officers, just as he ignored the other officers telling him to take down the crazed suspect. Paul's entire focus was on his safety, and trying to find out where Meredith was, and whether or not she was ok. By the way Aaron had spoken just minutes earlier, he hadn't found her, and she was alive. Paul could only hope that was true.

Aaron took another step or two closer before he looked past Paul and saw David. Something in his mind flipped and he lunged forward, grabbing Paul, dragging both of them to the floor in a heap of bodies, flailing limbs, and enraged howls. Before anyone else could react by drawing a weapon or running in to help Paul, they heard a gunshot, and retreated for their safety. They had no way of knowing who was shooting, and they weren't going to be able to get a clear shot at Aaron without risk of shooting Paul in the process.

In that moment, Meredith knew that Aaron was no longer in the room and she leapt out of the closet, the clothing she had been hiding under flying in all directions. She stumbled over the bed and pulling David's loaded pistol out of his bedside table. She hid behind the wall opposite of their open bedroom door and saw the two men tussling. Another gunshot was heard and she saw Paul's face tighten with pain before transitioning to fear. He knew he had been shot, but did not know the extent of the injury. He bared his teeth and continued fighting, even harder if that was possible. He knew he was in trouble now, with Aaron having the upper hand. He was fighting for his life, and that gave him the strength he needed to keep Aaron's hand with the gun away from his head.

Before she knew what was happening, Meredith leveled the pistol in her quaking hands and pulled the trigger with a slow, steady squeeze, just like David taught her during their countless hours of practice. With a massive adrenaline dump running through her system, Meredith's numb hand hardly noticed the minor kick from the handgun as it fired. The gun sounded quieter than she remembered it, too. Time also seemed to slow, with Meredith watching as the bullet left the gun's muzzle, flying through the short distance between herself and the two men, and entering Aaron's body. She saw him flinch with the impact and then fall. A split second passed and the fight was over - Aaron took one last ragged breath, then wasn't moving anymore. Blood began to seep gradually outward, soaking deep into the carpet.

Meredith kept the gun trained on Aaron, as she ran to Paul's side, falling to her knees beside him. He was breathing hard and raspy, his eyes closed. "Not you, too!" She was on the verge of panic, and for a moment, all her training left her. She was not prepared to see her closest friend like this. He was soaked with sweat, fighting against the pain that wracked his stomach.

"David! Aaron's down, Paul's been hit! Get my crew in here now! Aaron's down, Paul's been shot!" Meredith's voice was loud and commanding, belying a calm she didn't feel. David crashed through the front door with a ferocity that momentarily stunned Meredith. He knelt down beside his wife, trying to assess her for injuries.

"Stop that. I'm fine! He's been shot in the stomach. It's not looking good. I need my crew, we need to get him out of here." She pressed down hard on the gunshot wound and Paul groaned, opening his eyes and staring at the two of them, trying to focus his gaze.

"Hey guys…we got him. Thank God your girl is a killer shot." His voice was weak, just barely above a whisper. He attempted a smile at his awful attempt at a joke.

"You're not so bad yourself. We're going to get you out of here, ok?" Meredith's voice had a forced steadiness she truly didn't feel.

"I'm not sure I'm going to make it. If not, you make sure your baby knows how awesome Uncle Paul was." He tried to cough, but the pain prevented him from doing so. Dark red blood was staining his shirt, spreading out wider and wider from the bullet hole in his stomach. Meredith was full of blood as well, trying to stop the bleeding.

"You're going to be fine, Paul. You can tell the baby yourself," Meredith told him.

The ambulance crew followed cautiously behind the rest of the officers, who spread out to search the rest of the house, in case there was another suspect they hadn't found yet.

"Get that suspect cuffed!" a burly officer barked. Another officer immediately snapped handcuffs on Aaron and then checked for a pulse, shaking his head as he looked up at his supervisor.

"He's dead."

Paul reached up a bloodied hand and placed it on Meredith's abdomen. The baby decided to kick at that time, and he smiled. "You take…care of your…mama." He was struggling to get the words out, bleeding too much, skin too pale, too sweaty. It drew up awful memories of David's near-death experience. Meredith was crying softly, her composure at risk of breaking completely.

"You'll be fine, Paul. We've got you," Meredith told him as the crew finally arrived at her side.

Kneeling down, they carefully strapped Paul onto a backboard and with the help of Meredith and one other officer, carried him out to the waiting ambulance. Once inside, Meredith begged the EMT get them to St. Victory ten minutes ago.

She then asked the other medic in the back of the ambulance with her to get a baseline set of vitals, while she worked on getting two large IVs in place and began running fluid as fast as it would go. She was thankful their service carried tranexamic acid - a medication that helps the body to make clots with the intent of slowing life-threatening bleeding. She knew it would help, however slightly.

Looking at the monitor, Paul's vital signs were frightening to her. His blood pressure was too low, his heart rate too high. She pulled out the levophed to try and get his blood pressure up while the fluids replaced the blood loss. She knew he needed blood to survive, but they didn't carry it in the ambulance. She also knew that they weren't but ten minutes from the trauma center.

Calling quickly on the radio, knowing the other medic had his hands busy, she let the trauma center know they were coming in hot.

"St. Victory, this is Medic 302… St. Victory, this is Medic 302…"

Her voice was strained and full of emotion, and she was anxious, afraid that the trauma center wasn't going to answer her.

"Go ahead, 302," the voice at the other end of the radio told her with a collected demeanor.

"St. Victory, we're coming in hot, ETA ten minutes with an approximate 35 year old male with a gunshot wound to the right lower abdomen. We have two large-bore IVs established, running two liters of saline. We've given a bolus dose of TXA, and have started levophed at one mike per minute with little result. I have a heart rate of one-thirty-five, and a blood pressure of eighty over forty. We're going to need blood upon arrival. Again, we'll be there in ten." Her voice was tight, wrought with stress and fear. This was becoming too real.

"Ten-four, Medic 302," the voice concluded before the radio went silent. She was glad they didn't ask her a bunch of questions; she felt like she would cry if they had.

The monitor started to alarm for bradycardia, and Meredith felt for a pulse, trying to get a now silent Paul to answer her. His pulse was weak, thready, and slow. The bleeding hadn't slowed despite pressure dressings the other medic had wrapped around him, the tranexamic acid, and the fluids. Paul took a labored breath, exhaling with a shudder and then stopped breathing. The monitor alarmed for asystole.

"Get the big pads on him, now!" She didn't have the time for politeness. Meredith's hands went immediately to Paul's chest and began compressions as the other medic put the shocking pads on him. He pressed the "analyze" button on the monitor, which advised they could not shock him. Her compressions were methodical and precise, just the way her medical training had taught her. She focused on this, and tried to pretend it wasn't Paul who was beneath her hands, lest she lose all composure and panic.

"Get a new bag hanging and then take over. I'm going to intubate," she told the other medic. She knew she shouldn't be the one to make these decisions, but she also was afraid to let anyone else handle her friend's care.

The medic spiked a new bag of saline and hung it in the place of the empty bag, and then took over chest compressions as their monitor counted out two minutes of CPR. Meredith was able to quickly get her equipment together for intubation, and find Paul's vocal cords, passing the breathing tube into his throat. She secured it and began to breathe for him.

"Here, you look tired. Take over bagging and I'll take over compressions," she told him. They switched again and Meredith resumed compressions. At the end of the two minutes, the other medic told her to stop, and to check for a pulse. He had to tell her several times as she was so deep into compressions, she wasn't listening to him.

She looked at the monitor and felt for a pulse, and had a small moment of hope as the monitor told her "shock advised." That meant there was electrical activity in the heart that the monitor was going to shock in an attempt at resetting the heart back into a normal rhythm. Meredith pressed the "charge" button and waited for it to finish charging.

"Clear!" she yelled, and as soon as the other medic had his hands off of Paul, she pressed the "shock" button. Electricity ran through Paul's body as they were pulling into St. Victory, but he did not regain a pulse.

They wasted no time in getting Paul down from the ambulance and rushing inside, still doing chest compressions and breathing for him.

"He coded five minutes ago. Gunshot wound to the abdomen, I'm thinking liver with the dark blood. He's gotten two and a half liters of saline, and a bolus dose of TXA. He's one of our officers, he needs blood! Why haven't you gotten the blood?" She was close to hysteria again, furious that they had ignored her request over the radio ten minutes prior.

They continued CPR for several more minutes as the doctor looked at the monitor. It advised they could not shock him. They continued, and then hung blood, giving Paul every chance to pull through. Time passed quickly with everything they had going on. The doctor was grim when he told everyone they could stop CPR another twenty minutes later. There was nothing more they were going to be able to do for him. Meredith screamed at the physician.

"No! Don't you dare stop! He's not dead!"

Meredith jumped to the side of the bed and resumed CPR, tears pouring down her face. "Don't you die!" The doctor gently pulled her down from the bed. She was hysterical now, unable to be consoled, and turned, trying to hit him, but he was able to wrap her up in his arms, careful due to her pregnant belly.

"I'm so sorry...there is nothing more we can do," he murmured, knowing that nothing was going to console her.

David had arrived with several other officers and took her from the physician. "Meredith...it's ok. Calm down." He held her tightly, trying desperately to soothe her. He knew that Paul was gone. He could see clearly into the room. He was upset too, but was trying to soothe her. She was still sobbing, fighting, and in utter disbelief that Paul could possibly be gone.

"I'm so sorry," the physician told David, before quietly exiting the room to begin making phone calls for the autopsy.

She calmed slightly as David continued to talk softly to her, running his hands through her hair, and then pausing when she wrapped her fists in David's shirt. "David...the baby..." Her eyes were wide and terrified. It was still too early for him to come. He would be premature, and would have so many problems. What if he died, too? Meredith couldn't handle that sort of emotional blow right now. She began to hyperventilate.

David yelled for the doctor, who told them to go straight to OB, while a nurse got her a wheelchair. They rushed her up to the OB floor where they could better monitor her and the baby. She was in such a state of shock over everything, she was nearly catatonic now, breathing almost a normal rate, tears still streaming down her cheek.

Chapter 41

Once up on the floor, the nurses spoke softly and calmly, putting monitors on her and her abdomen. They monitored for contractions, and did an ultrasound to check the baby's placement, wanting to know if he was ready to come out yet. They were able to get a Doppler of his heart, which was beating without issue, and he showed no signs of having any distress whatsoever.

"It looks like everything checks out just fine, but I'd like to keep you overnight for observation, just to be safe." Her nurse was a large woman who had a maternal presence about her. It was no wonder she worked on the OB floor.

Meredith nodded blankly. She was too upset to truly have an opinion. The nurse received a call from the ER physician, and gave Meredith a dose of sedative to keep her calm. David sat beside her until she was finally asleep and then went to talk to the nurses.

"My best friend is downstairs in your ER, dead from a gunshot wound. I need to go make arrangements for him since he doesn't have family. Will you please try to keep her sedated, or at least calm, until I can get back? I don't think it'll take too long, but…just in case?" His blue eyes were pleading, and on the verge of filling with tears of their own. The nurse rested her hand atop his and nodded.

"Sugar, you go and tend to whatever business you need. We'll make sure your wife is ok. I'll write down the access code so you can get back in once you're ready." The nurse wrote down the code and handed it to David, who shoved it into his pocket.

David thanked her and went down to the ER as fast as the elevator would take him. Once there, he found the doctor and went into his office. He had to force himself to stay steady and calm as he spoke to the doctor about matters he shouldn't have to worry about. It was upsetting that Paul had no family, and even more so that he was dead.

"He doesn't have any family. It's just me, Meredith, and the department. Has the coroner been called?" He asked, voice flat.

"No, sir. We need to know what funeral home you want before we call anyone, if, of course, you're going to make the arrangements…? He will be going to autopsy first, though."

David nodded. He knew the protocol even if he didn't know much about the local funeral homes. He told the doctor he wanted a funeral home that he'd heard good things about to handle the rest of the arrangements, after the autopsy had been completed.

"Is it ok if I sit with him until they come for him?" David asked, tears still rolling down his cheeks. The physician nodded, sympathetic to David. With that out of the way, David went into the ER room and pulled up a chair next to his oldest friend.

"This isn't how it was supposed to go. You weren't supposed to die, man. What the hell are we going to do now? Who's going to tell my boy all those embarrassing stories you promised? Who's going to go and get him his first beer after I've told you a hundred times that he can't drink until he's forty? Damn you, Paul. Why did you go and do this?"

David rested his forehead on the bed near Paul's hand. He stopped trying to control his emotions and sobbed until he was emotionally spent. By that time, the tech for the autopsy had arrived. The man was patient as David took his time saying his goodbyes to his dearest friend. He assisted the man in putting Paul into a bag and then onto the cot, and transferring him into the van.

David fought back tears the entire time he was explaining to the man this was an officer, and that he should be treated with the utmost respect. He would be receiving full law enforcement rights and burial. He let the man know that Paul would be buried in his uniform, and he'd have to bring it by a little later.

The man nodded and shook David's hand. "I assure you that Paul would be treated carefully and with nothing but respect. Your supervisor already called me to make arrangements for him. You're welcome to bring his uniform to the funeral home that's been chosen when you're ready."

David waited until the van drove out of sight before he returned to Meredith's side, staying beside her through the night.

Several days later, they were both at the funeral for their friend. They listened as numerous officers gave their speeches after the eulogy. David wasn't able to give a speech due to his intense emotions, and Meredith was still numb and medicated from the entire ordeal. They followed the hearse to the cemetery and watched as they unloaded Paul from the back and stood stoic, hands raised in salute until TAPS played. There wasn't a dry eye in the entire cemetery. There was a twenty-one gun salute, and the folding of the flag. David received the flag and the gun casings in the absence of a wife or family.

The drive home was quiet and tense. Neither of them knew what to say, and without words, simply held each other's hands. They pulled into the driveway and sat there, not wanting to go inside and face the ordeal they had been through. They'd stayed at the hospital for the first night, as Meredith was there for observation, and had booked a hotel for the remainder of the days before the funeral.

There had been a team of crime scene experts who had done what they needed to do, gotten their measurements, and pictures, and had left while a restoration team cleaned up the area. They had scrubbed the carpet where Bullet, Paul, and Aaron had all bled, and had patched the hole in the wall where Aaron's rogue round had struck. While the house looked new again, there was nothing that could be done about the memories. The screams still echoed, bullets still boomed, and the fear still gripped them.

Steeling themselves, they walked into the house and tried to put the pieces of their lives back together the best they could.

Chapter 42

A month later, they walked back into the house with an extra bundle. The baby was sleeping in his car seat, his tiny breaths putting a smile on the faces of his parents. David went to the back yard and whistled, and Bullet came trotting into the house, limping with the cool, rainy weather. While the wounds themselves had healed, there were still long-term effects to deal with.

"Now, you need to be a good boy, ok? The little guy is your new brother. You need to protect him the same way you protected your mama. Got it?" Bullet wagged his tail happily and stared at David with a deep devotion evident in his liquid brown eyes.

Meredith sat the car seat down on a foot stool in the living room while she sat on the couch, poised to intervene if Bullet decided he didn't like the baby. David had the prong collar on him as well, in case a correction was needed. Slowly, Meredith pulled down the blanket to expose her child. The tiny baby's breaths didn't change and remained steady and even, a reassurance that he hadn't become cold with removing the blanket.

Bullet nosed the tiny bundle and sniffed at him, unsure of what to think. He wagged his tail with uncertainty. David gave him a scratch behind the ears. "That's a good boy. Bullet, this is your new brother, Paul David Price."

The baby woke and stared at the massive red and black dog with curious, unfocused blue eyes. He stretched his tiny little hands out toward Bullet as he yawned broadly. Bullet took only a second to make his decision. He extended his large muzzle and licked the tiny hand and sat in front of the car seat, resting his head on the edge. It was a bond that was sealed in that moment - the promise that even though he could no longer work as a K9 due to his injury, he would still protect his people from anything that dared to try and harm them.

Meredith smiled at the sight before her. Her husband smiled down at the child they had created, alive because of the large dog that was willing to give his all to protect them. Meredith realized how blessed she was to have a husband who loved her above all else, a perfect son, and a dog who would gladly give his life to protect their little family. With a full heart, she knew that there was no more perfect world than this.

www.ingramcontent.com/pod-product-compliance
Lightning Source LLC
Chambersburg PA
CBHW022015170626
46808CB00001B/420